# Flight of Fire

*The first book in the series:*

# Minorie Raine

# Trials and Tribulations

*by*

# Tara D. W. Tine

RED MANTLE

RED MANTLE PUBLISHING
Dundalk, Co. Louth, Ireland
redmantlepublishing.com

First published in 2017 in Ireland by Red Mantle Publishing

Cover design by Diogo @ Red Raven Book Design
Font by Cari Buziak

This book is a work of fiction and any resemblance to actual persons,
living or dead, is purely coincidental.

ISBN-10: 1979163030
ISBN-13: 978-1979163033

Check out carlinn.com for Minorie's world,
upcoming releases & lots of freebies!

.

# Contents:

# Acknowledgements

Firstly, I would like to express my deepest gratitude to Chris, the wizard, who was always there as a source of inspiration, to hold my hand during those long, dark nights of the soul and to remind me that my writing wasn't complete shit. There is much magic yet to be made, brother.

I would also like to give huge thanks to Martin, my editor, who helped kick my arse into gear more than once and who has ceaselessly believed in and supported me throughout the production of this book.

Finally, to the beautiful village of Carlingford, for being my muse. Thank you for inspiring and supporting me during our years together.

# Ꭺ Ꮼoᴄᴇ ꜰʀoᴍ Ꮼhᴇ Ꭺuᴄhoʀ

*"I will not serve that in which I no longer believe, whether it calls itself my home, my fatherland, or my church: and I will try to express myself in some mode of life or art as freely as I can and as wholly as I can, using for my defense the only arms I allow myself to use – silence, exile, and cunning."*
~ James Joyce.

It happened to me.

Home wasn't a safe place when I was growing up, though everyone around me pretended that it was. I wished I'd been brave like Minorie, able to run, able to break away and forge my own destiny.

But I wasn't, and that's okay too. When I did finally get to spread my wings, I travelled far and wide, and met many young women and men who *had* been brave enough. It had worked out well for some, and not so well for others, but they had all suffered the soul-crushing loneliness of exile.

It's hard to prepare for the big bad world, and no matter how ready we might think we are, the chances are it'll scare the hell out of you at some point, regardless.

So to all the young women and men who took a chance and ran, or took a chance and stayed, and to all who insist on carving out their own paths...this one's for you.

Tine, Flight of Fire

4

# Getting Out

Minorie danced slowly and sensually around the fire. Her wild red hair moved like one of its flames, gyrating and swaying with the rhythm of the music. She danced as though no-one was watching, although she was vaguely aware that there were crowds of people all around her, their voyeuristic gazes all focussed on her glistening naked skin. That kind of thing didn't matter in dreams though; she knew from experience it was much more fun just to run with it where possible. She'd had a few lucid dreams since she'd started experimenting, but this one was the most vivid by far – all her senses were tingling and telling her that this place was no less real than the one she'd been in before she'd fallen asleep, or at least no less important.

On the breeze she could smell sweet, musky incense and fireworks exploded overhead and Minorie grooved on. Nothing mattered now but the dance and the fire, not even the black shining snake which had approached her foot and was now winding its way up her leg….Her hips corkscrewed slowly towards the ground and her back curled and arched, and the bass line pulsed, met at its climax by thundering drums. The snake climbed higher still….A curious feeling, she thought, to have a snake wrapping itself casually around her thigh but to feel no fear. Its cool skin felt refreshing against her own, and she wondered where it meant to go as it slithered ever upwards. Actually, she *knew* where it meant to go, and was rather enjoying the sensation. She felt safe among the surrounding festival-goers and she knew there was something special about the fire which had captivated her so completely. Yes, she was safe here. There was a voice, rising from the crowd, shrill and penetrating. She'd been trying to ignore it, trying to hold onto the melody as it reached its crescendo – the psychedelic guitar line bent her spine like a liquorice whip and the snake was preparing to enter sacred territory…. "*Must be the sea-son of the wiiitch…*"

But the voice became louder, more persistent -

"Get out! GET OUT NOW, MINORIE!"

The sound of her name being called from a crowd full of strangers caught her off guard and her eyes jerked open.

The song she'd been dancing to was playing on her radio. She found the fire and the crowds had been replaced by her familiar things and a bed full of open books. The looming threat of upcoming state exams returned to the forefront of her mind like a black cloud filling her stomach with butterflies. For a moment the air seemed stale as if someone, or something had died. She hated it when awesome dreams were interrupted. *Another productive evening of studying* she mused, as she wiped the drool from her face.

"Get up and get out NOW, Minorie!" called *that* voice again, the one from her dream – much to her surprise, as she wasn't exactly used to having voices in her head when she was *awake*.

For a moment she sat on the edge of the bed staring at the rows of laces on her boots and wondering whether she had actually woken up at all. And then she heard it; the footsteps bulling across the downstairs hallway, the drunken ranting. *Dad must be home from the pub, and it sounds like he wants a fight.*

Her heart skipped a beat. She remembered Mam wasn't home. She'd made a rare evening-time excursion to a sick neighbour a few miles away. As his voice ascended the staircase, Minorie knew it would be her turn today. Dad only ever approached the second floor of their house to accuse her of something ridiculous. The topic of the day seemed to be the shopping bill. She could make out phrases here and there from the unintelligible bawling, phrases like "Where does my money go?" and "Where are *youse* hiding it?!"

Minorie's father had never quite understood that inflation of the economy also meant the increase of food prices and not just his wage packet. Occasionally, Mam found that he could be subdued if she managed to produce the receipt before he'd crossed the line to that place from whence he couldn't return, where his eyes took on a supernatural blackness and small dots of white foam would appear at the corners of his twisted mouth.

But more often than not it was neither answers or logic that he craved; Minorie had observed that it was his need to feel superior to someone and to vent his rage at someone scared who would not talk back. In short, he was a big bully. Unfortunately the bully was also fully convinced that his wife and daughter were conspiring to embezzle the food budget. Minorie had long since stopped trying to reassure him. A dark part of her reminded her that he was Mam's choice of housemate, not hers. But this time, Mam wasn't here to absorb the aggro.

Minorie stood up, feeling her adrenalin pumping and preparing her for fight or flight.

"Get out right now, Minorie. Grab your handbag and GO," rang the voice again from the air around her as clearly as if being spoken by someone in the room.

This time Minorie knew she was awake, and that this was no time to start arguing with disembodied voices. She slung on her coat and her handbag and marched to her bedroom door.

In the same moment she opened it, her father reached the top of the staircase, his steaming face looming several inches above her own, dilated pupils eyeing her as if she were his prey. He'd gone all *red mist* – she could see it in his eyes. Sure enough, he clenched his fist and gritted his teeth and went to swing a punch at her head. What she did next surprised her as much as it did him, but the voice was still echoing in her head telling her she had to get out no matter what. She lurched forward and grabbed the collar of his t-shirt, good and tight, so his yellow-tinted eyeballs bulged like squeezed grapes. He dropped his fist and looked at her with an expression she'd never seen him wear before. His usually deep furrowed brow rose high into an arch and the steely glare of his deep set eyes turned to uncertainty. She was quite sure she had his full attention now. She also noticed to her simultaneous relief and horror that her father, the terrifying man who dwarfed her in both height and width, was literally teetering on the edge of the staircase. *Just a little push*, she thought, *and we'd never have to fear him again.* But she wasn't going to kill him; at least she hoped she wasn't. The voice had just told her to get out, not to murder her father on the way. Besides, with no witnesses, she reckoned she'd have a pretty hard time proving it was self-defence. Best just threaten the old bollocks and get gone. She drew his face very close to her own, feeling fiery daggers shooting from her eyes to his and started in low and menacing tones.

"Listen to me, you paranoid old fuck. I could push you down these stairs right now but you're not worth the jail time. If you follow me, or if you lay a hand on Mam, I'll come back and smother you in your sleep. Understood?"

The confusion in his face twisted and morphed to paralyzing fear around the same time Minorie's legs turned to jelly.

"Good," she said without flinching, before hauling his huge frame onto the landing and out of her way. As she descended the staircase, his gaze burned into her back. *Please don't let him follow, PLEASE don't let him follow...*

For a moment as she reached the dark and cold night, she felt like Rapunzel escaping her tower after a lifetime of imprisonment. *Except Rapunzel had a knight in shining armour to defend her and he probably had an escape plan too. Bitch.*

At the bottom of the driveway, she stood still and seriously considered the idea of waiting for Mam to come back. It was October after all, the wrong time of year for running away from home. Maybe she could convince Mam to come with her and they could start again somewhere else. However, the undeniable fact kept rearing its ugly head and Minorie could only sigh in despair. She knew Mam was too scared to leave.

She'd begged her before when things were bad but the fear had crushed her spirit after all these years. Mam believed there was nowhere else to go and no safe way to get there.

Minorie choked back the onslaught of tears and forced herself to put one foot in front of the other, glancing back every few steps until she could no longer see the glowing lights of the house in which she'd felt captive for all these years. The thought of leaving her mother to pick up the pieces was enough to make every fibre of her being want to forget the whole thing and go back. She tried to think back to the last strong woman she had met, to ponder what she may have done in a situation like this.

Her mind led her to English classes with Miss Rocks in the classroom that smelled like feet and had green and yellow linoleum on the floor. In this room, Miss Rocks had meticulously deconstructed the character of Lady Macbeth, who asked the gods to take away all her womanly emotions and replace them with solid resolve. Of course, she did go on to participate in a heinous act of regicide, suffer a nervous breakdown and fling herself from a tower, but that was beside the point right now.

Minorie wondered if there were any gods listening to her at this moment, from the dark and rustling treetops perhaps, or from the twinkling stars when they peeped out from behind the gathering clouds. Maybe there were even gods in the rough gravel of the road beneath her feet. After all, who was *she* to say where a god may presume to live?

As her eyes adjusted to the black around her and the landscape grew even eerier, she figured it was worth a shot. Raising her eyes to the faces in the clouds, she tried her best to imagine someone was listening.

"Um, please take away my sad feelings so I can go through with this…"

She felt really stupid and more than a little frightened talking to the night sky like this. How funny, she thought, that if someone had actually answered her, she'd have turned tail and run home without a second thought.

Since the disembodied voices seemed to have vanished she thought she'd chance asking for something practical too, considering she'd just run away from home without even packing a bag.

"Also, please don't let me get my period, and please, please, can I have somewhere safe to sleep tonight?"

The only response from the night was the call of a distant wood pigeon which only served to greater emphasise the overwhelming stillness between breaths of wind.

"Uh, thanks," she finished, just in case.

Walking deeper into the night, she tried not to look at the half-ruined cottages and stable houses that punctuated the road to Findair. The remains of the cottages looked like many of the older inhabited houses along the way, except somewhere down the line they'd been abandoned by their owners, probably due to death Minorie imagined. Maybe grisly deaths that left unsettled or angry spirits behind….

And she was even more afraid of the abandoned stables, since the time she'd overheard Nan recounting the tale of a local 'lunatic' some years before she was born. (Minorie had managed to deduct that 'fits' meant the poor girl had suffered either from a mental illness, some emotional problem or perhaps even just epilepsy.) The girl's mother had died giving birth to her and her father had decided that the best solution for his newfound burden was to lock the girl in the stable beside the house. For years afterward, apparently, she could be heard wailing and moaning wordlessly at passersby through the boarded up windows.

"But sure, that was what they did in those days," her Nan had said, as casually and impersonally as if she'd been talking about some minor embarrassing trend, like wearing platform soles.

Minorie reflected that had she been born a few decades earlier her father would probably have built a stable especially for her.

As she reached the first fork in the road she began to take stock of the situation, searching through her mind for ideas on where to go next. Findair seemed the obvious choice, being the nearest town and the main hub of Minorie's social life. But it was twenty miles away and Minorie wasn't sure she'd be able to walk that far in this outfit. It hadn't occurred to her this morning, as she'd pulled her favourite steampunk corset/skirt combo out of the wardrobe, that this choice of clothing would also have to be suitable for a cross-country quest.

If she *did* manage to make it to Findair however, there was a good chance she could find Keith in one of the many party houses he frequented and he'd definitely let her crash with him. The thoughts of an unexpected night in his arms warmed Minorie from inside. She was sure he'd be just as delighted about the idea as her. Maybe tonight would even be *the night*...She'd been thinking about it for some time now but they'd never really gotten the opportunity of a whole night alone together....Suddenly, being out in the big world on her own didn't seem so bad.

*But*, she reminded herself, *I'll have to make it to Findair first*, and this seemed more unlikely every time she thought about it. The freezing fog was now unfurling it's tendrils into the lower lying fields through the high, messy ditches and onto the potholed road, doubling the chance she'd end up in a hospital bed tonight. *At least it would be safe, but they'd call my parents...*

Her mind wandered on through the myriad of ways that her journey could go wrong; getting knocked down because she was dressed in black from head to toe on a pitch black country road, spraining her ankle in a pothole then freezing to death in a ditch, being unexpectedly dragged to hell by desperate lunatic ghosts...

And then a light appeared behind her, small at first when she glanced back, but growing large against the thick white screen of curling fog around her. The faint sound of an accompanying engine broke the stony silence. She stepped cautiously but briskly up into the ditch and hoped the driver would notice her and also that they wouldn't be a rapist.

The engine muted to a soft purr as it approached her, signalling that she had indeed been spotted. The prospect of now being interrogated by a stranger, or even kidnapped by one gave new cause for concern. And what if it was her father, here to finish the rage she'd interrupted earlier? Or her mother, here to talk her into coming home and forgetting the whole thing?

As Minorie stepped up into the ditch and turned to face the headlights she prayed it was no more than a kind stranger behind the wheel. The vehicle stopped right alongside her and its window rolled down to reveal a little old nun, wearing a warm smile and clucking concerns for her wellbeing and sanity. A giggle of relief escaped from Minorie's chest.

"Get in, get in," she said with dramatic hand gestures. "It's a dangerous evening to be walking the roads!"

"Yes I know," she replied, feeling a spiel coming on, "it's just that I need to get home for school tomorrow. You see, I was visiting my sick grandmother...."

"Come on, child, HOP IN," said the nun, whose gesturing was now bordering on frantic.

Minorie grabbed the door handle and grinned. Perhaps the gods were listening after all. As she climbed into the passenger seat she could hear that the old nun's driving soundtrack of choice was 1960's era surf music of the thrashy variety, which surprised her greatly. Having been taught by nuns she assumed they all listened to church hymns and Gregorian chant when they were off duty. Neither was she prepared for the old girl to take off at top speed as soon as she'd pulled the door closed behind her, but away they went anyway, zooming around break-neck bends and bouncing over hills. Minorie remembered being in cars with joy-riders who were safer drivers. She looked over at the figure of the nun, hunched atop the wheel under her strange brown veil, straining to see the road with a row of white knuckles gripping on for dear life. The whole scene was surreal and Minorie looked forward to recounting it later to Keith and his friends.

There may even be some drinks and weed to look forward to. Oh, it was all coming together nicely now....

"So your poor grandmother is sick?" asked the nun, averting her attention away from the road for an alarming length of time in order to make polite eye contact with Minorie.

"Ah...yes," she said, forgetting for a moment that she now had a pretence to keep up. "She needed me to help her around the house and, y'know, look after her an' stuff..." She was usually a superb liar when cornered but the reeling emotions of the past forty five minutes were taking their toll.

"Well! What a terrific young lady you are, coming all this way on a night like that to help your grandmother. Let me bring you home dear. It's Findair, isn't it?"

"Oh, that'd be great. Yes, I live in Findair."

"Good. That's where I'm headed too. We'll be there in no time at all!"

The surf song kicked back in for the final pumping refrain. Minorie felt a pang of remorse for lying bare-faced to a nun. However, she reminded herself it was nobody else's fault that this woman had chosen to see the world from a distorted and overly-moralistic perspective, which rendered her out of touch with the modern world of teenagers. Feeding her a fabricated story was really just protecting her from the kinds of harsh realities she had long since denounced. The car roared on through the night like a jet-ski on open water. The old nun swerved occasionally to dodge small animals and other cars which threatened to impede her path.

As the orange glow of Findair appeared on the horizon, Minorie's excitement grew. The surf music had ceased for the moment and a familiar song that sounded like a lullaby tinkled from the speakers and made her think gushy thoughts about Keith. Her visions of their future together, living on the run, or off in the woods somewhere were cut short by the last line of the verse - "*And the darkest hour is just before dawwnn….*"

"Whereabouts is your home- ah, what is your name?" asked the nun, squinting again in her direction.

*Shit. Where would he be?*

"My name's Minorie Raine," she said, making a split-second decision to try Keith's last known whereabouts, "and I live in Brewer's Lane."

"Nice to meet you, Minorie, my name's Sister Xavier," she replied in her best schoolteacher voice.

Minorie could hear her silently jumping to conclusions upon the mention of Brewer's Lane – a famed drinking spot in a low-brow part of town. She would probably assume that Minorie's parents were unfit, which upon further reflection wasn't really a million miles from the truth.

"It's really nice of you to bring me home, Sister; only, when we get to Brewer's Lane, could you just drop me around the corner please? You see, my mum's not well. She….suffers with her nerves…." *Might as well be hung for the sheep as the lamb.*

"Oh? Well I can just watch and make sure you get in ok. Will your father be around?"

"My father's dead," she said, feeling a little sick as she did so, "and my mother gets terrible migraines and the headlights really upset her and…"

"Ok, dear, it's ok. I can just drop you around the corner, no need to disturb your mother."

Minorie wasn't sure if her story had convinced Sr. Xavier but she didn't really care. Even if the old nun guessed she was lying she'd probably presume Minorie was pretty messed up to have created such a huge and sinful story and she'd feel really sorry for her. Either way, she'd achieved the desired effect. As the car rounded the corner towards the top of Brewer's Lane, it bounced up onto the footpath outside a row of sleeping terraced townhouses. Minorie prepared herself to face the icy cold once again. Sr. Xavier turned to her with a heartfelt and meaningful look in her eyes and held out a gift for Minorie. It was a cross of silver with four equal-sized arms encased within a circle. It struck Minorie that it looked far more like a Celtic cross than the typical Christian crucifix. Its surface was intricately carved and polished, though it hung from a piece of mere twine.

"Take this, girl. It'll keep you safe."

Minorie couldn't help but be humbled by the nun's touching act. Forgetting herself, she timidly asked, "Can I wear it?"

Sr. Xavier just smiled and nodded in response, and pressed it into Minorie's hand.

"Thank you, Sister. It's beautiful. And thanks again for the lift."

"Now now, off you go. Make a nice cup of tea for your mum when you get in."

"I will," said Minorie, feeling like a really bad person. She climbed out of the car and it sped off up the tree-lined avenue past the sleeping town houses. Turning the corner for Brewer's Lane, Minorie paused to tie the cross around her neck. Its weight was comforting on her chest. She noted the street was quieter than usual for a weekend. Sister Xavier had left the fog behind them a few miles outside town and so once again Minorie could see the star gods watching over her. There was a drunken domestic happening inside the house on the corner which made Minorie's stomach turn. It made her wonder if Mam was home yet and what lies her father would have told her about the evening's events.

Her heart sank as she reached Sal's place. All the lights were off, which amongst the partiers was code for 'Party is elsewhere tonight, dudes'. *But where?*

She'd only been out partying with Keith's gang once – Mam didn't often let her spend nights in Findair and she'd have killed her if she'd known where Minorie was really going.

It was to that guy Pig's house, and Mam would probably have been right to kill her for going there. Minorie had disliked him and most of his friends immediately on sight and even more so when he'd asked her if her wearing a corset meant she was 'open for business' that night. She had informed him that even if it did, no amount of money would buy his way into her pants. He then promptly rebuked that he wouldn't take her pants if she offered them for free, in that most demeaning way that only a smarmy, entitled eighteen-year-old can. This had made her so furious that she wanted to punch him, or cry, or both, but she had known better and had tried to swallow it. All the same, Pig and his friends got a great laugh at her purpling face.

Keith had just laughed and told them both to play nice and Pig just snorted even harder in delight at his victory. She hoped that if Keith were there tonight, Pig would let her in the door with no bullshit.

She headed for the bottom of Brewer's Lane and the harbour road beyond it and prayed she would be able to remember which house Pig lived in; she'd been pretty drunk the last time. She didn't pass a single person. She wondered if the zombie apocalypse had happened without her knowing. She wound her way through the grid of alleys and lanes until the stink of the harbour filled her nostrils. When the tide went out it always left behind a huge, brown bed of what adults called 'silt', but which looked and smelled to Minorie like shit.

Finally she reached the row of decrepit and dingy houses. Sure enough one of them was jumping. This had to be it. She had a sick feeling in her stomach as she banged the door hard with her fist. She really hoped Keith would be there, and that someone would hear her over the blaring metal music and let her in. She had begun to knock a second time when the door swung open and she nearly fell in after it. Catching herself just in times she was greeted by a bubbly blonde with pink satin bunny ears on her head.

"Would you like some acid?" she said, as matter-of-factly as you'd offer someone a cupcake.

"No thanks. Is Keith here?" said Minorie. Trying psychedelics before losing her virginity just seemed wrong to her and besides, if she were going to try it, she could think of better places.

"Are you sure? It's got Marilyn Monroe on it...."

"I'm really just here to find Keith...." said Minorie, wondering if the girl really believed that taking acid with Marilyn Monroe on it was somehow more glamorous than taking regular old drugs.

Before the girl could answer, Pig jumped out in front of her eager to see who had come to his party.

"Ah, Red's back! We don't need any of your knickers today thanks." With that, he closed the door right in her face.

She could hear him laughing that phlegmatic, sleazy snortfest of his on the other side. *A pig indeed.*

The door opened once again. "Still here?" he asked, "Jeez, you must be really desperate."

"Pig, I'm just looking for Keith, is he here?"

"*Pch!*....Yeah, yeah, he's in the kitchen," he said, surrendering. He didn't need to wind Minorie up tonight; there were plenty of other unwitting victims in his lair.

The hallway was lit by the same dull, electric bulbs which give accident and emergency rooms that extra-depressing vibe. It didn't smell dissimilar to one either. Everywhere there were bodies, some were dipping in and out of consciousness due to one substance or another, some were giggling hysterically at each other's jokes. In one or two darker corners, the customary pre-mating rituals were being fulfilled by writhing shadows that had long hair and wore waistcoats and skinny jeans. Minorie squeezed past all of them in the bottle-necked hallway. The stench was a cocktail of beer and sharp fruity spirits, weed and unwashed hipsters. A few faces she'd met once or twice before lit up as she passed, and greeted her as though they were besties. They weren't besties though. *Not one of these people would offer me a sofa to stay on tonight.*

All the same she found herself pulling expressions of over-stated excitement in response, though she couldn't remember one of their names. She quietly gave thanks for the overwhelming throb of shredding metal music and wondered if they all listened to it just so they wouldn't actually have to speak to each other. It was quieter as she entered the kitchen which hadn't stopped a couple of vampiric-looking girls from moshing privately in the corner.

She could hear Keith engaged in a passionate discussion about the politics of the border regions as she entered. He was so serious and sexy when he talked about politics. His chiselled jaw line would stiffen when he had a point to make and he'd run his hands through his dirty blonde hair when he was conceding to a debating partner.

He didn't notice her, but she didn't mind.

"Yeah but there's a whole grey area there around Carlinn that's neither north nor south, and neither side would touch it with a ten-foot barge pole..."

"And who'd blame them," said the long-haired stoner for whom Keith was holding court. "The last guy who tried to represent that place ended up losing his mind and then his house burned down."

"True that," said Keith, as Minorie snuck up behind him and put her arms around his neck. *His hair smells so earthy and lived-in....* "But they have the best parties," he concluded, probing her soft arms with his fingertips and deciding it was time to wrap up the debate.

"And who do we have here," he said, turning to inspect the owner of the soft arms.

She could have sworn she detected surprise in his eyes when he saw it was her. But it had been a rough night and she was probably just being paranoid. All that mattered now was that she was here, with him.

"Hey babe, what are you doing all the way in here?"

"You're not going to believe what hap-"

"Got two dates for the night now, huh Keith? AWKWAARRRD! What d'ya want me to tell Nikki?" said Pig, bursting into the kitchen, clearly delighted with himself.

"Tell her you wana ride her, Pig man," said Keith.

"Who's Nikki?" said Minorie in his ear, as discreetly as she could manage.

"She's just the blonde bunny, babe," he said, with no discretion at all. "She told Pig she was into me and obviously I'm not interested." He pointed his thumb towards Pig. "He is, though, but he's choosing to act like a child instead of DOING SOMETHING ABOUT IT," he finished, turning to launch a bottle cap at Pig's head.

"Alright man, I'll do it, but you owe me big time!" Pig replied, watching the bottle cap sail past him and hit Bunny Ears, who had just entered. She had intended to open the beer can she'd been shaking in Pig's face but the bottle cap knocked off her aim and sent a geyser of beer foam skeeting around the room.

Pig squealed with glee. Keith laughed too, wiping beer from his face. He'd shielded Minorie from the worst of the spray, so she smiled too when he looked at her. He leaned into her and whispered "Hey girl, you wana go somewhere a bit quieter?"

She smiled for real now and nodded a resounding "Yes". He took her hand and led her out of the kitchen and up the staircase, stepping carefully around its many inhabitants.

The landing, too, was crammed wall-to-wall with hippies and metallers, and a layer of thick smoke hung heavy in the air. All Minorie could see was hair and faces and black t-shirts on a backdrop of peeling, piss yellow wallpaper, and Keith, leading her to their private heaven.

On the landing stood a set of rickety fold-away stairs, which led to a darkened attic space on the floor above. Keith began to climb and Minorie cringed at the inevitable. As she'd expected, the ladder wasn't skirt-friendly and her skirts kept wrapping around her boots making her ascent up the creaking ladder much less carefree-looking than she would have liked. Thankfully, none of the stoners below seemed to notice.

At the top, she stood up in the only part of the room in which it was actually possible to do so. The steep rafters sloped down over a double bed and a familiar-looking stack of books stood on the floor beside it. *Aren't those all Keith's books?*

"Welcome to my new digs," said Keith. He lit some candles on the stack of books which was serving as a makeshift bedside locker and then he hit play on the vintage cassette player sitting on the makeshift book sideboard beside it.

"You live here now?" she asked, trying not to sound intrusive, though she was surprised he hadn't mentioned the move when she'd spent the afternoon ditching school with him in Sal's earlier that week.

"Yup. Sal's getting kicked out so his landlord can sell the house. Me and Pig are going to start a band together anyway so we figured it made sense. Plus, I haven't had my own room in ages; it'll be a nice change...." He kicked off his boots and lay back on the bed.

She'd dreamed about this night for so long but she felt too agitated to enjoy it. *It's all wrong.*

"Do you have any weed?" she asked, unlacing her own boots and climbing carefully onto the bed. She hoped she wouldn't accidentally sit up in the night and crack her head open. He shoved his hand under the edge of the bed and produced his carved wooden rolling box from which he took a small green bud and proceeded to roll.

"So what's happening? Are you 'staying in Myrtle's house' again?" he said, doing one-handed quotation marks and smiling sarcastically. 'Staying in Myrtle's' was Minorie's own code for 'partying all night with older boys'.

"Nope, this time I've run away. Like, for good. My dad went to punch my face in and I threatened to push him down the stairs, then I ran away and now I'm here," she said, smiling and keenly awaiting his gushing response.

"Holy shit, girl," he said, pausing dramatically to lick the tip of the rolling papers, before the corners of his mouth curled up in that cheeky way that drove her wild. "That's bad-ass."

She loved it when he said things like that, though it wasn't very often. She was usually awkward and erratic around him and his friends, and she loved when he saw that she could be powerful too, and not just innocent, silly Minorie from the countryside. She loved that he found her sexy.

"So do you really not think you'll go back?"

"Do I look like I have a death wish?"

He laughed and asked "So what's the plan, then? Like, I'm sure you could stay here for a few nights, but Pig prefers a girl-free zo-"

"I want you to go with me," Minorie burst out, unable to contain her longing any more.

"Go where?" he asked, sounding mildly surprised.

"Anywhere! What about that place you were talking about downstairs, with the best parties? You said it was on the border and that's only a few dozen miles away."

"Where, Carlinn? Didn't you hear what we said after about that guy who lost his mind there? You don't just *go* to Carlinn…"

Minorie had overheard the whisperings of superstitious adults talking about Carlinn over the years. When she'd asked Mam about it, Mam would just fob her off and tell her that the place was bad luck and not to worry about it. Girls in school would relay fantastical stories of possessed children and zombies but Minorie's rational mind knew this to be the exaggerated chattering of pre-pubescent girls. She didn't take any of it seriously.

"So what if he lost his mind? It's probably just a coincidence; people go crazy all the time."

"Yeah but not like *this!* Man, he went missing for a week and was found up on the mountain, miles from the village, on his hands and knees in a bramble bush, crying for his mother. They reckon someone in the village put a curse on him."

He raised the fresh-rolled joint to his lips and lit the end, taking a long, slow drag which turned the top into a blazing red cherry.

Minorie hoped that wasn't fear she detected in his voice. She hoped he was just toying with her like he always did.

"Not that I'm saying we shouldn't go there," he added, deciding that his uncharacteristic prudence wasn't at all cool. "In fact, they do this whole 'Festival of the Dead' thing; it's around this time of year. Like Halloween, but it lasts for a week and from what I've heard, they really take it to the max..."

"Now you're talking," said Minorie perking up noticeably. "Tell me more."

"Well," said Keith, handing her the joint and rolling onto his elbows, "you know the way nobody ever actually *goes through* Carlinn....?"

"Mm-hm," she said, inhaling deeply on the sweet strong smoke and smiling seductively at him through the gathering smoke.

"I mean, if you wana go north from here, the most sensible way is to go by Carlinn. Look at any map and you'll see that, right?"

"Uh-huh," she said coyly, as if she suspected where he might go next. She loved it when he engaged her.

"But nobody. Ever. Goes there. Have you ever actually met anyone who's been there?"

"Nuh-ah."

"Exactly. They all go *around* it. They're scared shitless of the place. From what I can make out, it's because there's magic there."

"Like....magicians?"

"No, not magicians, with rabbits in hats and that....But magick with a 'k'."

"Right, now you've lost me," she said, taking one last, deep drag and making a big, pouting O-shape with her mouth before passing the joint back.

"Like, *real* magick," he said, with a twinkling in his eyes that she'd only seen once or twice before.

"What, curses and spells an' stuff?"

"Yeah, man. They say magick workers from all over the world go there to live."

Minorie could see he was being serious, so she resisted the urge to erupt into nervous laughter, but with the weed rapidly taking effect, it proved difficult.

"I've heard stories of people who went there and never came back and of some really freaky noises coming from the place at night. Some guys I know camped on the mountain above the village once and they packed up and drove home in the middle of the night. Could have broken their fucking necks coming down in the dark but they didn't mind saying it was worth the risk."

"Ooh, that place sounds awesome," said Minorie with a devilish gleam in her eye.
"Pleeease, can we go?"

"Sure baby," he said, suddenly noticing the cross around her neck, "We can go anywhere you like…" It was a beautiful piece and he felt himself getting lost in its centre for a moment. He rose to his knees and took it in his hand for a better look. "Where did you- "

"Don't ask," she replied, knowing full well that now was no time for talking about nuns, or how she felt bad for lying to them.

He could see the weariness in her face and raised a soothing hand to it.

His touch felt electric to her and sent shockwaves down through her body. She kissed him hard and pushed her body up against his. She'd wanted him so badly since they'd met and finally they were all alone with each other.

A hubbub could be heard on the floor below as fresh voices came charging up the stairs.

"You up there Keith? I'll keep this one running 'til that one falls asleep, yeah?" came the familiar oinking, followed by the high-pitched squealing and giggling of Bunny Ears, and some more excited animal noises.

Keith mumbled something that may have been an apology before going over to the hole in the floor and pulling the steps up through it. "We'll be having no more interruptions, methinks."

Minorie decided to ignore Pig's childish shit-stirring. He couldn't touch them now; tonight it was just the two of them in their cave, far above the madness.

She untied the cross from around her neck and threw it into her boot.

As Keith lowered the trap door, he caught sight of her on the bed, teasingly opening the top catches of her black satin corset one by one. It was his favourite so far – black satin just looked so sinfully delicious on the pale, soft skin of this young beauty. That mop of hair really set her apart from the others; she was like some gothic fire goddess, manifest in the body of half-girl, half-woman.

The thought that she was four years younger than him and not yet legal had crossed his mind, but she was very mature for her age, and no judge in the land could blame him for not being able to resist this particular offer.

28

*Besides, it is love, isn't it,* he wondered as he drank in the vision of her stripping on his bed. *She is like no other girl; surely she's what I truly deserve.....*

"Come to me, lover…" she said, replicating the same words she'd spoken every time she'd fantasised about this moment. "I've been waiting for you."

He approached the bed and knelt as though he were approaching an altar. He kissed her satin-clad belly, opening the rest of the corset's catches with one hand, holding her close to his mouth with the other. He kissed the skin of her body then, when the corset fell away, and it tasted better than any joint he'd ever smoked. She closed her eyes in ecstasy and felt his hands search beneath her skirts next, for that inviting pocket of warmth. He found her fishnet stockings and let out a deep, lusty grunt.

From a bedroom somewhere below them, the frantic yelps of adolescent sex could be heard, even over thundering drumbeats and screaming vocals.

Minorie swung her hair back over her shoulder as she pulled him down onto the bed. She climbed on top of him, feeling powerful and afraid all at once. She leaned down to kiss him and rose up again. She wanted to make him wait; she wanted to make it last forever. He grabbed her and flipped her down onto the duvet, which was damp from the cold.      Her   knees   went weak; he was taking what he wanted, and what he wanted was *her*....She knew it and it felt so good, even on the cold, moist bed sheets….He slipped off her skirts before wriggling free from his own fabric restraints. He'd hit the rafters with his head and elbows more times than Minorie could count during the course of his de-robing frenzy, but she figured laughing would only embarrass him and wreck the mood, and she'd heard that was a strict no-no in the bedroom. She crawled under the blanket and eagerly awaited him.

Finally, he lay down next to her. The all-over feeling of skin on skin was like a comfort blanket to Minorie. Her body surrendered completely beneath his and she wrapped her legs around him, allowing herself to get lost in the bliss.

"Keith?" she said, in a whispery breath.

"Mm?" he replied, kissing her neck ravenously.

"Do you swear you don't like that girl?"

He sucked her ear lobe softly and whispered back, "I'm going to tell you a secret….This is my first time too….That means you're very special to me, Minorie."

That was all she needed to hear. With all the girls who'd ever thrown themselves at him, that he was still a virgin too was indeed, very special.

She kissed his lips and moaned softly as he entered. It was a strange thing to think about, one body part fitting into another like that. But thoughts had no power over her now. The feeling of two becoming one was amazing, unlike anything else she'd ever felt. She felt complete, like something had been missing from her life for the past sixteen years. She wanted this feeling always….

And then it was over. She had just begun to feel a rising sensation, coming in waves from both her chest and her knees at the same time, on their way to meet halfway in her lady garden, when a barely audible moan escaped from Keith's lips and his eyes rolled back behind closed lids.

He lay his head down on her chest for a moment and she held it tenderly, picturing all the nights to come when they could do it all over again, maybe even under the eyes of the star gods somewhere…And it would last more than ten seconds.

He shimmied off her and removed the rubber appendage as discreetly as he'd applied it beforehand. She reached over and relit the joint, truly appreciating for the first time what they meant on TV about smoking after sex. She was a woman now and she felt like one.

Keith crawled in beside her and stole the joint from her, mid-toke, with a cheeky grin. She lay down and nuzzled her face into him.

"Make sure and get some sleep, babe," she said, from beneath the blankets, "I wanna get to Carlinn before my parents track me down tomorrow."

He leaned over and kissed her head. She heard him pull out his drawing pad from beside the bed and begin to scratch away at a new picture. The smoke that filled the room was filling her nostrils too, the music could still be heard downstairs, although quieter now, and sleep came upon her like a steam train.

In the dark of the harbour outside some swans preened themselves and did laps around the edge of the rising tide, searching in the fog for a midnight snack. Others slept on the pitch black shore, like rows of perfect white rocks.

Some hopped up stragglers from the party made their way to the water's edge with a pellet gun.

A blanket of freezing white spread over Findair town.

Tine, Flight of Fire

# Gecting In

When Minorie awoke Keith was nowhere to be seen. The trap door was open and the stairs were down. From it emanated the only hint of daylight in the otherwise shadowy room. The pungent smell of damp was more obvious now in the dim grey cold of the morning and Minorie did her best to get dressed beneath the sheets, though it didn't stop her from shivering. When she'd made it down the ladder to the landing she could hear a low drone and some stupefied laughter coming from the living room below. Most of the partiers seemed to have left, though there was a couple spooning on the stained carpet beside her. The girl lay curled up tight like a cat, fast asleep inside her thick hood. The boy wrapped around her looked at Minorie with big saucer eyes and a stunned expression, as though she'd just interrupted him in doing something he shouldn't. She didn't want to know what it was. She was too busy praying Keith had just nipped off to the kitchen to wake her up with a steaming cup of tea.

As she stuck her head in the doorway of the living room, she saw him lying in the middle of a blanket nest on the floor. Using him as a pillow was Bunny Ears, except the bunny ears had somehow made their way onto Keith's head, which was lolling around, taking in every detail of the fascinating mould formations on the ceiling.

On the table beside them lay a half-consumed perforated sheet with a picture of Marilyn Monroe on it.

A strange, crushing feeling coursed through Minorie. "Keith? KEITH? Can you even hear me?" she said in an increasingly panicked whine, feeling the tears coming fast and hard.

His eyes managed to locate her and he smiled a big childish grin at her. "Minooooorrriieee….Magick Minorie with a 'k'….Come into the nest, Minorie!"

"Yay, Minorie, Minorie," chimed Bunny Ears, "Come into our nest!"

"But Keith, what about Carlinn?"

"Ooh," he said, screwing up his face, "scary there…"

"Huh??" said Bunny Ears, feeling genuine terror for a moment before they both lapsed back into ridiculous smiling at each other.

A hot tingling came rushing over Minorie, and a terrible sickness churned in her stomach. She ran for the front door and felt the explosion rise just as she opened it. It splattered, steaming, all over Pig's front step. She took a moment to wipe her mouth and eyes and then she ran some more. She had to get away from that house. Keith just expected her to hang around waiting for him to come down from his trip with Bunny Ears, probably hoping she'd forget the whole thing. And what would she do when she'd outstayed her welcome at Pig's? Did he even care? She found herself standing in the freezing cold of a harbour morning, unsure of what to do next. Between great huffs of tears and uncontrollable wailing, she decided it was best to get out of sight until she'd calmed down, lest someone call the police to report a disturbance

Walking towards the small grove of trees along the harbour's edge, she mentally scanned Findair again, trying hard to think of places she could go. She had a few relatives in town but she didn't know any of them well enough to go dragging them into dramas, especially involving in-family death threats and violence. She'd have felt too ashamed to tell them what had happened with Dad. Odd, she thought, how she had felt so proud telling Keith just the night before how she'd stood up to her father. But then that was different.

She thought of Mam, and how she may never see her again. Suddenly she felt very cold and alone and a dark, chasmic blackness began to penetrate her. She spotted a lone rock almost totally white with lichen and frost. As she sat down beside the huddled group of leafless trees she saw the bloodied body of a majestic white swan laying right at the water's edge. The gruesome remains felt like a powerful metaphor for her life. Ordinarily the sight would have really upset her but now it just seemed to fit. Her gaze honed in on it completely. The plume of pure white feathers quivered softly in the breeze, tainted by the infrequent spatterings of dark red across its breast. Everything else around just faded into non-existence. It was like looking down the barrel of a gun. She never would have guessed it could feel so welcoming.

Just as she was beginning to wonder how long it took for someone to drown and whether she'd be able to stand the cold of the harbour, Minorie heard a rustle from the trees behind her. A quick glance over her shoulder proved fruitless, but as she turned to look again at the swan, a twig snapped among the trees and set her heart racing.

Her eyes searched harder now for any sign of movement – the snap had sounded more deliberate than a scurrying fox or squirrel. Her gaze moved as if being pulled to one particular tree with a wide trunk covered in deeply cracked bark.

For a moment, the trunk seemed to widen, then it wrinkled a little. She blinked a few times in the hopes it was just light playing tricks with her eyes. The trunk ruffled again now, and this time revealed itself to be the skirts of a lady, whose dark face peered out cautiously at Minorie who was fairly sure she was having some kind of stress-induced hallucination. *Nobody that exotic would ever be caught dead in Findair.* The woman stepped out from behind the tree and stood in such a way beside it that she appeared to be a part of it still – it was difficult to tell where tree ended and woman began. She could just as easily have been one of its more sculptured boughs, or the spirit of the tree itself perhaps, here to scold teenagers for leaving empty beer cans and dead swans around her grove.

But no, she was a flesh-and-blood woman; Minorie could see now that her nose was twitching as if she was smelling the air, though her stare never left Minorie. She was wrapped from head to toe in woollen layers the colours of a bleak winter landscape.

"You don't really wanna die, do you, Mamzelle?"

Minorie was dumbstruck. Had this woman been reading her mind or was she just guessing at the motives of a distraught young girl sitting alone at the water's edge in the early morning?

"Well, Mamzelle, you can stay here or you can come with me to la ville, your choice." With that, the woman directed her attentions and her stride towards the water's edge, stopping briefly to lift the dead swan by its leg as she went.

"Did you kill it?" asked Minorie, still not certain that this wasn't merely a prelude to a nervous breakdown.

"No, sha bébé," she said tenderly, "but if them couyons with their guns too stupid to collect their prize, I'll collect it for 'em."

Minorie could see her face better now in the light as she reached into the tide and began to pull at a rope there. There were curious markings tattooed on her forehead and cheeks, and her dark eyes were powdered with black. The rope she'd been pulling drew a small rowboat out from behind the brambly thicket which hung over the water. She carefully fixed the swans wings down by its side and placed it in the boat.

"Are you from Carlinn?"

"You could say that....It's where I live anyways. You comin' or no?"

The woman began to make "push, push" noises whilst untying the boat from its hitch. Minorie took a deep breath and looked at the harbour around her. The mist was pouring in thicker now. The place, decrepit-looking on even the sunniest of days, looked almost pretty when it was half-hidden in fog. She wished that the gods she'd prayed to the night before would send some kind of sign to tell her what she should do next. This woman could be a deranged psycho, maybe hopping into her boat and sailing away with her wasn't the wisest decision. She was, after all, currently talking to a cat that wasn't there.

On the other hand, she couldn't go home in case her evil father tried to kill her and Keith was too busy starting his stupid band with Pig and taking acid with Bunny Ears. *That settles it. There's nothing left here for me now.*

As she stood up to follow this strange woman, a brown and black tortoiseshell cat came tittering out of the grove. It had been as well camouflaged as its owner, who greeted it with "Sha, Menew," and a rub behind its ears. It promptly took a running leap into the rowboat and made itself comfortable beside the body of the swan. The cat's eventual appearance was a relief to Minorie. At least there was still a remote chance this woman was sane.

The woman turned to Minorie and offered her hand in assistance. Minorie took it, stepping carefully up onto the slick, icy rocks and into the rowboat. She'd never been in one before and was extremely unnerved by its erratic rocking, and by the two rope cages full of squirming crabs and lobsters sat at its helm.

The woman chuckled. "Sha, bébé, not five minutes ago you was thinkin' of jumpin' in that water, now you afraid of it, I swear!" She chuckled again at the irony. Her laughter was heavy and spare, as though she'd worked really hard for it and didn't want it going to waste.

"Now Menew sha, we got company, so shove up."

The cat seemed bothered to be disturbed, but nonetheless slunk dutifully to the space beneath the bench. Minorie put her hand down on the bench where she intended to sit, as though that were going to steady the boat to a standstill. Evidently it wasn't, and so she tried her best to put her ass on it instead. The woman took the wound-up rope and stepped expertly onto the boat. "Ok, Mamzelle, let's go home."

The boat cut steadily through the grey, stinking waters of Findair Bay and on around the edge of the peninsula. The coastline, barely visible through the stubborn freezing fog, consisted of cliff faces and stone walls, punctuated by beaches, some small and private, others large and full of shingle and rotting seaweed. Fishermen could occasionally be heard calling to each other in the distance and Minorie was certain she had spotted a surfacing seal at one point. The noise of the ocean was probably its most unsettling feature, especially on a day as ominous as this one. Every time an oar broke the surface, it produced a hollow echoing *clonk,* which emphasised the magnitude of the ocean's lonely, sinking depths. *That sea could swallow me whole and not even notice.*

Every now and then, the woman, who had revealed that her name was Na-Nan, would steer them towards a deserted beach or grassy bank and disembark to gather armfuls of the leaves growing there into a woven basket she carried on her arm. She offered some of them to Minorie to snack on and told her not to eat the others as they needed to be cooked before they were eaten. Minorie asked if she could help with the foraging but was told "Sha bébé, you've had a hard time, just let Na-nan do the work for now."

And so Minorie remained in the boat, stroking Menew and observing the futile struggles of her crustacean shipmates. She thought about home, and about how awful her mother must feel, waking up without her today; if she slept at all, that is. She thought about Keith on the living room floor, oblivious to the maelstrom of utter despair he had abandoned her to. She thought about the sweet little old nun who had been so kind, despite the fact that Minorie was a despicable, undeserving liar. Of all these thoughts, it was those of Sr. Xavier which made her face warm, tingly and tearful once again - her innocence and readiness to believe Minorie's half-baked story. *If only I'd told her the truth.* The nun probably would have brought her somewhere safe for the night, put food in her belly; she could have called Mam to let her know she was ok, and to tell her what had *really* happened with Dad....But no; Minorie had to have her way and she'd choose chasing after guys every time, wouldn't she? *Selfish, lying jezebel that you are*. She didn't deserve the nun's kindness and she certainly didn't deserve gifts-

The cross!

Her hand instinctively shot to her chest, though she knew she'd taken it off the night before. In the same moment, she became aware of a niggling pain in the sole of her foot, which, up until now, had gone unnoticed amidst her other concerns. She hitched up her skirts and removed her boot and found that yes, the cross was there! It brought her comfort as well as relief, as though losing Sr. Xavier's gift to her would just have been a step too far. It had bitten hard into the heel of her foot though; it seems it wouldn't be letting her forget *that* lesson in a hurry....

"I duno about protection though," she said to it, "Where were you when that asshole was taking my virginity?"

"Hidden away in your boot," said another disembodied voice, this time female.

"Huh??" she said, spinning around to find someone who wasn't there. *These voices are getting out of control. People get locked away for less.....*

"Mamzelle, get your boot on, else you get the frissons," said Na-Nan, returning suddenly with more green booty. "Them voices be botherin' you?"

"Just *how* do you know all this stuff about me?"

"Ah bébé, they talk to all of us who will listen."

"And what if I don't *want* to listen?"

"Then don't," she said, climbing back in and picking up the oars once again, "but don't ever forget how hard you listen when you on that dark, lonely road by yourself…"

*Could she possibly have heard me pleading with the gods last night? How could she know?*

Na-nan steered the boat back out to the open waters. She must have had fierce arms beneath those shawls to maintain the pace that she did. Minorie discreetly studied the swirling patterns on her face – the central motif on her forehead reminded her of a flickering fire. Dappled around that were shapes like little stars and arrows.

"Na-nan?" she asked, breaking an almost sacred silence.

"Yes, Mamzelle?" she replied, emitting great puffs of steam from her mouth as she spoke.

"How did you end up in Carlinn?"

Na-nan sucked in a deep breath with the next heave of the oars. "Well, let's just say I know what it's like to be the outsider. Folks on de bayou believed I was dealin' in black magic."

41

"Were you?" said Minorie, after an appropriate pause.

Staring off into the distance, Na-nan seemed to be lost in another time and place. "Ain' no such thing as black magic, Mamzelle, like there ain't no such thing as night and day, it all just depends on where you standin'…"

This wasn't exactly comforting.

Minorie began to re-evaluate her earlier to decision to get in a boat with a strange woman; indeed, probably the strangest woman she had ever laid eyes on. Maybe she had lied about everything and she was *really* going to sell Minorie to some foreign sailors. Minorie had heard there was great money in human trafficking. Yes, she could see it now – Na-nan probably lay in wait every morning for foolish young girls to come along and fall into her trap. And there was Minorie, so fragile and eager to run away from it all, now facing a life in the international sex trade. On the other hand, what if she was telling the truth, but only half of it, and she was secretly planning to use Minorie for some dark purpose of her own? Minorie hadn't had much opportunity to study the ways of black magicians, but her imagination more than made up for her lack of expertise on the subject. The rising fear was surely and steadily convincing her that Na-nan would be dragging her to some hidden cave to use her corpse as a life-sized voodoo doll.

Na-nan chuckled again and shook her head. "Gots the fear, I see."

"Right that does it, *how* do you know what I'm thinking?" said Minorie, becoming enraged by this intrusion of her headspace.

"Haven't you ever been in a room with a really angry person and suddenly felt angry too for no good reason?"

"I guess," said Minorie, wondering if this could have anything to do all those fights she'd had with her father.

"Or seen someone out of their mind with the grief and started crying for 'em?"

This one Minorie had definitely experienced – she'd just thought it was because she was an emotional mess. Even a half-convincing performance in an otherwise rubbish movie could start her off sobbing like a baby.

"So, it's the same thing with fear. When you've felt it enough, you start to recognise it when it shows up. If you got your eyes open, that is. Some people too wrapped up in their own misery to see outside their little bubbles of pain to the bigger picture."

Minorie had always felt that there certainly *was* a bigger picture, and that she'd like to see it.

"So," she said, hesitating. *No, I just* have *to ask,* "What exactly *is* the bigger picture?"

"Much like the smaller one," said Na-nan cryptically, "except bigger, and heavier."

Minorie decided that was enough questions for now.

She had no idea how long they'd been rowing when they reached Carlinn. It could have been days. Her backside had gone numb and so had just about every other part of her body. In real time, she guessed it to be lunchtime. Around the bend of a low-hanging crag, a small exposed sand bank at the water's edge appeared. At one end of it was a rickety wooden ladder leading to an equally weather-beaten jetty above. Na-nan pulled in as close as she could and threw the rope over a low-hanging tree branch before throwing Menew out onto the shore. Menew shot towards the ladder and up it, as though she didn't even notice that it was vertical, then she disappeared. Na-nan motioned for Minorie to follow Menew. Her leap from the boat was heroic, but she still managed to land in seawater deep enough to wreck her boots and cold enough to send a violent shiver rumbling through her whole body. She hoped Na-nan knew the kinds of tricks Mam did for things like rescuing ruined boots and getting blood out of stuff. *And I hope it's warm....When was the last time I was warm?* The half-frozen sand crunched beneath her feet as she made her way to the jetty. *More ladders*, she thought, *because my life isn't hard enough already.* The rungs were coated with frozen green slime and Minorie slipped and almost smashed her face against one no sooner than she had begun to ascend. She made a mental note never to leave home wearing floor-length skirts or ridiculous slippery boots again. Then she remembered that she no longer had a home and this was now the only outfit she owned. *Balls.* As she clambered onto the jetty, she could make out the outline of a most curious cottage through the swirling haze. There was a cluster of ramshackle huts around it made from various scrap metal and timber and everywhere could be seen plumes of sprawling brambles and other miscellaneous greenery. The fog was still so thick that Minorie could see no farther than the large willow tree which stood like a guardian behind the house. *So far Carlinn gets full points for mysteriousness. But magick? We shall see....*

Na-nan appeared over the edge of the jetty last, expertly carrying her basket of leaves on her shoulder. She quickly sniffed the watery landscape, which was barely visible behind her before heading for the cottage, woollen skirts trailing on the frost-tinged ground.

As if out of nowhere, a dark-haired boy with sad eyes and bulky shoulders passed them. He glanced at Minorie just long enough to gather the necessary details, but not so long as to appear inappropriately interested in her presence. The condition of his clothes and his purposeful walk told her that he'd been hard at work and had no intentions of stopping now.

"Hi," said Minorie, but he was already gone and almost halfway down the ladder. He crossed the sand bank and began unloading the rowboat's cargo.

"Come along, Mamzelle," came Na-nan's voice from the cottage.

For probably the first time in her life, Minorie ignored the prospect of a mysterious boy and followed immediately after Na-nan. *Later. Na-nan isn't the sort you keep waiting.*

As she approached the cottage, she could make out a few more of its distinctive details – the driftwood windowsills and rafters which had been sunk into the whitewashed walls to adorn the porthole windows and the weather-beaten door. A large L-shaped porch joined to the end of the jetty and wound around the gable end of the cottage. It was overlooking another, similar dwelling, though the second was smaller by half or more. Both had thin streams of white smoke rising from rough stone chimneys. *Mmm….fire…..*

"No point talkin' to that boy. This month he's learning the value of silence."

"Who's teaching it to him?" said Minorie as she stepped onto the porch and began removing her boots.

The way Na-nan had said that last bit reminded her of the strict Catholic nuns who had taught her in the girl's school. They were always banging on about the *value of silence*, which always struck Minorie as being extremely unfeminist and backward.

Menew had returned and was sitting on the windowsill anxiously awaiting her reward for summoning the boy. Na-nan came out of the door and gave her a fatty lump of skin from some bird or other, which Menew took gladly in her teeth before disappearing again.

"Every person and situation we meet is our teacher, Mamzelle, when we are awake. Everything is medicine. Though, I guess you could call me his teacher; I'm guiding his path for the moment."

"And you told him not to speak for a month?"

"Yes I did," she said, turning to go back inside. "He was talking for all the wrong reasons."

Minorie immediately began flicking through everything she'd said to Na-nan since they'd met, wondering what she would say about *her* reasons for speaking…

"Come inside, Mamzelle, we'll get you warm and fed."

The interior of Na-nan's cottage reflected the coastal landscape of Carlinn as much as her clothing did. Everywhere was textured with reclaimed wood and stone, with scatter-cushioned timber steps built in against the walls, making it difficult to tell where the wall ended and the floor began. The aged driftwood ceiling beams were hung with bunched herbs and garlands which mingled their sweet smells with the smoky undertones of the fire, which was burning inside a hearth so big Minorie could have sat comfortably on a chair inside it. Branches of driftwood stood in every corner and alcove, holding up collections of lanterns of all shapes and sizes. The kitchen space had at its centre a timber table which seemed to be made from old shipping crates. The counters were really just a jumble of free-standing wooden boxes and large cable spools which Minorie guessed to have been pulled from the sea, but they seemed to be serving their purposes quite handsomely. They gave the place an eclectic feel and a warmth that could not be matched by even the plushest designer units.

Na-nan plonked her basket on the table and disappeared through a heavy-curtained doorway to another room beyond. Minorie pulled her handbag off over her head and hung it on the back of the nearest mismatched dining chair.

Na-nan reappeared carrying a woolly pile which she handed to Minorie.

"You can change in there, Mamzelle," she said, nodding towards another brightly coloured curtain in a shadowy corner doorway. "And don't worry about them voices. Sometimes they serve their purpose and sometimes they don't."

Wondering what the hell that was meant to mean, Minorie stepped through the curtain and her eye was immediately drawn upwards to the rows of books on shelves which formed a canopy over the bed. *So this is where she keeps them,* she thought, noting that all wise and exotic people seemed to own mountains of books about subjects she probably couldn't even comprehend. The room wasn't much bigger than the bed, which was constructed from stacked wooden pallets with a rough-looking handmade mattress on top. As with most other surfaces in the house, the bed was laden with patchwork throws and cushions and Minorie wondered if there were any chance she'd be sleeping in it that night; it looked so inviting, despite its Spartan qualities. She didn't dare dream that this place would become her home though; her luck had been pretty fifty-fifty these past few days.

When she sat down to take her socks off, she saw that every wall in the tiny room was a bookshelf – even down behind the bed was crammed with dusty volumes that probably hadn't seen the light of day in several years. The room even *smelled* of books; and the titles….*Possession & Exorcism in the Rituale Romanum, Teas for Your Moontime, Daydreams & Other Dangerous States;* there was even a huge old volume of European fairytales similar to one Minorie'd had as a child. *Before my father burned them all.*

That was the time she'd answered him back and he'd told her that *children should be seen and not heard*. She'd replied by telling him that she was no longer a child. *Not after what he'd put me through*. His response was to burn her story books, all the friends that she had kept so well over the years, never scribbling on them or tearing them. The tales had always kept her company on the long evenings after the arguments, when it was important to stay quiet and hidden until her father's loud snoring could be heard. He'd taken them all and thrown them on the fire that day, dowsing them in petrol to ensure their destruction. "Only little girls need fairytales," he'd said, with the red can poised in his hand, "but you're a woman now!"

When she opened out the clothes Na-nan had given her, she found them to be a knitted floor-length nightdress and matching knee-high socks, in a yarn that was as soft and green as moss. The nightdress was a little too big, which made it all the cosier, though the patterned neckline stretched almost over her shoulders. At the bottom of the pile was a matching shawl with tassels on each corner, which Minorie draped around her like those women in high society movies did, always with their sunglassed noses in the air.

Unfortunate, she thought, that there was no mirror in the room, although something told her there may not be a mirror on the entire property. Na-nan didn't strike Minorie as the 'checking-herself-out' type.

When Minorie re-emerged, Na-nan had put the kettle on to boil above the roaring fire and was busy ladling porridge from a crockpot hanging above it. She had lifted down the shawl she'd been using as a hood, revealing her shock of long, dreadlocked hair. Here and there were singular dreads wrapped in colourful threads and pretty beads of carved wood and stone and clay. Her beauty had been breathtaking in the dank and gloom of Findair's harbour, but here amongst her own things she looked just right, almost motherly, for a woman with occult symbols tattooed on her face.

"Na-nan, did you make these clothes?" she asked, twirling the nightdress from one side to the other.

"No, Mamzelle, that was Audra," she replied, handing Minorie a steaming bowl with one hand and adding a splash of what looked like whiskey to it with the other. "She come on a fishin' boat from the east of Europe to get away from her mean-ass husband and she left the very same way to go back to him, yes indeed."

Her sigh betrayed her matter-of-fact tone. "Boy, could that girl knit. Used to get the wool from them sheep on the mountainside, dye it up herself; even got herself a spinning wheel. It's still in the shed, Blaise says he gonna fix it one of these days…."

Minorie was pleased to see sultanas, banana, honey and a pile of cinnamon mixed through the gooey porridge. She had never tried it before and she hoped Na-nan's choice of flavourings would make it go down easier. Her appetite had returned with a vengeance and she couldn't even remember the last time she'd eaten a proper meal.

"Why did she go back?" said Minorie, still stuck on how someone could be so brave and so stupid, in that order. Mam had tried to leave Dad a few times when Minorie was little, though he'd stopped her each time and threatened to kill them both. She wondered if Mam would have gone back, had she been in Audra's place. *At least Audra'd gotten away….*Mam seemed to have completely given up trying.

Minorie tried a cautious bite of porridge and was relieved to find it delicious. Soon her chest felt as hot as the skin on her knees, which were as close to the fire as she could get them. *That was definitely whiskey she spiked me with.* Minorie wasn't complaining though, and she shovelled in another spoonful.

"Well," said Na-nan through a mouthful of porridge, "some people just can't accept failin'."

"Failing at what, marriage?"

"No, failin' at fixin' the problem," said Na-nan, suddenly ringing a large bronze bell which hung from a rafter above her head.

Blaise appeared almost immediately, silently taking a bowl of porridge from Na-Nan and vanishing back out the door. He didn't even glance at Minorie.

"But wasn't her husband the problem?" she asked when he'd left, feeling that this wasn't a conversation to be had in the presence of a boy, particularly one who couldn't speak up to defend his sex.

"Yes he was."

"So she went back to turn an abusive person into a non-abusive person?"

"Mm-hm," Na-nan nodded, "Course, she'd never actually *say* that. In fact, her mind don't think that's what's happening at all. It's convinced her that she's been a bad wife, expecting her poor husband to put up with her. That's demons at work, Mamzelle."

Minorie wondered what she meant by that, but she couldn't bring herself to ask. If Na-nan had been speaking figuratively she'd sound stupid, believing in demons. *But this is Carlinn, after all.* "So were you teaching Audra too?"

"Yes, she stayed for almost four seasons. She liked my kinda magick, how it works in the shadows and dark places – very like the magick of her homeland. But she'd been thinking about him a lot; I could feel the guilt and the shame of failing eating her from the inside out. Then one morning I got up and she was gone, though sometimes she still sends me nice new socks," she said, standing back from the blazing fire and wiggling her socked toes gleefully at Minorie, bowl in hand. Her large pearly teeth twinkled in the light which poured in from the window. Smiling did a strange thing to her otherwise serious, almost fearsome-looking face.

The patterns on her forehead rose with her eyebrows and her intense eyes softened and gleamed.

"Very nice," said Minorie, shifting around her position on the cushion-filled bench. This was the warmest she'd been since she'd left home. She thought about Mam again, probably distracted with worry by now.

"Are there any phones around here?"

"No, ma'am," said Na-nan, with more than a hint of pride. "Locals said they don't want them lines goin' in and affecting their senses. Say they still gettin' over the electricity lines they put in decades ago. But I can help you get a letter to your Mama if you want."

"You're doing it again," said Minorie, certain she hadn't mentioned who it was that she'd wanted to call.

Na-nan clucked in amusement and disappeared out the front door momentarily, returning with a bucket in one hand and two small knives in the other. Keith would have loved this whole scene, and Minorie felt a bittersweet shade of smug that he was missing it. *No. He's an undeserving scumbag, remember?*

Na-nan sat down again at the fireside and presented Minorie with a knife.

Minorie hesitated, wondering what exactly Na-nan meant her to do with it. She thought it might be some kind of weird 'blood-sisters' ritual and was simultaneously terrified and curious.

"Now we scrape."

*That sounds even worse.*

Na-nan placed the bucket on the floor between them along with newspaper and an empty bowl. From the bucket she lifted a shellfish that Minorie guessed to be a mussel – a bluish-purplish ovular shell with a pearlescent shine – and began scraping the tiny white barnacles from their host, in much the same manner as if she were peeling a potato. She finished the first one and flung it into an empty iron cauldron at her feet, causing a DING so loud it made Minorie jump. She snapped back to reality and prepared herself for the task at hand. At home she had avoided peeling potatoes whenever possible. There was a good chance blood was about to be shed.

Starting slow, she began to find her rhythm with the knife, slicing carefully towards her thumb for the easy ones, and hacking away from herself when she got a stubborn one.

Na-nan got up after a few minutes and brought a tray from the kitchen which contained all the necessary equipment for tea. She placed it on a small upturned crate and filled the teapot, which looked more like a ceramic genie's lamp than a casual bit of crockery.

Minorie filled a weak cup for herself first and heaped in two spoons of sugar from a well tarnished silver sugar bowl which stood upon three legs. The milk was in an old-fashioned glass bottle, like those her mother's mother had used when milk still came fresh everyday from nearby farms. Mam loved to tell her what life had been like when she was young, and Minorie loved to listen. She always felt she understood Mam a little better after the stories.

"You ready yet?" said Na-nan, after a long, meditative silence, where only slurping of tea and the crackling of logs could be heard, along with some infrequent clattering from Blaise pottering around outside.

"Ready for what?"

"Ready for talkin'," said Na-nan, resuming with the mussels. "No doubt you left trouble behind you and found more when you tried to leave. Tellin' Na-nan'll make you feel better."

Minorie picked up her knife again, and took a mussel into her other hand, knowing Na-nan was right. She craved the release of sharing what had happened. The tempest of emotion had been raging inside her all day; the guilt, the fear, the anger, the despair, all of it was sitting on her chest like a sickening, lethal weight, threatening to destroy her.

A voice called from inside her though, a quiet, snarling one which didn't need to shout to get her attention. *She will judge you for threatening to kill your father. You are a spoiled, selfish little bitch who deserves no mercy or sympathy.*

At that moment, the knife slipped and made a thin line of rich red across the knuckle of Minorie's thumb. "GodDAMMIT!" She shoved her thumb into her mouth, just as the salt from the shell began to penetrate the wound. She squealed again and rushed to the basin full of slightly muddied water which served as the kitchen sink.

Na-nan chuckled somewhat inappropriately, "See, Mamzelle, it's just dyin' to get out!"

"Can't you just read it from my mind??" snapped Minorie, feeling herself growing very agitated.

"Ain't no healing in that, chile," she said, rising to check the wound. "You gots to speak those words. And besides, my energy is better spent than just reading people's minds all day…." She reached behind Minorie and opened the drawer of a bedside locker which apparently the first aid cupboard. From behind the mysterious bottles and jars she pulled a handful of rags and found the smallest one to wrap around Minorie's finger.

When she was satisfied Minorie would survive, she gathered up the ingredients necessary to complete the meal of mussels and brought them to the fireside.

"Well, *go on,*" she said, hinting that she wouldn't be asking a third time.

Minorie, feeling the rage coming with every wave of stinging pain, paced the floor a few times before her story began to tumble out, muddled and manic and unabridged. Telling it took so much of her energy and concentration that she forgot about the stinging in her finger.

Na-nan finished preparing the shellfish and hung the small but impressive cauldron above the fire. As she poured and stirred, and the smells of spices and fish began to mingle and rise, Minorie told her everything - about Dad, about Keith, even about Sr. Xavier. At times, reliving it was too much, it was still too raw. The familiar wet streams irritated her already swollen eyes. But she soldiered on, giving every detail she could remember.

Her back was turned to Na-nan when she'd finished; she'd been pacing the same strip of floor the entire time and only now she noticed how worn it was. She wondered how many people had paced it before her, spewing their depressing life stories at the strange tattooed lady.

She turned around sheepishly to resume her seat, expecting an expression of surprise and disapproval to await her.

Na-nan wasn't even looking in her general direction. She was more concerned with her mussels, which were just about ready.

"And what about dreams, I suppose there were some of those too?" she asked, carrying the pot to the table and summoning Blaise from outside.

Minorie had almost begun to say 'No' when she suddenly remembered the dancing and the fire...

"Yes, actually, there was one, right before my Dad went all psycho....I was dancing around a fire at some kind of, like, street party, or a festival....There was a snake going, um, up my leg, to my-"

She couldn't say *pussy* to Na-nan, and she totally refused to say *vagina*, and so she settled for pointing and hand motions instead. Blaise walked in just as she was pointing less-than-subtly at her nether regions. This time he looked right at her before setting about preparing the table for the meal. Minorie felt her face turn purple.

"There was a snake making its way to your *coco*," offered Na-nan helpfully, getting great sport from Minorie's squirming. Only uptight westerners squirmed so easily.

"Yeah...but it never made it that far. I woke up because some guy was shouting at me, telling me to get out." She gasped as the pieces fell together. She'd completely forgotten the voice telling her to get her handbag too; they'd been warning her about her father.

"Who *are* these voices?" Minorie asked demandingly, feeling a panic gush through her, bringing with it unsettling terms such as *schizophrenia* and *possession*.

"Depends. Mostly it's our ancestors, or parts of our own deeper mind comin' to the surface. Sometimes it's the spirits of the nature around us, or guides come to help, but sometimes it's somethin' darker."

"Darker, like what?"

"Darker, like them demons that carried Audra back to her wife-beatin' husband. And like them ones that be tellin' your daddy that the women are up to somethin' evil and that he'd better do somethin' about it."

"And how am I supposed to know which voices to trust?" said Minorie, feeling that even asking such a question sort of made her eligible for committal into some kind of asylum.

"There's a few different ways, all of 'em work much better with experience mind you, and with havin' your head in the right place…" Na-nan said, spooning out mussels and sauce into the three earthen bowls Blaise had laid out for them.

As Minorie took her seat and saw no cutlery, she realised she had no idea how to eat mussels. Blaise must have noticed her ignorance of the etiquette and wordlessly showed her what to do. From the first shell he'd ripped the fish by hand and plopped it into his mouth. Using the empty shell like a tweezers, he then proceeded to pluck the rest of the fish from their respective shells, which he flung into the large empty bowl in the centre of the table.

Minorie smiled a silent *thank you*, and followed suit. The first one was tricky but the skill came easily afterwards.

Na-nan said a quick *thank you* out loud to the sea for feeding them before tearing into the bowl, stopping every few moments to soak up some of the broth with a chunk of the fresh-made bread that filled the basket at the centre of the table.

Minorie felt she should have thanked the sea too, for feeding her and also taking her to Carlinn, but the moment had passed and Na-nan didn't seem to mind. Besides, it was Na-nan who had done all the rowing and fishing and cooking, not the sea.

A soft scratching sound came at the door.

"Oh, sha Menew, bébé; she always knows the exact minute the food's ready," said Na-nan as she got up to let Menew in. Menew purred around her legs in rapturous expectance of the inevitable plate of scraps set aside for her by Mama Na-Nan.

Minorie doubted there'd be much left. The bowl for empty shells was fast filling up and Blaise was already on his second serving. The spices in the tomatoey broth were as warming as the whiskey-laden porridge had been. Minorie found herself converted to another new food, although the texture of the mussels was a little strange. They were as rubbery as they looked, but surprisingly moreish. The bread was plain but fresh and wholesome, and Minorie suddenly felt very grateful to have her needs so amply fulfilled by kindness of strangers.

"This is really delicious, Na-nan. Thank you," she said, as humbly as she could, whilst still shoving mussels and bread into her mouth.

Na-nan nodded at her and smiled as she chewed.

"So are you going to stay for our festival, Mamzelle?" she asked, glancing discreetly at Blaise too, watching for reactions.

Blaise only raised his bowl and lowered his face to it, slurping out the remainder of the soup.

Minorie wondered if Na-nan's question had been an invitation to stay with her at the cottage until then, but she didn't want to seem presumptuous. "I heard something about it alright…it's soon, isn't it?"

"Oh yes, the local couyons be startin' with their *bangers* and beach fires this weekend, and the devilment be comin' with them. They like to mess with everyone. Last year they overheard old Alewise tellin' his workmen they could paint The Mussel Inn with seashells for all he cared, as long as it was finished in time for the feast, and when he woke up the next afternoon, the place was plastered roof-to-floor in purple mussel shells, I swear…." said Na-nan slapping her hand off the table and snorting. "Don't mind sayin' my mussel shells have never been put to better use!"

"So what's the feast about, then?" asked Minorie, eager to hear more about Carlinn's secretive traditions.

"Well, Mamzelle, we gots people from all over the world here, and they all gots different traditions and different feast days, heaven knows we couldn't celebrate 'em all….But the one thing everyone's got in common is their dead. They all make a point of honouring their ancestors, and they all agreed that the ancestors of Carlinn oughtta be feasted too. So every year, as October turns to November, the whole village turns out for feasting and dancing and dressing up and games….and *magick* of course," said Na-nan with a fiendish look in her eye.

Minorie's lips formed a small 'o' as she went to ask *what?* or *who?* or *why?*, but she wasn't sure how to begin in deconstructing the non-magickal reality she'd been living in for the past sixteen years.

"That reminds me, we gotta get that message to your Mama...." she said, rising from the table and leaving Minorie no wiser about magick than she had been before. "Blaise, better get clearing up."

He sucked the last of the juices from his fingers and set about tidying away the dishes and mess.

Minorie sat awkwardly as Na-nan scuttled about the kitchen and Blaise clattered dishes in the sink. *Best to stay out of the way until instructed otherwise. Children should be seen and not heard*, and asking the mute boy for a tea-towel was liable to cause a fuss. *Just stay out of the way, you fucking nuisance.*

Instead she watched Na-nan open the latch on the small window near the sink to make an impressive *cawing* noise out into the mist-choked afternoon.

This grated on Menew's patience and she made an insistent chirping noise at Na-nan and looked at her accusingly from the floor with huge yellow eyes.

"Menew, sha, how could I forget you?" she cooed, stooping low to pick Menew up and rest her on her hip whilst she gathered the last few morsels of fish into a bowl. Menew struggled, keen to get at the scraps, all the while looking into Na-nan's face and making burbling, agitated sounds.

"Yes Menew, I know you could do it faster than me, if only the creature that made you had seen fit to give you thumbs....."

Menew chirped again in agreement.

"And thank heavens they didn't, huh?" said Na-nan, placing both Menew and her bowl of goodies on the floor and stepping over them back to the window.

This time, when Na-nan opened it, a huge black crow swooped in and landed on the sill. Na-nan had kept a mussel aside for its arrival, which she placed before it, stroking its head gently with her knuckle.

"Where yat, Misyeu Crow?"

The crow regarded her briefly before lowering its beak to the mussel, which was gone when he looked up again. Na-nan tittered and placed another mussel in front of him. This one was still in its shell. The crow pinned it down with his claw and prised out the fleshy fish within and then that was gone too. Na-nan looked pleased.

"Alright, Misyeu Crow. You ate my food, now you gots work to do!" she said, removing a thin bracelet of braided leather from her wrist. This too, she placed in front of the crow. This time, when he picked it up, he hopped from one foot to the other, turning himself around towards the open window. "Go on. Tell the old man he's needed."

With that, Misyeu Crow took off into the mists. Minorie had never seen anything like it.

Na-nan called for Blaise and set about putting the kettle on to boil again. Minorie hadn't even seen Blaise leave; she'd been too engrossed in the messenger crow and his near-human mannerisms. *He moves like a shadow, mysterious boy that he is….*

"He's been practicing his invisibility," said Na-nan, so nonchalantly that Minorie didn't even bother telling her to get out of her head this time, nor did she ask how exactly one might go about practicing invisibility.

As she considered the idea, the door opened.

"I need the paper and the p- " Na-nan began, until she noticed that her young protégé was one step ahead of her. Blaise carried a ballpoint pen and some sheets of thick, rough paper with dried flowers pressed into them.

He placed them on the table, keeping his face down in a poor attempt to hide a smug smile.

Na-nan smiled too; a knowing smile, with her lips pursed tight. "See boy? Now you starting to notice what's going on around you."

She leaned forward and slid the pages in front of Minorie, not taking her gaze from Blaise until he had left the room. He'd looked delighted with himself as he'd left. Minorie sensed that if Na-nan were the kind of teacher who gave out gold stars, Blaise might just have earned one, though she wasn't entirely sure why.

"Alright, Mamzelle. You write your letter to your Mama and we'll get it sent off. I'll just be outside. If the kettle boils, lift if off. But for heaven's sake, don't burn yourself again!"

And with that she was alone. The noises of footsteps and tinkering came from outside the cottage and the fire crackled invitingly within. Minorie took a deep breath. *What the hell am I going to say to her?* With her finger she traced the outlines of the flowers pressed in the paper. Should she say sorry for almost killing her father? She wasn't sorry for that though. Even more than that, she intended to follow through on her threat to smother him in his sleep if she found out he'd hurt Mam afterwards.

*Sorry for what, then?* Sorry for leaving her alone with him? That was only half true. She pitied Mam being left behind, and she knew that was largely her fault. She couldn't say she was sorry for leaving though, not truly.

No, Mam had always spoken the truth to Minorie. She respected her enough to leave out the sugar coating and half-truths which would have been so easy to employ when discussing her father and his raging. Rather, she had always stated things just as she saw them, and allowed Minorie to make up her own mind. *All I can do is return the favour.*

"Dear Mam,
  I miss you and I love you. I am safe.
            'Til we meet again,
               Minorie xxx"

She had considered including her arrival in Carlinn, but she knew that would achieve nothing. Her father might intercept the letter and come looking for her. Otherwise, Mam would have to live with the secret, perhaps even wrestling the idea of coming to find her herself. But Mam would never stay with her in Carlinn. It had been obvious that she feared the place for its reputation. *But I need to be here,* thought Minorie, *I'm* meant *to be here....*

Instead she had just released a great heaving sob. Her lip quivered first and took her breath away as the tears flooded her eyes and drip-drip-dripped on the page below her. Outside, it was lashing too. The heavy slapping of rain could be heard on the corrugated iron roof and the porch outside. Seagulls squawked off into the distance. The harder it rained, the deeper and more all-consuming the sobs seemed to become. She thought of Mam left behind. Mam who tried to protect her from Keith, and from Dad. But was Mam really the one being left out, or was it Minorie who had been excluded? *I couldn't play their game any longer, I had to get out, for my life....* And now she was alone and small and afraid, and the grief was pulling her down and down and down.

When she lifted her face to try and catch a breath she noticed a face at the window and froze still, mortified. Her face must be swollen to the size of a watermelon with all the crying she'd done. Her eyes were sore and her face was awash, and the face at the steamed-up window was cupping its hand around its eyes and peering right at her.

The door opened then.

"Our Misyeu Messenger has just arrived, Mamzelle. Got your letter done?"

At that, the kettle began to scream boiling point and Na-nan set about making the tea.

When she looked to Minorie for an answer she said "Don't worry, Mamzelle. Your father won't see your letter. Christy's very good." She didn't seem to notice Minorie's face, nor did the man who presently entered the kitchen, though he looked right at her and nodded his head solemnly.

"This one makes it rain, I see," he said, turning at once to Na-nan and handing her back her bracelet.

"She's one brave catin, Christy. Our lovely Minorie Raine."

"Figures," said Christy, looking to the rain-soaked window and then back to her.

"See her Mama gets the letter," said Na-nan. Then she made tea for them and Christy asked Minorie some questions about the best place to leave the message for her mother. She was surprised at some of the locations hinted at during the conversation, places in and around a home that most men would rarely be found, if they were aware of their existence at all. *Does she empty the lint drawer straight after a wash, or just before the next one? Which make-up compact does she use most regularly? Where does she keep her lady towels?*

She found his choice of term for that last one endearing, especially since he'd said it with such familiarity and sensitivity. She wondered if Christie's wife had ever sent him to the pharmacy to buy lady towels. She found it hard to picture the sort of woman who would wake up every day with his face on the pillow next to hers, never knowing what he would say when he awoke. For all his insight to the female species, there was no overlooking his enduring *strangeness.*

He seemed to be a little beyond the halfway point in his life, with his salt and pepper beard and his wrinkled, lived-in sort of face. A black beanie cap covered most of his head and his clothes were ragged and smelly. He looked, for all intents and purposes, like a homeless person and Minorie couldn't help but envisage the fallout of him accidentally running into her father whilst snooping around her house.

"They all think I'm mad, young one. They take no notice of me. Even if they catch me and threaten the police on me, I always get the message delivered and I'm back on my bike before I've time to fart. They rarely catch me though," he said, allowing himself a cheeky wink of his eye.

She could see how his backup plan might work. The wild and strangely vacant look in his eyes, and the erratic nature of his speech could easily turn aggression to lenience once he'd been categorised as a harmless lunatic, she guessed. *Still, if Dad caught him....*

All the same, Christy and Na-nan seemed confident, as though he'd done this a million times before and Minorie decided not to argue. Instead she found herself trying to figure out if all the crazies on bikes who frequented the streets of Findair were secretly undercover messengers ferrying communications to and from Carlinn.

"Can you bring messages back?" she asked, certain that a few words from Mam could make all the difference in the world in settling her sick stomach and paranoid thought streams.

"No, Miss Raine. Too much risk in getting caught. One-way service only, I'm afraid."

When Christy had formed the bones of his plan, Minorie gave him her letter, folded twice in half and Na-nan gave him a packed lunch and a promise of dinner when he returned.

"There'll be a plate of swan waiting for you, Misyeu Messenger. May Misyeu Solé keep your bones warm." As she said it, the whole cottage lit up in a brilliant glow. It was the first sunbeam Minorie had seen since she'd arrived, as intense as it was unexpected.

"Cycling like a lunatic to the far side of Findair will keep my bones warm, woman. Mister Sun can piss off," said Christy, saluting resolutely to Minorie and slipping out the door.

Na-nan had called Blaise to bring the swan. He had plucked and gutted it and looked quite proud of himself when he slung it onto the table. Minorie couldn't help but notice his warm, yet dark features. She would have described him as the brooding type even if he hadn't been doing his vow-of-silence thing. His sort seemed to be a particular weakness for her, cryptic and deadly.

Keith too had come slinking into her life, barely saying a word. Yet it was obvious that he'd wanted her to pry, to draw from his depths the pain and suffering he'd held inside for so long. He could get her to listen for hours, just by starting with those magick words, *I've never told anyone this before, but....*

She liked to think her attraction to such men was as simple as wanting to avoid explosive, rash men like her father, but she suspected it was something much more sinister. After all, it hadn't done her any favours so far....

"Go present yourself to the mountain, Mamzelle," said Na-nan suddenly, whilst massaging the swan's naked body with some sweet-smelling aromatic sauce.

Minorie froze. *Am I being asked to leave?* Then she remembered, *Carlinn has a mountain.* She hadn't yet set eyes on the landscape of the place and so had no idea how far it might be or even which direction. Her mouth bobbed open and shut like a goldfish at the thoughts of setting off again in the cold. At this time of year, the sky would be black within the next two hours.

"Outside, Mamzelle. Just go outside," Na-nan prompted, smiling and shaking her head, without so much as looking up from the swan. "See what she's got to say to you." With that, she thrust a pole through the carcass and began prodding at it with an iron claw.

Minorie pulled her woollen layers tight around her, hoping Na-nan would remember that she wasn't properly attired for, *for what? For stepping outside? What exactly would the* correct *attire be, then?*

"Go *on*, girl. Mamon ain't gonna wait all day for you and she don't *care* how you dressed...." she said, crossing the kitchen to the hearth and sitting the pole into a sort of spit that Minorie hadn't noticed before.

There was nothing else for it. *Why am I so afraid to go outside?* She ignored the voices telling her that Nanan might lock the door when she went, or that Blaise might be waiting to tie her up and stuff her into one of the small tin sheds in the garden. She adjusted her shawl and opened the door, stepping from the cosy kitchen out into the crisp air of an October afternoon. The mist had vanished completely and the sea had changed from the murky grey of the morning to a vivid green, striped here and there by rich shades of deepest blue. The sky was a pale indigo, fading down into the slightest hint of peachy pink, and the cool salty air filled Minorie's head and lungs. *Now, just where* is *that mountain?*

As she followed the path of the driftwood porch, allowing her palm to slide along the smoother parts of the impressively shaped handrail, she rounded the gable of the cottage and came face to face with Mamon.

The sight of it stunned her at first; she hadn't guessed that such an ethereal scene could be found so close to the place where she'd spent her whole life. The backdrop was a swirl of neon pinks and purples and oranges, which further emphasised the dramatic silhouette of the mountain itself.

In actual fact, it looked more like two mountains, one great peak and one lesser, joined by a ridge which was almost saddle-shaped. The lesser peak was shaped much as one would expect a mountain to be, but the greater peak, well it was something else.

Its climax was distinctly V-shaped, which Minorie knew from geography classes probably indicated the path of a glacier from hundreds of thousands of years ago. But she still couldn't help noticing how uncannily *vaginal* it looked. *And didn't Na-nan call it a she?*

She remembered then that Na-nan had given her instructions. "See what she's got to say to you," she'd said. *And how-in-god's-name am I meant to do that?*

Just then, a little breeze rose, although it seemed to be completely localised to the clump of willow trees at the edge of the property, which began whispering and vibrating suspiciously. In a moment of absentmindedness, her feet had begun to take her down the steps and off the porch, and down a seashell pathway which led around the willows where Na-nan's garden fell away to the sea. The further away from the cottage she got, the more untamed the garden became. Either side of the path were huge bushes which smelled of mint and onion and perfume, and others which had flowers that looked like faces. Everywhere there were blackberries, cascading out of beds and winding around their neighbours, menacing and strangling the entire garden with thick jagged tentacles.

Approaching the willow clump, she noticed lanterns, collections of them, strung up in the branches of smaller trees and even one or two in some of the sturdier limbs of the shrubs. They lined the pathway too, as it split and encircled the willows. As she approached the trees, she saw that they had been lashed together to form an arched shelter above a raised driftwood bench. *The perfect spot for chatting with mountains.* She ascended the three cut lengths of tree trunk which served as steps and took a seat in the mossy-smelling structure, which allowed a full view of the psychotropic landscape. The tide lapped at the hollows in the rock behind her and made otherworldly murmuring noises. "So what now?" she asked aloud, to those same spirits who may or may not have heard her pleading in the dark the night before. "How do I listen to a mountain?"

As soon as the question had left her lips, a humongous seagull shrieked directly above her head, soaring away from her and on towards the sun where it was sinking behind the saddle of the mountain. *It's a start, I guess*. She followed the gull with her eye as it crossed over the roofs of Carlinn, between the poker-straight plumes of smoke rising from chimneys at the foot of the mountain, and from those which sat perched just below the tree line. Marking the boundary of the village was a thick smattering of birches, sheltering the homes below from the arid wilderness of the mountain. Minorie recognised them from their vibrant foliage.

In truth it was the only tree she could identify easily, which had become a source of great amusement to the few other young people who'd lived near her in the countryside. Her late arrival to the area, and her ignorance of even the most common local species had set her apart from the beginning, and made her the butt of many jokes, practical and otherwise. But Minorie always knew birch, even from this distance. The scarlets and plums and golds were unmistakeable. They were like the fireworks in an autumn landscape.

She fancied she could hear the seagull screech again as she watched it rise above the birches, before swooping down amongst them and disappearing. When it did, a sudden wind seemed to lift from that very place, stronger than the one which had beckoned her to the willows. The gust roared through the canopy and whipped up leaves from its boughs with such ferocity that the wind itself seemed to materialise before her eyes as a living, breathing creature, made of multi-coloured dead leaves.

Though it hadn't yet reached her, the whirling creature sent a chill through her bones and set her hairs to standing, bringing with it the distinct feeling that there was another being in her presence.

*It's as natural as autumn leaves,* a voice said, clear and humanlike and unfamiliar, although she knew it hadn't come from a person. She *hoped* it hadn't come from a person. The wind was headed for the sea now, sweeping down the mountainside and across the sleepy village, its tail dragging in some foreboding-looking clouds of charcoal grey which were slithering around the V of the mountains summit like the snake which had wound its way towards her *coco* that night…..

"What does it all mean?!" she shouted into the wind as it roared down over Na-nan's cottage and off to sea. It set all the trees in its path to furious lurching and convulsing. The magickal and serene landscape had suddenly taken on a much more menacing personality. Leaves began to lash at her face and the icy gust pulled at her shawl and nightgown. *As natural as autumn leaves,* it seemed to whisper….

She pulled the wool close and considered running for the house, but the path back was lined with ominously animated greenery. Long loose brambles waved about wildly, like the flailing arms of a man on fire. Around them, bushes careened into each other like a panicked and helpless crowd looking on. *You can't be afraid of the wind,* she reminded herself. *You're a woman now.*

"It's natural as autumn leaves," called Na-nan as she appeared from behind one of the frenzied bushes.

"So you *are* reading my thoughts," Minorie answered, raising her voice to be heard above the hiss of the wind and the crash of the waves.

"No Mamzelle, I'm reading Mamon's thoughts," she cried, ushering Minorie back to the path, back to the warmth of the fireside. Minorie took a deep breath and scuttled after her.

Back at the cottage, Minorie's cheeks flushed red when kissed at the doorway by a sigh of warm air. The gale squealed through cracks around windows and roof tiles. Blaise was seated at the hearth chopping vegetables and flinging them into a small cauldron over the fire. Na-nan inspected his work and gave the swan another turn on the spit and a quick baste with a brush made from a small bunch of dried herbs. A mouth-watering smell of wholesome food filled Minorie's nostrils and made her belly rumble. Even though she'd been fed well since arriving, the sea air was making her ravenous, and made the strange and mingling aromas of new foods seem even more alluring.

"So is Mamon the mountain?" she asked, resolving to find out whether Na-nan was supernaturally gifted, a master at mind-control or a little of both. And there was still also the outside chance that she was just plain nuts.

"Mm-hm," she answered, reaching up to a shelf of salvaged wood to fetch down plates and other assorted pieces of dinnerware.

"And how do you know its Mamon talking to you and not just voices in your head?"

Her response wasn't quite the spurious string of reasoning Minorie had expected. Instead, she simply eyeballed the cross which still hung around Minorie's neck and said "That right there looks like it's made for the job."

"This? It's the one Sr. Xavier gave me…."

"Yes, it's the right shape alright. You can check 'em with that."

Minorie raised an eyebrow and searched again through what Na-nan had just said, looking for some obvious conclusion she had clearly missed.

"Just ask your thoughts, Mamzelle, or your voices, whatever you're dealing with, *are you here to work for my highest good*?" Her hands were gesticulating gently to signal the need for caution when sussing out the true intentions of disembodied voices. "You gotta allow your mind to give you a clear picture of what they look like…..When they answer you, you can picture your cross there travelling right through 'em. If it pass through 'em just fine then they're telling the truth."

"And what happens if they're lying?"

"They explode," she replied nonchalantly, laying the dishes out on the table, "or they gets dragged off by the shadows. Sometimes they turn to smoke; then you gotta be careful."

"Why?" asked Minorie, suddenly forgetting that she didn't strictly believe in magick or occultism, particularly the kind that came with crucifixes.

When school masses dictated a visit to the local cathedral, Minorie couldn't help being spirited away by the heady smoke of frankincense and the epic echoing drama of the place. The services were always desperately boring but the ambience inside the great gothic monstrosity meant she had almost looked forward to her class visits there.

"Smoke can get back inside you when you're not looking, Mamzelle. Gotta keep it out with smoke of your own," Na-nan said, producing a huge, cigar-shaped bunch of herbs from a pocket hidden somewhere in her skirts. She brought it to the fire and lit one end from the weaker of the flames and began to move it around Blaise as if she were swatting a persistent fly.

When she finished, she took the bundled herbs back to the table and motioned for Minorie to rise from her chair so she could repeat the process on her.

"What are you doing?" asked Minorie, feeling the suspicious thoughts creeping back in. "Is this some kind of voodoo?"

"No, chile," she answered, in a tone lower and deeper than her usual one. "What I know is much older….." She seemed to drift off with the waft of smoke currently tendrilling its way around Minorie. It smelled sweet and musky and Minorie could have sworn she could *feel* it, like a breeze that could penetrate skin and bone and rustle the leaves that lay rotting within. "Mind you," she said, returning to her normal matter-of-fact voice, "When the Christians back home found me using the red man's sage for cleaning peoples spirits, I might as well have been calling the dead up outta the ground for the way they treated me!"

"So they thought you were a witch?" said Minorie, imagining what her father would say if she were publicly accused of sorcery. *He'd probably tie the noose himself whilst loudly proclaiming that he'd known all along that his daughter was Satan's handmaiden.*

"Something like that, except they didn't have the decency or the courage to come knocking round my house with pitchforks and torches like folk used to. No, they had their own ways of getting me to leave," she said, placing the smoking herbs into a large clamshell on the windowsill and taking a seat by the fire, where Blaise presented a sample of swan for her approval.

"So that's when you came here?" asked Minorie, who found herself hanging on Na-nan's every word. It was as though her story of being cast out gave weight to Minorie's experiences. It made it feel a little more ok.

"Oh my, no….when I left New Orleans I was a scared mess," she said, still noisily sucking meat slivers from between her teeth. "Worked as a nanny around Louisiana for a few years- " Minorie's expression of mild horror stopped her mid-thought. "Of course I didn't have tattoos all over my face back then; I was as respectable-looking as anyone else."

That made a little more sense.

"You can only hide it for so long though," she said, suddenly staring intensely at Minorie. "They could always sense there was somethin' different about me, and most folks don't trust what they can't put their finger on. I got accused of lots more things and called lots more names before I was led to a place where my heart could relax and be happy," said Na-nan, placing her palm on her chest and remembering.

"And what? You're saying this is going to happen to me?"

"Now you're reading *my* mind, Mamzelle," she said with a knowing smile. "You got the call in your dream; Misyeu Snake and Misyeu Fire are wanting to make your acquaintance. Dreams are very important. You know this."

Minorie took a moment to consider it. *I'm sixteen and homeless, and now this crazy tattooed lady is trying to tell me I'm going through some sort of magickal rite of passage, which seems to mean signing up to be a social outcast forever.*

On the other hand, there was a voice deep down in her belly telling her that it was right, that it was *real*....And quite frankly she didn't have anywhere else to go.

"So would you teach me?" she asked in a pitiful voice that even she hadn't expected.

Na-nan gave the cauldron a stir and puffed with exhaustion. "Chile, we been teaching each other since I found you bawling your eyes out in the docks! Ain't you been listening to a word I've said?"

Minorie smiled awkwardly, becoming noticeably embarrassed.

"But you can stay here, if that's what you mean," said Na-nan, letting her off the hook. "You can have your food and that room," she said, gesturing vaguely to the room Minorie had changed in earlier. "In return for help with whatever needs doing."

Minorie sealed the deal with a nod of ecstatic gratitude. "Thanks, Na-nan."

The meal of roast swan and vegetable stew had been rich and filling, and much more enjoyable than Minorie had anticipated. Na-nan had filled her in on some more of the traditions associated with the upcoming festival, and Blaise had taught her the way of the compost toilet out back before carving a pendulum for her from the bone of a sheep's jaw. Na-nan had said that sheep was a good bone to dowse with because sheep's minds were empty, like a human mind should be when asking for answers from the other side. Minorie had floated off to bed with thoughts of supernatural conversations and festival frolics dancing in her head. Her final thoughts before drifting to sleep had been of Mam, which made the tears come again, and of Keith, which stabbed a pounding pain through her heart and a sickness through her belly. But she'd had no energy left for mourning and had soon passed over into the dreamspace without trying at all.

When her eyes flashed open, she was in darkness. *Where the fuck am I?* More importantly, she wondered what had woken her, until it came again. A shrill howl cut through the night, which was otherwise silent but for the gentle swish of waves. *It's right outside.* Minorie's rational mind knew all the wolves on the island had died out thousands of years ago, but her just-awake mind was in a strange house in a village reputed to be magick, and she was taking no chances.

She shuffled from beneath the blankets to the window beside the bed. She opened a chink in the thick curtain and peered out into the moonlit night. On the jetty at the bottom of the garden, a figure was convulsing and pacing and gesturing at the moon, its breath pluming in the formation of words she couldn't hear. *Na-nan.* Minorie couldn't begin to imagine what she could be up to out there in the freezing night. *Maybe it's a test,* she thought. Perhaps Na-nan was testing her dedication to learning, checking to see if she would run away like Audra.

And so Minorie began to don her clothes, a mixture of her own black garb and the knitted green nightclothes

Na-nan had given her, and made her way to the kitchen. As she entered, a slow, sinister, beastly laugh came bellowing from the jetty. *That couldn't have been Na-nan.* Just when her heart skipped a beat, she heard heavy footsteps approaching on the porch and it skipped two more. She quickly hid behind the door and watched the door handle turn. As she had suspected, the figure who walked through was neither Blaise nor Na-nan and when the opportunity came, she scrambled out the door behind it and across the garden to Na-nan.

Na-nan didn't seem to notice her coming, although Minorie's darting footsteps weren't exactly stealthy. As she approached her, Na-nan was crouched down low with her legs wide, like a spider, and she seemed to be scolding the sea in a language Minorie had never heard before, punctuated here and there by faintly animalistic gurgling noises and nasal whines.

"Na-nan?" Minorie whispered, just loud enough for her voice to carry. "Na-nan there's someone in- "

When Na-nan spun around, her face was contorted beyond recognition, and her eyes were glossy silver pools. She was softly repeating the word *Atabey* between hissing breaths, and sidling up to Minorie like someone possessed, her fingers straining and stretching like a cat's paws. Minorie opened her mouth to scream but only a whimper came out. The smirking face that Na-nan was wearing began to flick its tongue over its lips and laugh a hissing, inhuman cackle.

Minorie turned and ran and didn't look back.

# Secon∂ Sunrise

Jolly music babbled through the steamed-up porthole windows of The Cat Dragged Inn and grizzly-looking old men leaned over its half-door smoking noxious tobacco. Some sailors stood ashore, leaning on barrels and drinking spirits from bottles, whilst others were busying themselves with preparing to sail. Minorie did her best to shrink into the shadows behind some abandoned cargo, which wasn't easy considering her chest was heaving and catching and making her want to cough up gobs of phlegm. *Man, I wish I had a smoke right now.*

She considered presenting herself to some of the less shifty-looking sailors to ask nicely for a lift back to Findair. *They'd definitely rape you and dump you in the sea. And even if they didn't, where would you go? Nobody wants you.*

The warm glow from the windows and the lively music wafting out into the cold night air made the tavern seem welcoming and the crowd of patrons seemed almost friendly compared to the partygoers at Pig's house the night before. *Jeez, that seems like weeks ago...*Dread coursed through her momentarily as she envisaged running into Keith or one of his crew. *No, they're all too chicken shit to come to Carlinn. Keith and Pig and fucking Bunny Ears....All wimps.*

She summoned her strength and managed to keep the tears back. When she was sure none of the sailors were looking, she strode out from the blackness and followed the light cast by the street-lamp overhead to the door of the tavern. One of the smokers had put his pipe away and tipped his hat to signal his departure. As he was saying his goodbyes to his fellow smokers, Minorie slipped past them in the doorway, nodding a greeting as she went. One of them nodded back and said "Ev'nin'" and the questions and objections that she had worried about never came.

Once inside the door, the scene had changed to one of tangled bodies and merriment, and one huge nook in the corner was awash with instruments being plucked and squeezed and stroked and beaten. Around them on one side stood a crush of drinkers all elbowing in to get closer to the music. Everywhere there were people sitting on stools around small tables, or dancing where they could find a space. There were old men with dark-coloured pints in their hands and peak caps on their heads and sailors in beanie caps like Christy's, who drank beer from jugs. Here and there she spotted others who stuck out like sore thumbs and guessed them to be locals. One looked like a wizard and had even brought a giant carved staff which stood in the corner behind him. Another was made up like a sexy vampire, but Minorie was certain she was really a man under it all.

She decided to make her way to what was probably the only empty stool in the place. It was at a table next to the musician's nook and the fire. It was already occupied by two very drunk sailors who were clapping each other on the back and pouring shots of vodka from a bottle. When she sat down they both grinned at her and filled an empty glass for her. They held up their drinks and then each of them shouted a short toast in their own languages. Minorie said "To Carlinn" and gulped the searing liquid. The sailors banged their glasses on the table when they were finished and went back to smiling and nodding and laughing at each other. Minorie gathered that they had no mutual language other than the sea and the bottle of vodka they had almost emptied.

She turned on her stool to observe the crowd around her. The wizard was sitting at the next table. His friend had returned to his seat – another wizardy type, less flamboyant than the first in a brown woollen robe, but no less dramatic. Minorie allowed herself to stare at them, hoping some magickal beacon might mark her out as a potential student. *It's either that or freeze to death at closing time.*

For a moment, the second wizard looked right at her and pointed a finger in the air, before turning to finish his thought to his companion, who sipped at his goblet and rolled his eyes. *They didn't even notice you. I told you, nobody wants you...*

She turned back to the sailors. The older-looking and more tanned of the two filled another shot for her. They made their salutations and drank again. This time when they banged their glasses, one of them looked like he'd had a light bulb moment and produced what looked like a joint from under the edge of his beanie cap. The other sailor's eyes lit up and he smacked his buddy on the back and made excited noises of approval. They beckoned Minorie to follow them outside and she was powerless to refuse. *Thank the gods, a smoke at last.*

Minorie now took her turn at leaning on the half-door, puffing delightedly on the weed, which felt to be much stronger than what she'd been used to in Keith's. *No more shitty weed for me, no sir....*Her whole body relaxed, although her heart was racing, and the older-looking sailor was saying "Many thanks, many thanks," as she passed him the joint. She looked out to the dark harbour and the bobbing boats, getting lost in her thoughts and clouds of sweet-scented smoke.

"Now there's a girl who looks like she's in the wrong place," called a voice from just behind her. *Shit. Rumbled.* She looked over her shoulder at her accuser. It was a sailor who was more well-spoken than he had a right to be. He pulled a pipe from his pocket and filled it.

"So what, boys only tonight, is it?" she said, turning back to look at the boats. "Or is it because I'm so young and impressionable?"

The man chuckled and put his elbows down on the door next to hers. "Oh my, I was right about you," he said before sucking a long draw from his pipe.

When Minorie's fury forced her to look at him, he was no longer a sailor, but the plainer of the wizards she'd seen inside. She hadn't realised his beard was so long, but now she could see it was trailing well out over the door towards the ground. She tried not to look surprised. *Maybe the weed is just playing tricks.*

"Yes, the red hair gives you away as a bit of a firecracker. Ms. Merryweather's going to have her work cut out with you."

"*Who?*" She'd had enough of being patronised by her father and the nuns and everyone else, and she didn't care if he *was* a wizard.

"You can't miss her, on the side of the mountain. Just look for the sunbeam," he said, and he was gone. This time Minorie did a full three-sixty, but there was no trace of him at all. *Floated back to his sunbeam, it seems.*

Inside, strangers sat at the table where he had been, and his companion's staff had vanished too. Luckily, her sailor friends had somehow got their seats back and were beckoning her over for another shot of vodka.

The band struck up a tango, slow and grinding and punctuated by loud clapping, where everyone joined in. The crowd parted and the vampire lady strode in to take the hand of a short man in a pinstripe suit and gangster hat. Minorie threw back her drink and her head began to spiral with the building climax of the song.

When she awoke there was a man standing over her, although he was far away, and the ground beneath her was rocking.

"You're lucky you survived that one, lassie," he said in a thick gravelly voice and she realised why when her body began to shake and tremble violently. Around her face, her hair was frosted and she couldn't feel her hands or feet, though someone had at least thrown a blanket over her. When she tried to sit up, her clothing made a disconcerting *crack* and she saw that it was white with frost. The ground began to rock harder and her head was pounding.

"Careful how you go," said the man above, extending an arm to her. *Christ. I'm on another fucking boat....*Even though she was now more experienced at manoeuvring in rowboats her feet would not come easily to her. Between the deadly cold and the hangover, Minorie reckoned there was a good chance of her ending up in the sea. *It's where you belong. Nobody wants you. Even the sailors didn't bother to take advantage of you.* She could just about see in the vague light of dawn, yet somehow she managed to stand up and, keeping her frosty blanket wrapped as tightly around herself as she could. With some difficulty, she even made it to the top of the salt-eaten ladder, where the man handed her a hip-flask, from which she gladly took two swigs. It tasted a bit like whiskey. Ordinarily she wouldn't have been able to keep down more alcohol when suffering from a hangover as monstrous as this one, but something told her stomach that its heat might yet save her life.

"We have to sail, lassie," he said, taking the hip-flask back. For a moment Minorie hoped *we* might have included her. "Are you sure you'll be alright here?"

She wasn't sure of that at all and she didn't remember saying so. But reading between the lines, she knew it meant there was no room aboard for sick little girls. *Nobody wants you.*

"Where are you sailing to?"

"We'll be heading north to fish."

"Oh. Uh, yeah. I'll be fine," she said, eager for him to leave now so that he wouldn't see her cry. He nodded politely in gratitude that she'd let him off the hook and he walked off into the mist. Behind her, the half-door of The Cat Dragged Inn was shut up tight and its windows were dark. Her trembling had slowed somewhat after the slug of whiskey, and her hands and feet ached as the feeling returned to them. She sobbed softly, which made her head hurt even more. She sat on the nearest stone bollard and held herself. "Hey gods, I need you again," she said, to the misty sea.

She heard a dull *whomp* noise in the distance. Another, slightly louder one followed it. This one made a movement in the mist, which curled and twisted furiously after the third *whomp.* After the fourth, a great set of white wings came into view, flapping awesomely above the water. When the swan rose and began to climb high into the sky, the clouds suddenly parted, revealing a rosy sunbeam which swept across the dim horizon. *Look for the sunbeam.*

She wasn't sure if the sailor or the wizard had said it, or how much she could trust either of them, but it was all she had to work with for now. Or was it? She put her hand into one of her pockets and found Sr. Xavier's cross and her sheep bone pendulum. She held the cross up in front of her, aiming it just above the horizon, as Na-nan had described, and she imagined it passing through the pink sunbeam. At that moment, the beam seemed to explode as a purple grey cloud moved aside to reveal a neon sunburst. *Wrong sunbeam, I guess. And didn't he also say something about the mountain?* Minorie turned to find the great vagina in the sky and could barely make out its outline through the lingering clouds and mist. *At least the sun's up. I might still live.* She rose from the cold of the bollard and began to take small limping steps towards the harbour's exit. The road was a tunnel of bare branches from which the dawn chorus of birdsong was just beginning to swell. The cottages Minorie could make out were still sleeping. *Just as well. I must look like such a mess.* Another, quieter voice in her mind said, *You* are *a mess…*

Juicy bunches of blackberries dotted the hedgerows along the road. She feasted on them by the handful, silently pouring out her thanks to the gods of ditch food. The berries stained her hands purple and their pips stuck in her teeth, reminding her that she must find a toothbrush somewhere, and soon. *Oh yes, Madame Minorie must have her modern conveniences. Spoiled bitch....*

Just as she reached a familiar-looking opening in the road, the sun began to chase off the mist and the clouds, illuminating Carlinn like a newly-fed flame. Minorie could hear shutters opening nearby, and the chattering conversations of the village merchants. The medieval stone gatehouse at the southern entrance to the village had a jack-o-lantern head on a spike in its window. She'd almost forgotten about the Festival of the Dead. It seems the rest of the population of Carlinn had certainly not.

Each crooked-looking little shop and inn was apparently trying to outdo the last in decorative displays of carved pumpkins and creepy dead branches draped over cobweb-laden bales of straw. One particularly grizzly display even featured a live black cat wearing a witch's hat of patchwork velvet and feasting on a breakfast of fresh animal entrails. *At least I hope they belonged to an animal....*The doorway in which that display stood was one of the few on the cobblestoned street which was already open and Minorie could hear the bustling sounds of life within. She poked her head in and saw a portly woman wearing a patchwork apron and hat that matched the cats. She was sweeping the floor with an old-fashioned broomstick and humming a lively tune. She seemed to sense Minorie almost immediately and spun around to catch her.

Minorie showed only her face to the witch, hiding her blanket and mismatched layers and her sticky, purple hands on the other side of the threshold. *No point hiding. Even your face will give you away as the useless bitch you are. Nobody wants you.*

The witch coughed nervously and made an effort to straighten up her own clothing for her first customer of the day. "Ah welcome, welcome. Come in, dear girl. Please excuse me, I'm not used to early morning callers, you see."

Minorie pursed her lips and stepped through the door, waiting for gasps of disapproval. Instead, the witch placed her broomstick aside and said "Rough night, I see," before disappearing through a red velvet curtain to a back room. "Have a look around whilst I'm making us some tea!"

Minorie couldn't help but grin like a fool. *Tea sounds so damn good right now...*

Whilst the witch clattered about in the back, Minorie inspected the contents of the shelves around her more closely. One contained the skulls of small animals, whilst the one below contained pipes and flutes made from various bones. In one dark corner was a glass-fronted display cabinet containing miscellaneous glass bottles of all colours with labels reading *Abortifacient* and *Venereal Restorative* and *Consecrating Oil*...Minorie wondered if they were given complicated names because they did embarrassing things.

In the centre of the shop floor was a collection of clothes rails marked by a sign reading "Finest Festival Apparel". She had a quick rifle through them. Ordinarily she'd have been keen to try on every dress in the place, but today it was hard to be excited. The silks, feathers and velvets would have to wait until she'd acquired the important things, starting with a place to stay, followed soon after by a hot shower, she hoped.

"Now, dearest. Come sit and have some tea and bread, this morning's batch."

Minorie took a seat behind the counter, where the witch had a small electric fan to blow hot air onto her shins. Minorie thought she'd died and gone to heaven as she sunk her teeth into the soft brown bread, which was still warm and piled high with creamy butter. She sweetened her tea with two sugars and poured in a little extra milk, so she could gulp at it immediately. It felt as warming as whiskey or vodka, but without the unpleasant taste. There was even a ginger biscuit on her saucer to dip into it. The witch had thought of everything.

"Thank you," she said, managing to remember her manners as she reached sheepishly for a third biscuit.

"Huh? Oh, yes," said the witch, through a great ball of half-chewed brown bread which was tumbling around in her mouth like a beanbag in a washing machine.

"I like your shop. And your cat."

The witch simply nodded, not even trying to push another sentence through the bread ball in her mouth, which currently seemed to be winning the struggle for territory.

"How did you get him to wear the hat?" asked Minorie, who was aware of the fundamental un-trainability of cats, as well as their total disdain for wearing clothes.

The witch's jaws expanded and contracted once or twice more before Minorie saw the bread ball go down her wrinkled throat in one monstrous lump. "We have a deal," she answered.

"I didn't know you could bargain with cats," Minorie said pondering the sorts of terms and conditions a cat may propose. "Would you teach me?"

"Oh no, dearie. I'm no teacher, just a simple seller of goods the teachers need. Besides, my house is barely big enough for my own children, without taking in a clatter more," she said, laughing to herself and envisaging the carnage.

*Nobody wants you. You're a parasite. Run home, foolish girl.* The rejections hurt more every time. But Minorie wasn't prepared to give up just yet.

"The wizard told me to look for the sunbeam. I came from Na-nan's but- "

"Lovie," the witch cut in, "you mustn't talk about your teacher, or what they taught you. The teachers don't, well, they don't all *approve* of each other's….methods. It can be a touchy subject. Best not to bring it up." Her face lightened then, and she had a nibble at a ginger biscuit. "You'll find Ms. Merryweather's more easily if you go before the sun climbs high. Just follow the smell of bread to Madame Neige's bakery on the hill. You'll see the sunbeam clear as day from there."

Minorie took the hint and gathered her blanket about her once again. She stalled a little so as to soak up a few more hot blasts from the fan. She'd been so desperately cold outside and was only now beginning to thaw out. The thoughts of facing the icy air again made her want to cry. But she was finished with tears. *You're a big girl now. Suck it up.*

Finally, when she couldn't prolong it any more, she began to make for the door, where the costumed cat was cleaning its whiskers.

"Thanks again for the tea and eats," she said, forcing a courteous smile.

"Not at all, dearie. Come back to me when you're sorted and we'll get you dressed for the festival. Shop rules, you know. Festival virgins get a free costume!"

*I only wish I was a virgin,* she thought as she stepped out into the piercing cold. Though she knew that wasn't true. Even though Keith had proved himself to be an ass, she was happy to have tried sex. She felt somehow more like a woman now, even if she was a silly homeless one.

The low sun illuminated the grey cobblestones of the Carlinn's square, to the point where they could have been made of gold for the sparkle they gave off. It made Minorie's eyes and head feel as though they were about to explode.

She emerged from the mouth of the street onto a large, rounded plaza. To her right stood The Mussel Inn, complete with its purplish-navy pearlescent seashell cladding. It really was quite a remarkable sight. At the centre of the plaza, Minorie saw a huge bowl-shaped structure made of black stone, with ornately carved skulls covering its outside. The square was lined with more pokey, interesting-looking shops with imaginative displays in their windows and doorways. Minorie had dreamed of finding such a place when she was a child, playing around with wands made from twigs and potions made from muck and leaves. As she passed Mrs. Birch's Broom Shop, Minorie caught the sweet, homely aroma of freshly baked bread rolling gently down the sloping mountain road on the other side of the square, and she knew she was on the right path. She started across the plaza and up the hill to follow the scent

Whilst passing another shop she averted her eyes from two men who were struggling to manoeuvre a cauldron so big that either one of them could have fit quite comfortably inside it. Perhaps even both of them, if they'd been neatly butchered first. She could feel them looking at her as she hurried past, and she couldn't bear for them to see her face. Neither did she answer the man who wished her a cheery good morning from the threshold of his music shop.

With a glance, she could see the bakery ahead, its bouquet of fragrances becoming more intricate as she approached. Along with bread now, she fancied she could make out the smells of cinnamon and stewed apples, chocolate muffins and thickly iced cupcakes. No doubt she'd have been able to buy herself a comforting treat to fend off the headache if she'd remembered to lift her damn handbag before she'd given up the comfort of Na-Nan's. *Dumb, broke, silly bitch.*

Beyond the bakery there were only tree-pocked ditches and stone walls as grey as the clouds which were utterly refusing to move on. The broken concrete of the road was smeared with slimy, decaying leaves of the early autumn falls as they melted back into the ground.

She began to wonder about this sunbeam she was meant to be heading for, and the house it would bring her to. What would this Ms. Merryweather think of her showing up at dawn, wrapped in a skanky blanket? And was she really to suppose that the door would be opened wide to her? After all, she'd been so lucky to meet Na-nan the way she did, what right did she have to expect such hospitality a second time?

And then it appeared, just as she rounded the corner on which Madame Neige's Bakery stood. It looked like a second sunrise; golden pink at its base, fading up through fiery reds and oranges – a spotlight from a sun that wasn't there. She couldn't yet see where it touched down to the earth and so she quickened her pace along the road. Its gradient took her a little higher up the mountain before it levelled out and gave her a clear view of the house nestled quietly in the sunbeam.

She hadn't expected it to look so *unnatural*. In truth, she hadn't thought much about what she *should* expect from Ms. Merryweather's; she'd been in a daze since seeing Na-nan in the moonlight the night before. She felt somehow unprepared for the sight of citrus trees in full fruit amongst an icy landscape of dying leaves and bare branches. As she drew nearer, she saw that it wasn't just fruit growing in Ms. Merryweather's frost-free garden. There was a huge vegetable patch to the side of the house, with rows of lush edibles growing contentedly in their personal, permanent sunbeam.

By the time she reached the gated entrance of the quaint yellow house, the true sun was well above the horizon, making the supernatural shaft of light around the house seem less surreal. Ms. Merryweather's was built in a slight dip on the side of the mountain, so the contrast between it and the autumnal landscape was not so stark. Minorie could see from here how one could easily convince oneself that this was a never-ending summer rather than a questionable manipulation of the laws of physics. She gulped hard and stepped up to the door.

It didn't open immediately when she knocked. In the moments she stood waiting, her mind scrolled through a selection of grizzly outcomes. Voices told her she was doomed, others told her to run, or to go back to Nanan's. She told them all to shut the fuck up. When she did, the top half of the door opened.

There stood a woman in a bright pink dressing gown, rubbing sleep from her eyes. "What?"

"The wizard….he said to come here," she said feebly, looking down at the ground.

"Oh," said the woman, unlocking the bottom half of the door and pulling it open. "Come on. You can have Lisa's old room."

"Thanks," she said, but the woman had already turned away from her. Minorie entered the house, which was inexplicably shadowy for one that was permanently sunlit. She gingerly followed the woman she assumed to be Ms. Merryweather through a dark living room, across one corner of a kitchen to an even darker corridor, at the end of which, a door was opened before her. No sooner than she had stepped through than the door was shut again and she was left alone in overwhelming blackness, broken only by the faint crack of light where the blind had crept away from the window. She noted the singular click of the latch. *At least she didn't lock me in.* She made her way towards the window and lifted up the blind. The room was flooded with warming sunlight, revealing its contents to be a single bed, a bedside locker and a huge old armoire, which filled one whole end of the room and almost touched the bottom of the single bed, but for the space in which Minorie was standing. She sighed as she fiddled with the cords of the blind to raise it a few inches from the sill. She was glad the night was finally over and a little sunlight would remind her of that as she drifted to sleep.

She shrugged the cold, damp blanket from her shoulders to the floor. The air in the room was warm, as warm as Na-nan's fire-lit living room had been. Except there was no fire here, just the artificial sun outside, warming the house and its contents like a heat lamp over day-old sausage rolls. Minorie sat on the end of the bed and slipped her boots off, wriggling out of her top next, then standing up to lift her nightgown over her head. Her muscles ached in their exhaustion. Her mind was numb, yet running at the speed of light. When she'd cast the last of her garments into their pile on the floor, she squished her toes into the carpet beneath them and did her best to stretch out her limbs. The last time she'd been naked was in Keith's, where she'd shuddered with the cold almost constantly, and the damp had caught hard in her lungs with the deep breathing of their lovemaking. She was pleasantly surprised now by how good it felt to move, liberated, through the warm, clean-smelling air of her new digs.

When she lay down on the sheets, they were crisp and cool and smelled of lavender. It brought her right back to crawling into bed after Saturday night baths and the first time she'd discovered sleeping without her pyjamas on. As her head sunk into the puffy pillow, she thought of Mam. But she was too tired to miss her, or to feel guilty or angry. She was too tired to wonder if the letter had reached her, or what she must have felt when reading it. She was beyond musing over how lucky or unlucky she'd been at The Cat Dragged Inn the night before, and too drained to be thankful for still being alive and relatively unharmed. Deeper and deeper she sank and sleep took her almost at once.

She dreamt of a thick wooden pole in a fire pit, and the fire licked at her feet and dress, and tight, scratchy ropes bound her sweaty ankles and wrists. The people looked on intently but nobody stepped in. Nobody spoke up as the fire got closer and hotter, as it began to sizzle her shins. Nobody seemed to hear her screams. *Nobody wants you.* She smelled burning hair and meat and her whole body felt as though it were being stabbed by a million searing knives.

She awoke still bound, rolling and struggling and gasping for breath. The sheets had coiled around her in a claustrophobic embrace and Minorie panicked more with every moment she was unable to free herself. She could still feel the ropes around her limbs and the fire….

When she'd finally pulled the sheet from around her sweating body, she sat up sharply, disturbed from her frenzied dreams and wondering how long she'd slept. She reeked of sweat, filth and stale beer. Her head felt tight, though not as sore as it had been. The light from outside looked more like that of an afternoon sun now, rather than the rich sunrise hues it had been displaying when she'd arrived.

From the other end of the house she heard a door open and voices were laughing and chatting. Minorie looked to her sad pile of stinking clothes and sighed. By the time she'd pulled them on again, she felt so dirty that she wasn't sure even a hot shower could fix it. She opened the bedroom door and found the corridor outside still in darkness. She couldn't remember which door had brought her from the kitchen and accidentally opened two wrong doors leading to more pitch black rooms. Her wandering hands had found no light switches, and for a moment she imagined she might never find her way.

Her cheeks were flushing red from embarrassment by the time she'd turned the correct door handle and found herself in the slightly brighter kitchen, before two girls who looked to be of an age with her.

One was pale and gaunt-looking and her hair had been shaved very close to her scalp. Minorie wondered if it was cancer from all that excessive sunlight. She was dressed in plain, loose garments of green cotton which rippled softly when she stepped forward and said "Hello and welcome" in much the same manner as a disingenuous tour guide would. She even had the same half-assed smile. *I guess cancer will do that to you,* Minorie thought as she allowed the girl to take her hand in a cold, clammy handshake that would have put a dead fish to shame. "My name is Grace," she said, before turning to the other girl. "And this is Omelia Varley, a Priestess of the Serpentine Sisters of Heart Hill."

"*Soon-to-be* Priestess," the girl objected. "For now I'm just Omelia," she said, smiling a warm and full grin. She too took Minorie's hand, but startled her by lowering her lips to meet it. She kissed the pale flesh on the back of Minorie's hand and said "Enchanté". When she'd finished she looked expectantly at Minorie, who was stuck for words.

"Minorie," she managed after a moment of staring at Omelia. "My name is Minorie Raine." Minorie had never had her hand kissed before, let alone by another female.

"Beeaauutifulll," said Omelia, who was dressed in a floor-length kaftan with a teal and turquoise kaleidoscopic pattern on it. Her eyes twinkled green like emeralds and her fair hair was bunched up in a matching jewelled headscarf. She looked every inch the High Priestess, despite her young age. "Minorie Raine," she said slowly and carefully. As she did, her fingers were wiggling in the air and silver glitter streamed from them like rain.

"Isn't she amazing?" said Grace to Minorie, who was awestruck. "Come. Mary can't wait to meet you!" she said, gleefully beckoning Minorie to follow her through the back door to the garden beyond. *Mary now too…How many girls* live *here, exactly?*

The garden outside was like a fairytale. Rosebushes faded to honeysuckle and lupins, which faded to perpetual primroses and black, velvety tulips. Wisteria and grapevines lined archways and encircled the windows of the house. Everywhere were little nooks and hidden pathways, marked by lanterns and sculptures and decorated trees.

"Every girl who's ever stayed here has left her mark on this garden," said Grace, as she led Minorie and Omelia past a huge, white-painted gazebo and down a corridor of bamboo plants. It opened out suddenly into another, more intimate little garden, with a golden statue of some fat, cross-legged deity sitting at its centre. "This is the meditation garden. It was mostly my work, with a little help from Scarlet."

"I told you not to mention that name," called a voice from beneath a tree at the rear of the garden. The words were noticeably musical, like that of someone who didn't want to be perceived as nagging, but who very clearly *was* nagging…

As they walked on and the speaker came into view, Minorie saw that it was Ms. Merryweather, reclining on a sun lounger in the shade of a tree. As she sat up, she took a sip from the glass at her side and shifted her sunglasses onto the top of her head.

"Minorie!" she exclaimed in an exuberant manner that took Minorie by surprise. "I want you to forgive me for my little *mood* this morning, *so* unlike me….I *do* hope we can start again. I'm Mary Merryweather, as I'm sure you'd gathered, and I see you've met my daughter Grace and my other lodger, Omelia."

"Of course," said Minorie, massively relieved. "It's so lovely to meet you all and to be here. Thank you so much for letting me stay."

The girls beamed at her, and Omelia took a seat at a nearby bistro table, gesturing at Minorie to join her.

"Grace, love, would you be a dear and fetch us a nice bowl of strawberries." Grace turned to do as Mary had bid. "Oh, and please fill up Mummy's drink for her," she added, making a pouty face and wiggling her glass in the air.

"I told you, *Mary,* I want no part in your addiction, and enlightened beings don't have *mummies*," said Grace, turning again and leaving.

"Grace? GRACE!" called Mary, to no avail. "*Do* excuse me," she said politely to the girls, breaking into a slow awkward run after Grace, empty glass still in hand and flip-flops slapping wildly beneath her feet.

"Of course," Minorie found herself saying again, though she couldn't remember when she'd even begun using the phrase.

When she was safely out of earshot, Omelia turned to Minorie and said "They're both mad, you know." She puffed out a sigh and sat back against the intricate curved back of her wrought iron chair.

The tone of her voice told Minorie she was being deadly serious. *How should I react to that?* What if this were some kind of test, to determine if Minorie would fit in here? Or what if Omelia was just shit stirring and wanting to pull Minor into her twisted game?

"I mean, I love them both to *bits*," Omelia continued. "It's just that…..well….you'll see for yourself soon enough anyway. Just, whatever you do, don't bring any boys around…."

"Boys?" asked Minorie, confused.

"Ooohhh!!" squealed Omelia, without warning. "Now I can have company for the festival! We simply *must* go shopping for costumes….Have you got yours yet? Have you heard about the Procession? Mary and Grace would never- " She calmed down noticeably when Mary reappeared, stomping across the meditation garden in her swimsuit and sarong, muttering to herself.

"Omelia, you missed half the broccoli this morning, are you going to let the carrots rot back into the ground too?" she asked unceremoniously as she threw herself down onto the sun lounger.

"Oh, you're so good to remind me," Omelia answered cheerily, completely ignoring Mary's snarling tone. She stood up at once and discreetly twitched her head at Minorie, who followed suit.

Omelia didn't speak until they were well out of the meditation garden, midway down another winding pathway, which had a little stream running alongside it, and a trellis tunnel above it that teamed with succulent-smelling lilacs. "Changeable like the weather, you see," she said finally. Her voice had taken on a more melancholic ring. She had stopped now to sit on a little bench carved from a hunk of driftwood. From her sleeve she produced a large joint. The match seemed to appear, already lit from a pocket on her hip that Minorie couldn't see, despite her best efforts. "But, mother always said that watching the weather is as powerful as talking to the goddess herself."

"What?"

"Weather prediction.....you have to practice to get good, see? But it's a *very* worthwhile skill. One of the basics, I'd say."

"Don't the carrots need....something?" Minorie asked, half-terrified that Mary would appear around the corner, and half-ecstatic at the smell of the fresh-sparked ganja.

"She doesn't really care about her carrots," said Omelia, trying not to exhale. Smoke stole from her mouth anyway like S.O.S. signals. "Besides," she continued, allowing the clouds to gush from her lungs now, "If they wanted them, the people would be breaking the door down at this stage. But even Mr. Savage hasn't dropped by," she said, handing the joint to Minorie. "Usually he's too sickly to take his goats up the mountain when the weather is poor and so he gives them vegetables instead. However, it's been so mild recently, and with the ample straw harvest this year,

Mary's lost a lot of bulk orders that she was depending on, poor dear," she finished, remembering her manners.

Minorie sucked a long draw from the joint before passing it back to Omelia. "How long have you been here?"

"I've lived in the sun for three years now," she said somewhat wistfully. "Mother decided I should learn the ways of weather and to harness and utilize it. To become a Priestess of the weather," she said rather proudly.

"And have you?"

"Do you think I'd still be here if I had?"

"Maybe. Who wouldn't want blazing sun twelve months a year?"

Omelia just giggled. "Oh Minorie, you sweet thing. Come on. Let's get you a wash and some clean clothes."

She stubbed out the joint and led Minorie back into the darkened house, through one of the doors she had accidentally opened earlier.

Inside, Omelia sent the blind hurtling upwards, revealing a charming bathroom, furnished by a standalone bathtub and matching antique fixtures.

"What's the deal with the black-out blinds?" asked Minorie, when she was sure no-one was listening.

"It's the only way to stay sane, really," she said, turning the bronze faucet and waiting for the water to steam before she put the plug in. "Plus we'd broil alive in here if the house were to be stewing in constant sunlight. We come inside when it's getting dark for everyone else, to try and stay on local time," she said, laughing breezily. She sat on the edge of the tub and added a thin line of rose-pink potion to the gushing water, along with a small sack of dried herbs that she had produced from one of her hidden pockets.

"Thanks," said Minorie, sitting on the lid of the toilet to remove her boots. "It seems I've hit it lucky ending up here."

Omelia turned very serious for a moment, and stared intensely into her eyes. "All that glitters is not necessarily gold, Minorie." She broke her stare to rise from the tub and approach a little door that was midway up the wall behind her. Inside were piles of fluffy towels, which Omelia rifled expertly through, producing one to place upon the rail for Minorie. "It won't be a free ride. There are vegetables to be pulled every day of the year. Your body won't thank you for that. And the psychological effect of living in a permanent daylight….Well, neither your body *nor* your mind will thank you for that."

She looked again at Minorie and smiled. "Are you shy?"

"Huh?"

"Do you always bathe fully clothed?" she said, positively grinning now. "Oh go on, get yourself ready and I'll find you something to wear."

"Thanks," said Minorie, now smiling too. *Clean clothes. Another prayer answered.* She began stripping immediately, to show Omelia that she wasn't shy. *Why should I be, after all?* Though she couldn't remember the last time she'd been naked in the presence of another female.

Thankfully, Omelia had gone by the time she got that far. The bath was still filling up, but the hot, misty water looked inviting. Minorie dipped a toe in. The warmth embraced her foot like a brand new fleece sock and so she slid the rest of herself into the tub, releasing a long, growling sigh of pleasure as she did so. The bubbles didn't quite cover her boobs, and so when Omelia came twirling back in, Minorie instinctively moved to cover herself with her hands. *Why are you shy?* a quiet voice asked her from within, compelling her to put her hands back down beneath the bubbles.

"I found this for you, it's perfect," said Omelia hanging a draped lace creation on the door. Through the bellowing swirls of rising steam, Minorie could make out a pretty dress with thin straps at the shoulders and layers of dusty pink and cream cut asymmetrically to give it the bohemian edge. Wearing it anywhere else in Carlinn at this time of the year almost certainly would have ended in pneumonia, but Omelia was right – it was perfect for living in a sunbeam.

"So will I learn magick now that I'm here?"

"Magick is hard, Minorie," answered Omelia in an unexpectedly patronising tone.

"Obviously. Hence the teachers, right?"

"It's not that simple. Learning to actually *do* magick is one thing…..Having the magick learn about *you* is quite another. It brings you to the brink of insanity, takes away everything you think you know, and everything you *think* you love…."

"There's nothing I love, except maybe my Mam, and she's already gone." Minorie reclined against the high back of the bathtub before continuing. "As for insanity, the last two days of my life have brought me as close to that as I reckon I'm gonna get without falling over the edge."

"You're confident," said Omelia, grinning again. "The universe is going to just *love* you!" They both giggled then, even though Minorie wasn't quite sure she'd gotten the joke.

When the bath was full, Omelia turned off the water and opened the window, glancing cautiously outside. Minorie had expected her to leave, but she once again produced the stubbed joint from an invisible pocket and began puffing at it, sending the smoke out the window amongst clouds of flowery-scented water vapour.

"She was in one of those laundries, you know," she said, passing the joint to Minorie.

"What laundries?" asked Minorie, hunching forward and trying her best to get at least some of the smoke to go out the window as Omelia had done.

"You know the ones that were run by nuns? The ones where they sent the *fallen women*?" answered Omelia. Minorie wasn't sure she knew what a fallen woman was, but by Omelia's eye-rolling and air-quotation marks, she guessed it was an unfair title.

"I guess I've heard of them…." she said, though she was fairly certain she hadn't.

"It was easy to end up there in those days. They'd send you for getting pregnant in your teens, or for getting pregnant by a man who wouldn't marry you. Sometimes they'd just send you for being too pretty."

"Which one was Mary?"

"I suppose she was a little of all three. The local priest had taken a shine to her, being such a gorgeous young thing. Have you seen the photographs of her, by the way? She really *was* something…."

Minorie shook her head and passed the joint back.

"Well anyway, after the good padre had invited her to perform his *special errands* for him, she found her belly began to grow."

Minorie was wide-eyed and embarrassed. *Why is she telling me this?*

"That was when they shipped her off to the laundry. The nuns seemed to especially hate her because they *knew* the baby belonged to the priest. They would take her outside and tie her to the statue of the virgin and leave her there all night, in the rain or even in the snow."

"Didn't she just tell them that he'd raped her?"

"Pfft. Nobody cared. They maintained that she'd seduced the good man from his oath and that she would burn in hellfire for all eternity."

She offered Minorie the joint, but Minorie declined. Her head was starting to spin.

"Why are you telling me all of this?"

"So that you understand her a little better, and maybe not judge her so harshly…"

"I-I wasn't….But you said- "

"What I said earlier is true, about them being mad. But wouldn't *you* be after that? Wouldn't *anyone*? In truth I think she's really brave. She's survived so much…" With that, she stood up to leave. "So, lazy bones. You have guest rights for your first day, and tomorrow, we harvest," she said, smiling as she closed the door after her.

Minorie's mind was reeling. She felt guilty for what had happened to Mary and guilty for judging her, though she wasn't sure why. She also felt guilty for having been called lazy and wondered if the option to drop out of work and take a luxurious bath had been a test of her willingness to earn her keep. But above all the feelings of guilt and inadequacy, her outstanding thought was, *How could so many horrible things have happened to someone with a name like Mary Merryweather?* The irony was almost palpable.

She decided she'd had enough of bath time, but she could still smell smoke and sweat and dirt in her hair. Quickly, she gathered consecutive handfuls of the other bottled potions Omelia had assembled by the bath for her, and lathered and smoothed them through her hair and onto her skin. Everything looked to be handmade and smelled of various flowers and essences. The sticky humidity of the bathroom was intense, and rinsing herself off had felt somewhat similar to drowning in heat. She gasped momentarily at the fresh, slightly cooler air from the window as she scrambled out of the tub and allowed the swirling air currents to dry her skin. When the room had stopped spinning, she shimmied into the delicate-looking dress and spent a few minutes posing in front of the mirror in the corner. *I wish Keith could see me now. Bunny Ears wouldn't have a look in. And she doesn't know the first thing about magick....*

Minorie gathered up her hair in the fluffy towel Omelia had left for her and unplugged the bath. As the water gulped loudly and eerily down the drain, Minorie stepped from the sunny bathroom into the cool and darkened heart of the house. She felt her way back to the kitchen where Grace was preparing food.

"Oh dearest, Minorie, won't you have some sprout salad and cold soup?"

Minorie was mildly horrified at the prospect but she was starving. She hadn't eaten since the bread and biscuits the witch had given her that morning. *Or was it yesterday morning?*

"Uh, yes please. I'd love some," she answered somewhat unconvincingly.

"I see we have a carnivore in our midst," said Grace, turning away from a worktop full of glass jars which were each full to the brim with various green sprouty things.

Minorie glanced around her to make sure they hadn't been unexpectedly been joined by a leopard.

"I mean *you*, silly meat-head," grinned Grace. Even her smile was condescending. "It's only vegetables around here, I'm afraid. But I know the secrets to making them delicious."

Minorie forced a smile back at Grace, whose gaunt face and shaved head she found rather unnerving. "I've been meaning to try more vegetarian food," she said, cool as a cucumber. "I can't wait to taste it."

"Great. Well you can join Mary in the garden until it's done," she said, flashing one more smirk before turning back to her sprouts. As Minorie stepped outside, she'd have sworn she could hear her speaking to them.

The warm air enveloped and caressed her once again. It even smelled of sunshine. She was transported back to long rolling days in July and August at home, when Dad had stayed late at work. Afterwards, he'd often go drinking until well into the night, and Minorie and Mam would have the whole place to themselves for the day. On those days Mam would potter around their large, vivacious garden and prepare delectable salads and hamburgers for dinner, and Minorie would laze around in the shade of the tree-covered mound of rock in the corner of their field, which she'd named the Fairy Rock, for the armies of bluebells which overcame it every Maytime.

There were bluebells in this garden too, but they were all mixed up with foxgloves and lupins which, at home, bloomed long after the bluebells. She found the sight of them all fighting for the same spotlight to be simultaneously spectacular and unsettling.

In the small courtyard just before the bamboo corridor she came across Mary sitting in the gazebo, still sipping from her misty glass and doing a crossword. She'd surely heard Minorie's footsteps crunching along the gravelly portion of the pathway, but she hadn't looked up from her newspaper. *What's that supposed to mean?* Another voice answered, *It's obvious; you're not wanted here.* She pivoted instead in the direction of the meditation garden, intending to leave Mary to her puzzle, but as she approached, Mary looked right at her. *Is that annoyance in her eyes?*

"Minorie! I trust you enjoyed your bath?" Her tone was more welcoming than Minorie had expected.

"Oh god, yes," she answered, stepping up into the gazebo and taking a seat across from Mary. "I felt like I hadn't washed in a month!"

Mary scrunched up her nose and twisted her lips into a polite smile.

"But of course," Minorie continued, realising how common she'd sounded, "Omelia laid out all the toiletries a girl could ever want."

"Oh good. She makes them all herself, you know. Naturally, she still has a lot to learn, what with her young age, but she *does* try…I can't use them myself; they make my skin all blotchy. When I tried her oatmeal exfoliation paste, my face positively ballooned. I couldn't go outside for a week!"

Minorie's hand shot to her face. She'd shovelled the stuff on in great squelching handfuls. She hoped the red glow it had produced was just that of freshly-scrubbed skin. She didn't think she could handle a fully-fledged break out on top of everything else she'd just been through these past few days.

"So have you been to the vegetable garden yet?"

"No, not yet. I saw it from the road, though. It's very impressive."

Mary scoffed at that. "Oh a few years ago maybe. This year it's in ruins. I tell you, those girls just don't give a damn about carrots and onions rotting back into the ground. I even saw some giant hogweed taking hold in the bottom corner!" She sat back in her chair and adjusted her robe. "They don't know how good they have it, you see. They don't know what it's like to go without. You know when I first moved here, people survived the winter on those deplorable, chewy velvet shank mushrooms from the forest and whatever foul, vinegar-soaked leftovers they had from the summer. By February, the only vitamin C they were getting was from the last of the fuzzy strawberry jam. I'm surprised the scurvy hadn't wiped them out years ago. When I arrived and coaxed in my little sunbeam, they called it the Vegetable Revolution." Her face beamed as she said that last bit.

Minorie hid the desire to giggle behind an air of fascination. "They're really lucky you came along."

Just in the nick of time, Grace appeared soundlessly carrying a tray which she laid on the table before them. From it she lifted a bowl each for Mary and Minorie, along with two large serving bowls. One was full to the brim with the tangled mess of dreaded sprouting things, swimming in a swamp of oily liquid; the other was half full of indistinguishable cubes of vegetable, smothered in thick pink goo. Minorie might have savoured their appearance more had they been dolloped on top of a juicy steak.

"I'm sure Mary's been regaling you with glorious tales from the Vegetable Revolution," she said, as she slopped great piles out into the bowls for the diners.

"If it weren't for my vegetables, you'd have starved years ago," was her mother's reply. She said it in a way that at first seemed playful as a kitten, but slowly revealed a lethal edge, as if the kitten had been hiding a samurai sword behind its back.

"This looks really good, Grace," Minorie interjected, hoping that a little mannerly small talk would be enough to melt the tension, which was currently thicker than the pungent pink chunks on her spoon.

"The cold soup is my speciality. I like to make it from the harvest of the day whenever a new girl arrives. Today it's carrot, radish and pea, with the gift of an egg from Mr. Duck thrown in for good measure. Of course, the *real* goodness comes from the sprout salad. I always say that vegetables grown to fruition are nothing but a waste of good energy."

Mary rolled her eyes and snorted.

"Didn't you bring a bowl for yourself, Grace?"

"Oh no. I eat very little, you see. My body no longer requires that kind of nourishment. I have progressed onto the nil-by-mouth stage of my evolution. Occasionally I consume some fallen hazelnuts or a cup of nettle tea, just to remind my body that it is human." She smiled enigmatically and lifted the tray. "Well, enjoy!"

When she had disappeared around the side of the house, Mary began to poke suspiciously through her mingling mounds of food. "She calls herself *breatharian.* I'm sure it is how we were all meant to live, like she says. But I told her, I just can't take that final step with her. I would have nothing whatsoever in common with my friends any more if we weren't sharing meals….And what would the locals say about a vegetable producer who wouldn't eat her own vegetables? No, it just wouldn't *do* at all."

Seemingly satisfied that nothing unusual was lurking in her bowl, Mary began to eat. Her face betrayed her surprise at the curious mingling of flavours. In Minorie's first mouthful she could detect the sharp kick of pickled beetroot which gave the cold soup its neon colouring, and it was wrestling with something so earthy it could have been soil, except it crunched when she bit it. The recognisable whiff of boiled egg was grappling for its corner too, and gave the whole dish a distinctive undertone of fart.

"So Grace just doesn't eat?" asked Minorie. Having tasted her food, she believed she could understand why.

"She doesn't need to. Her body is completely sustained by *prana*."

"What's that?"

"Life force energy," answered Omelia, as if from nowhere. "The stuff of creation. Some Christians would call it the breath of the Holy Spirit. But Grace isn't Christian, obviously." She seated herself beside Minorie and began filling a bowl that Minorie hadn't even seen her carry over.

"Well, Holy Spirit or *prana*, whatever you call it, it's obviously working for her. Doesn't she look so healthy? She works all day and meditates all evening and she still has the healthy glow of an athlete," said Mary, without even the faintest hint of sarcasm.

Minorie almost choked on her sprouts. "Mm," she found herself concurring, through splutters and strangled coughs.

"So Minorie," said Omelia, completely changing the subject, "Will you be joining us for our little ritual tonight?"

She wasn't sure what to say. '*Ritual*' could mean any of a number of things, all of which seemed to invoke images of hooded figures and blood sacrifice.

"Don't worry," Omelia reassured her. "It's really fun. It's just tea." She had a roguish glint in her eye.

"I won't be here," said Mary coolly.

"Oh what a pity. We had such fun the last time."

"Yes well, I have….things to do."

"Well don't worry. We'll be up good and early to get everything down for market."

Minorie made more agreeable noises and nodded her head. She intended to show Mary that she was a keeper. *If I have any say in the matter, this will be my new home. It's time to stop running.*

"I hear the pranks have started," said Omelia between giant mouthfuls of cold, wet food. She seemed to be completely immune to the cacophony of incompatible flavours, and was already closer to emptying her bowl than either Mary or Minorie were. "Jenny Magee called earlier for a bag of onions. She told me she intends to cover them in chocolate and leave them on a tray on her father's stall, just waiting for unsuspecting thieves to snatch them up. She also said that Mrs. Aldron's massive cauldron had been placed atop the highest tree in the village."

"Maybe she'll brag less about having the biggest one in Carlinn," said Mary, revealing more than a hint of jealousy. "Well once they stay away from my house, I don't care what they do."

"Surely *no-one* would be silly enough to try and fool *you*. The people of the village have such *great* respect for you, Mary," said Omelia with commendable sincerity for one who was so clearly pandering.

Mary knew it too, and she shot Omelia a look that would curdle milk, although her ego was satisfied at the compliment. "They know what side their bread is buttered on," she said, sipping authoritatively at her glass.

By the time Minorie had forced down as much of the meal as her stomach would take, the light in the garden had begun to turn crimson and gold. The sun was setting behind the mountain, whose crude peak had lost its suggestive shape at the angle from which it could be viewed in Mary's garden. From here it just looked like a regular-shaped mountain, pointy at the top with steep sloping sides dropping away from it like the swinging skirts of a fine velvet skirt, coloured in greens and browns and purples which intensified beautifully in the warm glow of the sunset.

Mary had excused herself and left the girls to go and prepare for an evening excursion, without ever disclosing to them where she might go. What was stranger still, was the fact that Omelia never asked her, or seemed surprised that she might leave them unsupervised for the night.

"She does it all the time," Omelia told her. "*You* can ask her if you like." But Minorie knew she wasn't that brave. Standing up, Omelia added, "Come on, you don't want to be out here when the sun sets. *Very* confusing for the brain."

In actual fact, Minorie *did* want to see what it felt like to stand in the only sunlit part of an otherwise black nightscape. She imagined it would be something like standing inside a rainbow. She wasn't, however, prepared to risk her place at Merryweather's to find out and so she obediently followed Omelia back to the house.

Once inside, the house felt like a different place. Far from the collection of dark and dingy rooms Minorie had awkwardly felt her way around earlier, it had been transformed into a cosy cave of ambience and comfort. Smoke from intoxicating incense curled gently around the room and filled Minorie's nostrils and, it seemed, her very being. Soft, warm light radiated from table lamps in every corner. Omelia led her through to the living room, which was also awash with candlelight, which made interesting shadow patterns across the walls. Omelia knelt and lit the pre-laid hearth fire, which began casting a flickering glow over the low coffee table in front of it, atop which there was an intricately arranged tea tray and place settings for three.

Grace entered behind them wearing a flowing ceremonial robe of indigo, with a sash of cerise pink across one shoulder. In this light she almost *did* look healthy. "So do you like what I've done with the place?" she asked them chirpily, like a little girl bursting to be told how good she is.

"It's….it's awesome," said Minorie, still drinking in the soothing familiarity of the scene.

"Marvellous job, sister," smiled Omelia, bringing her hands together at her chest in prayer position and bowing her head to Grace, and then to Minorie. "Shall I begin?" she asked, raising her hands into the air and closing her eyes with a deep inhalation.

"Actually," Grace interjected, "I thought *I'd* host this evening, considering I'm at such a powerful stage of *being* right now."

Without missing a beat, Omelia smiled graciously and said "Oh, of *course*, sister. You really *must*. I don't know *what* I was thinking of."

Grace beamed at her victory and closed her eyes as Omelia had done. As she raised her hands into the air she said, "By the power of the mountain and the sea, your humble servant beseeches you! "

"*Servants,* dear sister," corrected Omelia, raising her own hands and signalling for Minorie to do likewise. "We are three."

"Of course," said Grace, squinting one eye open to see if they were watching her. Minorie was. She'd rarely been around people who even acknowledged magick, let alone practiced it. *Finally, I'm where I belong.* She noticed there was no milk or biscuits laid out on the table and guessed it was going to be no ordinary tea.

"By the power of the mountain and the sea, your humble servants beseech you! Come sit by our fire, whisper to us in the winds and bless us with your presence this evening. Oh, spirits of the Fae, keepers of the magick, we ask that you open the door of knowing for us, and guide us through, that we might, without fear, carry out your work upon this earth with our hearts open and willing. Blessed be!"

"Blessed be," answered Omelia, opening one eye and winking it at Minorie.

"Blessed be," said Minorie, wishing she knew what it meant.

Grace lowered her hands to her heart and for a moment stood, catatonic, with a strange, vacant sort of grin on her face. Omelia lowered herself to the piles of cushions strewn about the coffee table and began making herself comfortable. As Minorie did the same, Grace seemed to come to and knelt carefully and purposefully in front of the table. She muttered to herself before lifting the lid from a canister of fine china, removing from it a large pinch of some dark substance that looked like spiders legs and placing it in a strainer in the top of Minorie's rose-patterned cup. Minorie tried to make out what it was. *Even for herbal tea it looks strange.* And then it hit her.

"Are those *magic mushrooms?*" she whispered furiously at Omelia. Omelia smiled at her and gave the faintest of nods as Grace muttered again and filled Omelia's strainer.

Minorie was in shock. She'd never had much of an interest in *real* drugs, but magic mushrooms had always held a certain fascination for her. That they just *grew everywhere* seemed to her as though the universe were perhaps hinting at something. Keith had always been talking about them, too. *Jesus, I'd barely thought of him at all today...I wonder if he's realised his mistake yet,* she thought, picturing him howling like a baby and tearing his hair out in mourning for his lost love. She'd thought they might do "shrooms" together this autumn, but she had secretly worried about the possibility of Pig and the others being there. If anyone was going to fuck with her trip, it was him. *But here I'm safe, aren't I? These girls are spiritual, and they understand magick.*

*They are inviting me in. All I have to do is walk through the door of knowing....*

Minorie looked to Grace, who had finished doling out the 'tea' and was now filling each cup carefully from the small cauldron which had been hanging above the fire. *Haven't these people ever heard of electric kettles?* When she had finished, she sat back and said "Now we brew," smiling that watery smile of hers. "You can set your intentions for development now whilst we wait, if you like."

Intentions for development sounded hard, and like something Minorie certainly hadn't prepared for.

"Don't mind her, Minorie," said Omelia, half giggling. "Shrooms need not be such a serious business. In fact, *the giggles* are one of their greatest gifts. What do you think, dear sister? Poor Minorie's had a dreadful time making her way here. Wouldn't you agree that what she *really* needs is a good old laugh?"

Grace didn't do a very good job at hiding the bitter taste this left in her mouth, though the watery smile barely broke at all.

"Of course, dear sister. I know not everyone is able to maintain the same dedication to their evolution as I am. Sometimes I forget to slow down and allow others to catch up."

Even Omelia wasn't going to jump for that one. She simply flashed her own sort of watery smile back at Grace. Minorie detected a tension hanging in the air like the bum note that brings a nervous musician to an abrupt halt. In the firelight, expressions on their faces seemed to change every instant, turning into a myriad of people, some who Minorie knew and some that she didn't. *Stop freaking yourself out. You're about to trip, remember?*

"Well, if you'll excuse me, ladies," said Grace, getting off the floor and lifting her cup in both hands.

"Oh sister, you're leaving us?"

"I feel an intensive evolution session coming on," she said, trying to sound humorous, but falling flat once again.

"Blessed be, sister. I'm sure you'll hold the space beautifully for us, said Omelia, raising her cup as though she were toasting to Grace. Grace reciprocated and left them.

"She often prefers her own company for magick," said Omelia politely when she had gone. "So…shall we?" she said, allowing her mischievous smile to return.

Minorie hesitated. "What will happen to me?"

"Sweet Minorie. You can just sip at first, if you like. There is no pressure. Then, with any luck, you will become deliriously happy and positively fascinated by everything around and within you." The way she said it made it sound so irresistible. "You might notice your heart rate go up or down a little, but it's important to remember that it will do you no harm. We are nature within and without…." she said, in a manner more profound than Minorie had ever heard spoken by someone her own age. *Even Keith and his philosophising friends don't get that deep…* "And besides, I'll be here with you every step of the way."

Minorie resolutely lifted her cup to Omelia's and *clinked* them together. "Bottoms up," she said, allowing the devilish smile on Omelia's face spread to her own face now too.

They removed the strainers from their cups and sipped, then sipped again, as though one were a mirrored reflection of the other. Then Omelia gulped back the whole cup and a moment later, Minorie followed suit.

She got up and beckoned Minorie to join her on the sofas. Omelia chose the large, squishy cream one and threw herself amongst a nest of cushions and throws. Minorie sprawled out on the green chaise longue facing it. It was a similar colour to the nightdress she had taken with her from Na-nan's, but it was softer, plusher. She lay back and looked at the shadows flickering around her. Her heart was racing already at the thought that she had put a foreign substance into her system, one that would, at best, leave her a giggling fool, perhaps even similar to the state in which she had found Keith and Bunny Ears the previous morning. The image stabbed at her heart. *How could he do it?*

"So, is there a special someone?" asked Omelia dreamily.

"Not anymore."

"Let me guess. He wouldn't come with you?"

That caught Minorie by surprise. *Am I really so transparent?*

"You'd be amazed how often it happens. Some kids get sent here. Many others come because they had no other place to go. Of course they will have begged their friends and their special someone to go with them, but almost always, the answer is no."

"*Almost* always?" asked Minorie, intrigued to know how many special someones in ten would have said yes.

"Well, sometimes a sibling will come, like the O'Mara twins. They were destined to never part. The locals say they will even die at the same time."

"Pity I didn't have a twin," said Minorie, with no attempt to hide her bitterness.

Omelia ignored her and went on. "And then there is the infamous case of Lady Marmaduke and her faithful darling, Orwell. Now *there's* a romance to be jealous of. The good Lady had been promised by her parents into a life totally devoid of magick and filled instead, with performing the duties of a wife to some dribbling old fool. Excuse me, some *rich,* dribbling old fool, to whom her father owed a great deal," she said, rolling up onto her elbow so as to look at Minorie. "Well Lady Anna and Orwell both knew that her inheritance would be up in smoke if she did not obey, but they threw caution to the wind anyway and crossed the country to come to Carlinn, where Lady Anna's innate skills would be nurtured and celebrated, and they could be together forever without fear of her father."

"Yeah that is pretty romantic," she said, not even believing her own words. It just felt like having salt rubbed into her wounds.

"Oh, but the true romance is in the tragedy, you see. Their journey had been long and hard. There were few cars in those days and hitch-hiking wasn't yet popular, and so they had walked every step of the hundred or so miles they had crossed. The little money they'd had had run out before they'd even made it half way, and by the time they arrived here, they were starving and emaciated. Poor Orwell had caught pneumonia and by the time they got to him, it was too late. They later said that he must have looked like an animated corpse as he led her through Findair and on to the village. They couldn't believe he had lasted the whole journey. Lady Anna was beside herself with grief, and truthfully, I don't think she ever fully recovered. She still wears all those elegant old gowns from the twenties. I think under it all, she wishes to remain in that time with him, the way he remained with her, until his last moment." Omelia fell back onto the sofa and let out a swooning sigh.

"You mean she's still alive?" asked Minorie, rolling over to see if Omelia was being serious.

"Oh yes, very much so. Apart from a few laughter lines around the eyes, you wouldn't even know that she was over one hundred years old. Her hair is jet black, and I'm *convinced* she doesn't even dye it. She's a good friend of my mother's family, you know," she said, rather proudly. "A total recluse, of course. But every now and then she sends for me and we have tea together. Oh Minorie, you simply *must* meet her. She has the most *wonderful* stories…"

"Yeah, sometime," said Minorie, suddenly feeling inexplicably anxious. Her heart began to pound and the butterflies in her stomach began to flap frantically, rising towards her chest and falling again, over and over, until she wondered if she weren't going to puke all over the expensive-looking chaise longue.

"The fairies are coming, I see," said Omelia, noticing the deathly shade of pale in Minorie's face. She rose from her sofa and sat at Minorie's feet, taking them in her hands and beginning to massage them.

Minorie shifted awkwardly and searched Omelia's face for signs of lust. *Is she flirting with me?*

"Just relax, Minorie. Focusing on your feet will help you forget about your heart. I used to do it for Scarlet too when the mushrooms made her jumpy. Close your eyes and be still until it calms down. You're going to be just fine."

Omelia's words were amazingly comforting and so she lay back and decided to let go of it all. *Who cares if she fancies me? Maybe girls make better special someones than boys anyway….And who cares if Keith loves Bunny Ears and Pig and acid more than he loves me? I don't need him. I mean, look at how far I've come without him. And who cares if Mam….*No. She still cared a great deal for Mam. The thought of her would have brought tears to Minorie's eyes if she'd let it. *But now isn't the time….Now I am letting go; letting go of anger, letting go of fear. So what if my heart's about to stop? So what if I die? So what if I live?*

Images from the past few days gave way to images of the supremely beautiful Mamon, as she had seen her from Na-nan's garden. The pinks and purples of the sky melted into the waves around her, which ebbed and flowed as steadily as the seasons and Mamon stood, like a proud chalice, overlooking and guarding all. Inside the chalice, it seemed that the flame of the setting sun had kindled a fire, which was burning passionately next to the clouds, like a torch on Mount Olympus, lighting the way of the gods as nightfall threatened. The chalice began to overflow with light as it oozed like liquid gold from Mamon's fount and down towards Carlinn, towards the sunbeam…..

When Minorie opened her eyes, the shadows on the walls were writhing like snakes. *Mr. Snake and Mr. Fire are wanting to make your acquaintance.* Another voice said, *So what?* She looked at Omelia, who was still holding her feet, though she had stopped massaging them. Her eyes looked larger and blacker than usual, but not sinister. She had taken on a more elfin demeanour, one which suited her roguish smile perfectly. Minorie grinned back at her. The snakes were now more like branches overhanging a secret fairy grove that they had stumbled into, or had they been born here? She couldn't remember, but she could *feel* the magick all around her, even *inside* her; there was no separation of the two. She and Omelia belonged to this place, as it belonged to them, and no-one could touch them here.

"They're *here*," said Omelia, in a high, sweet voice, like that of a child full of wonder.

"I know," said Minorie, hearing now that her voice had changed too. She began giggling uncontrollably, and she saw Omelia observing her giggle as it crossed the air between them and made its way into her mouth, down her throat and into her belly, where it began to rumble and shake in the heartiest laugh Minorie had heard in an age. She couldn't tell how long they'd laughed for, or how long they'd been in this special place, when she felt it begin to melt away. And now they were just Minorie and Omelia alone in Mary's living room. *Mary and Grace's living room. But Mary and Grace aren't here. They aren't here because of you. They don't want to see you high on their sofa. They'd have nowhere to sit. They don't want you here.*

"Did we do something wrong?" asked Minorie. Her voice still child-like, which gave her question a tone of such profound and innocent worry that even Minorie heard it. It was like watching herself at five years of age, crouched behind the bed, watching her father trying to strangle her mother, roaring at her "Which of us do you like best!?" and not knowing what her answer should be. She wanted to hug that little girl, to take her away from all that adult unpleasantness, and to show her the magick grove, where all little girls are welcome. She felt her face change to an exaggerated frown.

"Oh Minorie, we love you, Minorie," Omelia sang in the voice of a happier child. Her sympathy came back across the air towards Minorie and filled her heart, warmer even than the whiskey given to her by the sailor who had pulled her out of the rowboat. *Nice man who saved my life.* The darker voice followed up as always with, *Yes, but he didn't want you either.*

"Need music," said Omelia, squeezing Minorie's feet and getting up from the sofa. To Minorie, this separation felt as though Omelia had stepped off the edge of the world. And then she disappeared!

*I am all alone.* The *so-what?* voice had abandoned her now, to the snakes who were creeping back in along the branchy shadows. They were closing in on all sides. Minorie shot to her feet at what felt like lightening speed. She made her way to the world of the kitchen, whose electric light seemed vulgar by comparison to the living room, traversing its vast loneliness to the doorway, beyond which lay the *great freedom.*

When she opened the door, it was all wrong. She was standing in the blinding spotlight of sunshine, and the dark over Carlinn below was her audience. They were watching her, judging her. Perhaps even Mam and Dad were down there. And even they weren't applauding her. But she had stepped out onto the stage now and there was no way back. The audience had come to see the freak show, the sunbeam that didn't belong. *Nobody wants you. Nobody wants you. Nobody wants you.* As she began to sob softly, knowing the audience would probably dislike that even more, she could faintly hear someone calling her name from someplace backstage. It sounded like the voice that had summoned her from her dream of….*the fire!* Of course! She'd been happy in the dream when she had let the snake come, in fact she'd enjoyed it, and the fire too.

"Minorie!" came the voice again; much louder, much closer. It was Omelia.

Minorie turned to face her and saw that backstage was actually the house. *Merryweather's house. Merryweather's sunbeam.* Feeling the emotions drained from her now, she said matter-of-factly to Omelia, "I have no home." Again came the voice which made everything feel okay, saying, *So what?*

Omelia simply grabbed her and hugged her, deeply. The sensation was like being wrapped in a huge blanket that was made entirely out of love and thick fleece. "So it is, for us, Minorie," she whispered in her ear. "But never think that the universe will let you fall. It will not, even if things appear otherwise. I will not let you fall. We are sisters now, you and I."

"You and *eye*," repeated Minorie, pulling away from Omelia and pointing to her two actual eyes, and then to the third one she felt blinking in her forehead. That started them both to giggling again as Omelia led her back inside.

The kitchen seemed brighter and less cavernous than before, and the living room had transformed into a place of secret joy once again. Her body was getting too heavy to operate, and so Minorie flopped down on the big cushy sofa. It felt like falling into a cloud. There was music now too, some mystical and atmospheric noise that enhanced the fairy-like energy about the room. She looked around her, basking in the delicious temperature of the air and the snug, protective feeling of the shadow canopy overhead.

Time passed. How much, she couldn't tell. She watched the fire die down and grow again as Omelia periodically got up and fed it more wood. At some point, they smoked a joint, which at first had been a novelty experience – she had felt her lungs expand to accommodate the flavoursome smoke, and thoroughly enjoyed the head-rush it brought in slow-motion, as she had never felt it before – but it quickly became a mere distraction from the intricate cave of wonder which Omelia and Minorie had made their home for the night.

The music was spellbinding too; every crescendo and pause was breathtaking. One song, which had a heartbreakingly beautiful mandolin line, had even seemed life-defining. She rode the rollercoaster of song as much as her senses could manage, allowing it to take her plummeting from one exhilarating high of perfect understanding to the next crushing low of pure and beautiful sadness, and safely out the other side, where she sometimes allowed tears to roll from her eyes, down onto the softly smiling edges of her lips. One or two had dripped from her chin onto her neck and breast, like warm little streams trickling from Mamon's peak, and inevitably down to the ocean from whence they came. They reminded her that all things are really only going back to where they came from, in one form or another. *Dust to dust,* just like the nuns had said. *As natural as autumn leaves....*

As the cave gradually became just a room again, Minorie told Omelia all about herself; about Mam and Dad, about Keith and Bunny Ears and Pig, she even told her about Na-nan. Omelia hadn't stopped her like the witch in the shop had, but she had told Minorie when she finished that Na-nan was mad, a black witch who cursed people.

Then she had told Minorie her own story; about her cruel stepfather, who thought magick was ridiculous, and about her gifted mother, who had been a High Priestess of the Serpentine Sisters before she'd married, and who had wanted Omelia's talents to be nurtured and refined, which is why she had sent her secretly to Carlinn. Her stepfather thought she was in a boarding school on the other side of the country. Omelia's mother wanted her to be proficient in weather magick before he found the truth out, that way his wrath might be a little less ferocious. "I mean, who would *dare* take on a weather worker?" she had said. She was so *worldly* and cool....

By the time she started to feel sleepy, Minorie had decided that all her doubts about Mary and Grace were to take second place to revelling in her friendship with Omelia, which she hoped would spread to the Merryweathers before long. When she could no longer keep her eyes open, she felt Omelia throw a blanket over her and heard the hollow *clack* of fresh logs being thrown into the fire. *Oh, the fire. The sweet, warm fire.....*

# The Dams of Minorie

Somewhere in the room, a door opened abruptly and a woman's voice said "Oh yes, *all* ready for market I see…"

Footsteps marched across the room and then the voice, sounding surprised, said "Oh." Minorie's eyes shot open and for a moment she had no idea where she was. When the dim room came into focus and she remembered whose sofa she was on, she managed to deduce that the speaker had been Mary, and that she had sounded very displeased.

She threw back the heavy tartan blanket and stretched her aching muscles. When she made it as far as the kitchen, she found Omelia alone amongst the scattered evidence of meal preparation.

"Breakfast's up," she said cheerily as she put two plates of toast with scrambled egg on the dining table.

"Thanks," said Minorie, pulling out a chair for herself. It had a puffy, pristine white pillow on it, which sank when she sat in it. "Is everything ok with Mary?"

"She'll be fine," said Omelia, dropping her voice to a whisper. "She's often grouchy after her excursions, and I think she suspected that we'd miss market."

"And did we?"

"No we didn't, dear sister. I've already packed the handcart and with your help we'll get it there in fine time."

"Why didn't you wake me?" She couldn't bring herself to say *sister* back to Omelia. It felt too weird. She was an only child, after all.

"The sleep after your first trip should be enjoyed as much as possible. It gives the system time to come back to reality."

"Seems I came back with a bang," she said, between giant mouthfuls of eggy bread. "I feel like I've been hit by a steam train."

Omelia smiled knowingly. "Ah yes, your body has remembered how it is to relax. A rather rude awakening after the few days you've had, I'd say."

Minorie made agreeable *hm* sounds as she wolfed down the last of the breakfast and guzzled an entire cup of tea, which really wasn't a lot, since the cups here were those delicate porcelain types that came with saucers and not the huge mugs she'd been used to at home. If she was going to be pulling a handcart, she guessed she was going to need a second cup too.

"I've left a change of clothes on your bed, also. It's going to be quite chilly down there."

"Jesus. What time were you up at?"

Omelia just tittered to herself.

"No wait, let me guess. Um, your body no longer requires sleep because of all the evolution and *prana* and stuff…"

That actually made Omelia snort. Minorie could have sworn she saw tea dribble from her nostril. "Oh shush, Minorie. Later, later," she said from behind her hand, beginning to clear the dishes away and giggling as quietly as she could.

When Minorie made her way back to her bedroom, she found the clothes Omelia had laid out to be a stark reminder of the icy cold village she'd left behind her at the bottom of the mountain. There were knitted leg warmers which stretched to her thigh, and which she presumed were to be worn over the baggy thermal leggings. The long-sleeved thermal top was to be worn under the pixie-style woollen dress, and for over it all, Omelia had provided a Victorian-inspired double breasted blazer jacket, of thick, fine felt, which stretched all the way to her knees at the sides and even lower at the back, with a shorter hemline at the front, to show off the dress underneath. The whole ensemble consisted of navies and greys, and looked totally dashing when she added her own boots to the look. In the pocket of the jacket she found a pair of long, buttoned gloves which stretched to her elbows, and she pulled up the jacket's lengthy, pointed hood to admire herself fully in the mirror. *If Keith could see me now he'd cream his pants...* That familiar voice that she couldn't quite place wafted through her mind once more, saying, *So what?*

When the moment of sweet resignation it brought had passed, the longing returned, the physical ache when she considered the possibility of never seeing him again, never *being* with him again....She grasped for the *So-what* voice. She felt better when it was there. But *where* had it gone?

*Come back here!* she demanded. *Why should you be able to grab my attention like that, but not I yours?*

*Here I am, your loyal servant, as always,* it answered. It half surprised her, and half caused her to think it was simply all some elaborate construct of nothing more than her imagination. Either way, it helped.

*What do you mean 'So what'? Why shouldn't I want the boy who popped my cherry to get horny over me? I'm a sixteen year old girl, for fuck's sake.*

*True, that. But he is an ass and you don't need him to define yourself or your life. You know this. So.....what?*

Minorie felt a laugh ripple up through her chest, the kind of laugh she felt should be accompanied by exclamations of *Eureka!* The voice was right, of course. She was quite a specimen to behold in this pseudo-Victorian finery. She thought she might share her revelations with Omelia, so as not to forget their importance and their true nature, but as soon as the bedroom door opened and Omelia walked in, she forgot what she'd even been thinking about.

"Got the daydreams?" she said, smiling as ever. "Isn't it marvellous? Lady Marmaduke once told me that daydreams which interrupt one's daily activities should be considered more important than the activity itself. She credits dreams and daydreams alike with much of her limitless wisdom, although I can attest that they make her rather poor company at times. Shall we go?"

She spoke in hushed terms as she led Minorie outside. "I hope you don't find my fashion sense too disagreeable, Minorie. I tend towards the dramatic. It's the aristocratic blood, you understand." Her own garb was not dissimilar to that which she'd laid out for Minorie, except in place of navies and greys, Omelia wore rich emerald greens and earthy browns. She had rolled her hair up into an old-fashioned style which she said was called 'victory rolls.' She looked like one of those ice-skaters on the vintage Christmas cards Mam was fond of, but with some sexy modern twist Minorie couldn't quite put her finger on.

Outside, the sunbeam camouflaged almost seamlessly into the natural pink sunrise. It was even a little chilly, though not enough to warrant the woollen jackets, Minorie thought. However, Omelia expressly instructed her to keep it on, and she did.

As they rounded the back of the house, Minorie saw that she hadn't been kidding about the handcart. It looked ancient to her, a shallow wooden affair with a large rail across the front for pushing. Omelia had covered its contents over with sacking cloth for the trip. She lifted up the rail and stepped under it, and Minorie stooped down and squeezed in beside her. She'd imagined that old relics like this would be heavy and awkward to operate but on the contrary; it began to roll smoothly on the path with only the slightest bit of encouragement and they were soon on the road, heading for market. *How quaint. Omelia and Minorie, off to sell their wares.*

Instead of turning right, the way Minorie had come when she first arrived at Merryweather's, Omelia had steered them left, down a gentler slope which wound absentmindedly down the foot of Mamon. Even with the effort of pushing the handcart, Minorie found she was shivering before long. The natural temperature of Carlinn felt arctic compared to the morning haze which had been hanging around the cottage. There a spooky feeling in the air, which seemed to intensify as they descended the meandering mountain road.

They passed a small stone church, and several cottages, some of which lay right on the side of the road, and others which nestled down laneways and at the back of the fields they tended. Almost all of them had a display in their windows, or on the pillars of their stone walls, made up of dried branches and colourful leaves, with pumpkins carved into the shapes of witches on their broomsticks, skeletons dancing and all manner of creepy ghouls. Minorie appreciated each and every one. They all reminded her of the feeling that had washed over her upon discovering Na-nan dancing and hissing gruesomely beneath the moon, but not one came close to instilling in her that same sense of terror. By comparison, they just seemed pretty and artistic.

Against the brightening sky, Minorie could see the silhouettes of trees and hawthorn bushes which were bare and haggard and looked like bent old men and grasping monsters, though the stillness of the morning gave them no animation. They looked as though they were frozen into the landscape itself. Beyond the green was the contrasting greyish blue of the Lough. It seemed that the sea was calm also, with not a single pale crest visible anywhere.    Still half lost in the worlds of daydreams and nightdreams, which seemed to be bleeding into her every waking minute these days, the view of Carlinn from up here was like a tonic to her, especially at this time of year. The fear and trepidation she'd felt down there seemed insignificant and far away. She didn't at all mind facing the village now, because she was with Omelia, wise Omelia, who had taken her under her wing and would let no harm come to her. It was as though all the shattered pieces of her life were finally falling into some kind of recognisable shape. *Finally, I* am *wanted…*

Eventually the road seemed to level off and the dwellings became denser. Up ahead Minorie thought she could see the familiar shop faces of the square, and sure enough, before long, she could smell the freshly baked bread from Madame Neige's bakery. As they rounded the corner onto the square, a lively hubbub of market traders appeared, pulling tarps over the frames of their stalls and laying out their goods in presentable order.

Omelia pointed out their spot and they manoeuvred the cart into place, right between the man selling the detailed carved pumpkins Minorie had seen on the road, and Jenny Magee's father's stall. Jenny had left the chocolate-covered onions laid out on a tray, as promised. Arranged on all sides of them were delectable-looking confections; honeyed pumpkin slices, jars of spiced nut butter, and at least half a dozen seasonal treats which included rich-looking chocolate as their main ingredient. Along the back of the table was a selection of boiled sweets in different colours with odd-sounding names. Among them were *Bad breaths, Throat Ticklers* and *Bubble Tongues.* Minorie thought of the joke sweets which had been trendy for a while in school when she was little. She was, as always, the last to know about the opening of the local joke shop and so was the only one fool enough to take one when they were offered. She had wondered why the other girls were being so nice. She could still remember the bitter garlic flavour of the blue one she'd taken, and the hysterical laughing that seemed like it would never end.

Omelia removed the sacking cloth from their cart and asked Minorie to place an empty basket in the ground in front of it. She rolled down the tops of the bags in the cart, revealing one bag each of carrots, onions, potatoes and three bags each of lemons and apples. On a crate in front of the cart she placed a box of strawberries. It was a pitiful display, compared to the lush selections offered by the other traders.

"We'll run clean out of fruit," said Omelia, mostly to herself, "and not a single vegetable will move."

"You really think so? Won't everyone be needing them this time of year?"

"Mary still seems to think so, although in truth, many others simply grow extra in the summer and preserve the excess in bags of sand for the winter. I've told her she should go exclusively into fruit. I mean, all the summer berries she could provide….But it would require a lot of effort and she's somewhat…stuck in her ways." It was touching how she was always so diplomatic and kind when she was talking about Mary. *As if she was her own mother….Perhaps she'll be mine someday too.* After all, Minorie understood what it was to be a woman persecuted. Maybe Mary could teach her to forgive, to overcome, to thrive…

"Come on, let's go costume shopping," said Omelia when everything was ready.

"But the stall…"

"It will be just *fine*, Minorie. They'll put their money in the basket and take what they want." She chuckled at Minorie's expression of intense dubiousness. "Don't worry, dear sister. Nobody would *dare* try and cheat us. They know better."

Minorie admired Omelia's ferocious tone as she said that last bit, and made a mental note never to cross her. She trailed behind her as they crossed the square towards the shop with the dressed-up cat outside. It was truly a most magickal-looking market. Many traders had lit brightly painted glass lanterns around their stalls, which also were dressed for the season. They floated prettily like colourful fireflies behind the faint freezing fog which was tendrilling in from the sea. Smells of incense, and of sweet and spicy foods, and the familiar earthy smell of her father's beloved turf washed over her with the smoke from the great fire at the centre of the square. She savoured every second.

When they reached the witch's doorway, the cat looked up from between his legs to glare at them then promptly went back to licking himself.

"Ah, the red-haired one has returned!" exclaimed the witch from behind the counter as they stepped over her threshold. The two browsers in her shop turned to see what ungodly creation was stepping through the door.

"Now find the dress that speaks to you, and be sure to tell all your hip friends from Findair about how festival virgins get a free costume in The Witch's Cat!" She said that last bit extra loud, like a TV advertisement trying to casually drop their offers into a natural-sounding conversation. The browsers looked at each other and made for the door.

Minorie smiled and nodded in response, straining to remember when she'd told the witch that she'd come from Findair. *Christ, are they all bloody psychic?*

The witch disappeared behind the large red curtain and left them to their shopping. Minorie could hear her putting on the tea.

On the first rail she reached, Minorie found a black and red satin burlesque-style dress, whose skirt was short and bunched, like a tutu. She held it up against herself for Omelia to see.

"That's what the locals would call *an amateur's dress*. Remember, the best festival fun happens outside, in the square and in the graveyard. You'll have pneumonia by midnight if you wear that."

Right enough, that was a point Minorie hadn't even considered. When she looked again, she realised that the rail she was browsing must have been the amateur's rail and indeed, the one next to it was no better. Deeper into the shop, Omelia had found the *real* dresses. She was holding up a shimmering green, blue and gold creation which seemed to completely change its colouring as she swayed it lovingly from side to side, as if it were Prince Charming and she was Cinderella. Minorie blinked a few times in an attempt to work out what strange fabric could give such a paranormal effect.

"It's enchanted felt work," said Omelia excitedly. "I've never seen it worked so beautifully." With that, she scampered off to a curtained nook in the back of the shop. The witch's kettle could be heard screeching to a boil. Minorie turned her attentions back to the rail before her. There were all manner of gowns in all manner of fabrics, some with matching eye masks attached. Some had big puffy skirts with bustles on the back, some had flowing transparent sleeves, and some had lushly beaded detailing on the bodices and waists. *How could I ever pick just one?*

But then it called to her. As her hand fell upon the hanger she just *knew*…It had ravens wings around the collar and jutting out over the shoulders. She didn't even examine the rest of it before stealing away to the curtained nook with it over her arm. Once inside, she wriggled fervently out of her clothes and into it. She found the exquisite black feathered mask which accompanied it too, and she slipped it on over her eyes. *Man, I'm going to look bad-ass in this thing....*

When she stepped through the curtain and stood before the mirror, she saw that she had been correct. As she admired the perfect way it hugged her body, and twirled the wings which flowed from the sleeves, Omelia's reflection appeared suddenly from the ether. Minorie spun around and saw her standing there, clearly very pleased with herself.

Minorie could see now how the flickering colours of the dress may have been achieved. There was patterned stitching all over it, frequently punctuated by tiny glowing sequins and beads in the three rich tones of the fabric itself.

Omelia was now doing a slow twirl before the mirror, which caused her dress to look blue, then green, then to sparkle entirely in a golden glimmer, which almost momentarily blinded Minorie. The mask to match it was mounted on a long stick handle, and was cleverly decorated in the same fabric, and it seemed to change colours at precisely the same times as the dress. "And you look superb, Minorie. I think you've found *the one,* don't you?"

Minorie winked at her in agreement. She was changed back to her own clothes before Omelia, and went around to the counter, where the old witch was knitting furiously at some sprawling black thing, which looked as much like a squid as it did an item of clothing. "I think I've found it," she said, showing off her find.

"Oh yes," said the old witch, as if someone had just offered her a slice of double chocolate fudge cake. "Couldn't have picked better myself! Let me wrap it up for you. You *are* a virgin, yes? To the festival, I mean…" said the witch, tittering to herself as she rifled through a shower of coloured tissue paper beneath the counter.

"Yes, I'm a festival virgin," said Minorie, warming more to her jovial nature, now that she wasn't being turned out into the street by her.

"Good, good," said the old witch, slamming down a delicate sheet of purple tissue paper and folding the dress neatly on top of it. She glanced quickly around the shop then said, almost inaudibly, "Did you make your way up there alright?"

"Yes. Just fine thanks. Mary is so kind to let me stay."

The witch grumbled to herself and lowered the tissue paper package into a paper bag. "The grass isn't always greener, you know lovie. And sometimes it's better to go back to the first grass, if you get my meaning…" As she handed Minorie her bag, she added rather loudly "Now be sure to tell your friends, free costumes for festival virgins!"

Minorie saw that Omelia had joined them again. "I will," she said, blushing from her secret conversation with the witch and even more so at the fact that she had no idea what the witch was even talking about. Had she meant for Minorie to go back to Findair? Did she have some kind of prejudice against outsiders? *No, it's just you. You offend her very senses.*

"And you, lovie," said the old witch, turning her attentions to Omelia, "Are you a festival virgin too?"

"I am," said Omelia, as calm and gracious as ever. When the witch disappeared into the tissue paper again, Minorie furrowed her brow and made a little shape with her mouth. Omelia shook her head just a little bit, and smiled that devilish smile that meant she was up to no good. The witch stood up and Minorie swung towards the door to conceal both the delight and the shame in her face. She chanced an eye at Omelia, who was deadpan. It was too much.

"Thank you so much!" Minorie said hurriedly to the witch, holding the bag up in front of her face, before edging as quickly and naturally out the door as she could manage. Omelia came out behind her. "You are *evil*...." she said to her. Omelia grinned down her nose at her in a faux snobbish way. At least Minorie hoped it was faux. She allowed Omelia to take her arm, and the two of them fell about laughing the whole way back to the stall.

Omelia begged two unused stools from neighbouring stalls, and they huddled in together beside the cart. One bag of strawberries was nearly empty, and a whole bag of apples had been taken.

"Don't you feel bad about scamming that nice old witch?"

"Oh what she doesn't know won't hurt her, Minorie. It's a silly offer anyway, surely she expected *some* people to take advantage....And besides, maybe if Mary were to *pay* us....Really, how does she expect us to get by?"

Minorie shrugged, not sure what Omelia was expecting her to say. She hadn't really thought about the money end of things, but at this moment, surrounded with all the captivating and mouth-watering treats of the marketplace, she couldn't say she wasn't disappointed at learning that she wouldn't be getting paid any time in the near future. "Aren't there other ways of getting money?"

Omelia looked at her tiredly, as if it were a subject she'd given much weight and consideration to in the past. "It's really not that simple. For a start, there are few enough hours left in the day once all the work in Mary's is done with. I'm not sure one would be *able* for an additional job…" she said, rather forlornly. "As for the *availability* of work, what skills can one really *offer* to a village populated with magick folk?"

She had a point, albeit a rather depressing one. Omelia sighed with resignation, leaning over the cart to lift the money basket to count its contents.

"Omelia?"

"Mm?"

"Why Carlinn?"

"What do you mean?"

"Why did they all gather here? The magick workers."

Jenny Magee's father stuck his head into the conversation and his large ass onto Omelia's stool. His business day was starting at a pace that could have been described as *leisurely*.

"I'll take that one," he said, in a gruff, but amiable fashion. "Run into my shop and fetch us three cups of tea. There's a good girl," he said to Omelia, much as you would say it to a waitress, if you were some fat-cat businessman who thought women were your inferiors. Omelia looked at him like he'd just squeezed her ass, and went off across the square, mumbling to herself.

As she went, a man wearing only a loin cloth and a turban walked over to a small makeshift platform facing them and sat cross-legged upon it. He lifted some spectacularly complex-looking instrument into his lap and began to make long, ethereal notes with it, which sounded like sparks of magick pinging off steel and which threatened to drag Minorie off to the daydreams again. She was, however, acutely aware of the expectant old man at her side who was eager to tell his tale.

"It all started with the ancient tribe of Danú," he said, sitting up straight on the stool, and throwing his head back. *Of course it did,* she thought, wearily. Still, there was an art to storytelling, she knew. Perhaps this man was a true kind of bard and therefore worthy of her respect. Besides, it wasn't like she had anything better to do.

"They were a skilled and magickal people who once were the guardians of this whole land. Their high priests and priestesses could perform magick that we can only dream about today. Why, our very own Mrs. Aldron claims to be a direct descendent of the Dagda. I trust you know the Dagda."

"Mm-hm," said Minorie, knowing fine well she didn't.

"Of course you do. Well, he had the cauldron that never emptied and he would share with everyone around, but I daresay if you went calling on Mrs. Aldron in need of a meal, you'd find her cauldron quite empty and her curtains drawn shut," he said, with a sneer in his voice. "But anyway, the tribe was one day overcome by an army of invaders from another land. They landed in great big boats in huge, incalculable armies and caught Danú's people unawares, jealous of the magick here, no doubt. Now Danú's people knew they were in a tight spot, but they were still mighty

143

magick workers, after all. They ordered their own souls to march right out of their bodies and into the magickal underground caverns which spanned the whole land, where they vowed to live until their time should come again, and they would take back the land for themselves. The land was much larger then, you understand. Some believe it was even the fabled land of Atlantis, though there's others who would laugh at you for saying so. It has since split and cracked and, as far as we can make out, the magick and influence of Danú's people seems to have all surged into Carlinn. Well, to be more specific, it seems to be radiating from the mountain. It's a dormant volcano, you know."

Minorie didn't pretend to have known that last bit. She couldn't hide the surprise in her face. A shiver went down her spine as he'd said it, which felt eerily fatalistic. *The way things are going for me, that mountain's bound to be spewing lava all over Carlinn before the day's out...* A vision of last night's trip trickled through her mind and brought her back to the pleasant smells, sounds and sights from the market around her. *As natural as autumn leaves....* Almost as if her thoughts had commanded it, a breeze swam past them, taking with it a small plume of coloured leaves.

Omelia came back then, carrying a tray and all the necessary accoutrements for tea. Jenny's father leaned over to his table and lifted three thin ginger biscuits which were smothered in dark chocolate, handing one each to his new companions. Minorie poured steaming tea into three mugs.

"I was just explaining to your friend about the volcano."

"Oh yes, Mount Vagina, you mean," said Omelia, biting into her biscuit and maintaining a flawless *butter-wouldn't-melt* expression on her face.

The instrumentalist paused between songs at the exact moment she'd said it. Minorie nearly choked on her tea. Jenny's father didn't know where to look.

"That's the bit nobody ever mentions, Minorie; the fact that it looks exactly like a great big vagina." The music struck up once again.

"I wonder how he doesn't freeze to death," Minorie said, nodding at the man in the turban, not wishing to further embarrass the man who was giving them free tea and biscuits.

"Magick," he said distractedly, clearly grateful for the change of subject.

"*Mind* magick," said Omelia. "Mother studied with some famous yogis in India. It's *incredible* what a lifetime of meditation will get you."

"Never had much patience for it myself," said Jenny's father. "I'll stick to my sweets, I think."

"Quite," said Omelia, in that posh, passive-aggressive way she had. "Minorie I have a message to run. Would you like to join me?"

"Not just yet," she said, hoping there may be more free sweets and interesting stories, yet unsure of how much longer the storyteller's company would remain enjoyable. Omelia left and Minorie saw that she seemed to be heading towards Madame Neige's Bakery on the hill.

Jenny's father seemed very pleased that Minorie had stayed behind. He leaned in, a little closer than Minorie would have liked and said "You know, if things go south at Merryweather's- "

"Yeah, yeah, I know, go back to Findair," she said, getting off her stool and pretending to count the money to avoid his warm breath on her face and his unwelcome closeness.

"Oh you came from Findair, did you? Stopping in with that voodoo witch, no doubt!" Talk about out of the frying pan and into the fire! I bet Mary Merryweather doesn't know *that* little nugget...."

*Dammit.* She'd just spilled the beans to perhaps the only person in Carlinn who *couldn't* read her mind. And he was shaping up to be a bit of a creep, by the looks of things.

"I've heard they are rivals," said Minorie, instinctively not wanting him to know any more about the situation.

"Heh. You could say that. One's a *black* witch and the other is white. They go together as well as day and night. In other words, you'll never see them both in the same place at the same time," he said, rather amused by his own wit.

*Thank god for that. At least he's not racist, just sexist.*

"Would you like another biscuit? I could tell you another story...."

Whatever appeal the prospect of a second free biscuit had held for her was lost now, with the detectable hint of lechery in his voice. She felt a little dirty for having even accepted the first one. "Um....no thanks. I forgot I have a- " *How did Omelia put it?* "I have a message to run too," she said, edging out from behind the stall. The musician looked right into her eyes as she did, causing her to pause for a moment before scurrying up the hill after Omelia. His twanging music rang in her ears the whole way. It didn't even seem to get quieter as she got further away from him.

When she had almost reached Madame Neige's, she heard a *Pssst* noise coming from a nearby bush on the side of the road. It was one of those brambly, nettle-filled ones, but the gap was just about big enough to squeeze through.

When she emerged on the other side, she was met by a huge, gnarled tree with monstrous great branches drooping in their middles, in places almost as far down as the ground. Omelia was perched on a seat-shaped knot on one of them, speaking to Misyeu Crow, no less. She glanced up to make sure it was Minorie who had come, and offered her the joint she'd been smoking with an outstretched arm, before going back to fiddling with one of the bracelets around her wrist. Minorie sat on a hunched branch across from her, smoking and staring at the crow, who was staring back rather intensely. Omelia managed to pry the knot in her bracelet loose and offered it to Misyeu Crow, who immediately forfeited his staring match and took it in his ebony beak. He hopped off the branch to the ground, turning to look back at Minorie once more.

"Thank you, Mister Crow," said Omelia, flapping her fingers at him dismissively as though he were a butler.

"That bird is creepy," said Minorie, when Misyeu Crow was safely out of earshot.

"Some say he's decades old, or more…." said Omelia, lying back against the branch and closing her eyes. "So Mr. Magee ran out of stories, did he?"

"Ew. What a creep."

"I tried to save you," said Omelia, smiling with her eyes still closed.

"I know, I just…."

"You just second-guessed your instinct. We all do it when we start out. Plus, you thought there might be more free biscuits," said Omelia, breaking into an outright giggle now.

"No!" said Minorie, embarrassed at being discovered. "Well, yes……But I just- "

"You wanted to be *nice*. I know, sweet girl. I know. It's the scourge of women everywhere. It plays a big part in what I call The Catholic Hangover."

Minorie handed her back the joint and grunted a "Huh?" through a cloud of smoke.

"For guys it's mainly just the issues of having been born into 'Original Sin.' So from day one they are told they are sinners for so selfishly choosing to be born. It breeds a sort of 'In for a penny, in for a pound,' attitude. I mean, if they're going to hell already, why *shouldn't* they drink until they fall down; why *shouldn't* they rape their wife, or beat her bloody?"

Minorie saw her father's eyes in front of her own, bulging and boiling with fury….*You conniving little bitch*…..She pushed him out of her mind. *Carlinn is my home now*, she told him in her imagination. *And you don't belong here.*

"You can see where this is going," said Omelia, even though Minorie couldn't see anything except the joint sitting so perfectly between Omelia's lips. She looked so cool when she was smoking.

Minorie feared it didn't suit her quite as much. The roach always seemed to stick to her lips and make blisters there, and when she was taking a drag, her face would elongate and stretch, almost as if to distance the hot thing from her eyelashes. She knew because she'd watched herself do it in a mirror once.

"For post-Catholic women, things are even worse. We've been taught to *be nice*, and that having people *like us* is one of the most important survival skills we can possess. Which is complete and utter nonsense, by the way, though one *does* often catch more flies with honey than with vinegar….But above all, we have been taught that men *matter* more, that our needs are secondary to theirs, and our opinions too….I mean, the Vatican. Talk about a *boys* club…."

Omelia stirred something in Minorie that she'd only ever experienced with Keith. She was so passionate, so educated – like when Keith talked politics – except she talked about girl stuff…..Minorie could have listened to her all day.

But the exchange was cut short when the bushes Minorie had come through began to rattle and shake. A dishevelled black boot came through it, half-covered by a leg of tattered waders, followed by the top of a raggedy black beanie cap which was now covered in leaves and thorns and even the odd blackberry. It was Christy, looking decidedly nonplussed by the bush.

"Bejayzus, it's the rain girl," he said, placing Omelia's bracelet back in her outstretched hand. "Gave me some fright the other night, so yeh did. Running off like that. I just came in for my dinner and-"

Minorie suddenly realised it had been Christy she had pushed past that night at Na-nan's door. "*You* were frightened?" she fired back, "I woke up and saw the strange woman who'd *abducted* me dancing around the place and laughing like a demon!" She felt bad

149

accusing Na-nan of kidnapping her, but she was standing firm on her weirdness.

He was ready for her. "What Na-nan does is no stranger than- " His stare fell to Omelia when he paused, though he forced it back to Minorie, "No stranger than what some *other* people get up to around here…."

He held his hand open to Omelia before he tore his stare away from Minorie. Omelia produced a little rolled up piece of paper for him which he took and placed into his breast pocket. He held his hand out again and, to Minorie's astonishment, Omelia placed into it a fruitcake of such size that, by Minorie's reckoning, it could not logically have been concealed anywhere on her person. Yet there it was, sticky all over and thick with raisins. Christy produced a cloth bag from his pocket and placed the cake inside.

"Same place?" he asked Omelia.

"Yes."

"I'll be off then. Oh and rain girl," he said, pointing his finger at something above Minorie's head, "Na-nan says to remind you that all mountain roads eventually lead back to the village."

Minorie made a vaguely affirmative *hmm* noise, still baffled as to exactly where Omelia could have hidden that fruitcake. The message only began to sink in as Christy disappeared back through the gap in the bush. It occurred to her that she had no idea what the meaning of the message was, and that it could not have been a reminder, since she didn't recall Na-nan having said such a thing before.

"She's subtly inviting you back," said Omelia, inspecting her fingernails. "God forbid you'd get a little sunshine on your cheeks…"

Minorie held her tongue. Na-nan's place *was* dark and weird, especially when she'd been prancing around in the moonlight and howling to herself. But Minorie couldn't forget that it was Na-nan who got her to Carlinn and sheltered her in the first place. It was Na-nan who'd practically saved her life. And Na-nan wasn't as moody as Mary….*You're never happy. Ungrateful bitch.*

"What do you say to your mother?" she asked, desperate to change the subject.

Omelia looked up from her fingernails.

"When you write home. What do you say?"

"Oh, only as much as I have to. 'Still studying the sunbeam. Need more money. Glad you're not dead.' That kind of thing."

"Are you annoyed that she sent you here?"

"Not at all. I love Carlinn," she said, her face almost sparkling. Her teeth were so pearly and her skin was so clear and pink…..She stretched her arms back to the trunk behind her and lay against them. "But if my mother was really so concerned about what I'm up to, wouldn't she keep me closer to hand? Why bother writing an essay home when she can't be bothered to visit?"

So she *was* annoyed. But pointing it out wasn't going to do any good. Minorie suddenly missed her own mother terribly. She wondered if she could ever be convinced to visit Carlinn. She wondered if Mam would like Mary. She wondered if she'd found her note and what she was doing right now. And for a moment she wondered what would happen if she went home. Then her father's bulging eyes again. *No. I can't go home.*

"Let's go back," said Omelia. "No doubt Mr. Magee will be looking for his new friend," said Omelia, teasingly nudging her with her elbow as she stood up and straightened her clothes.

Minorie rolled her eyes and followed Omelia through the bush and back down the hill. The sweet, wholesome smells which wafted from the bakery made Minorie's belly rumble.

"We're due another lecture about the cost of hospitality any day now," said Omelia, drawing Minorie back from the fairytale vision of Carlinn's festival market.

The sky had the golden hue of an October noon. A slight wisp of the morning's mist still hung faithfully over the village square, which was actually not square-shaped but circular. The nestled stalls were in full swing now, being browsed by all manner of folk – the local witch and wizard types, with their long-haired children and grandchildren, and the tourists, the punks, goths, hippies and the odd normal-looking one too. None of the tourists seemed to carry a basket like the locals, but all carried cameras. A cheerful hubbub could be heard above the crackling of fires and the odd maniacal laugh. The turbaned musician had taken a break from performing and was drinking mulled wine from a cauldron beneath an archway of painted wooden barrels. Minorie couldn't believe she'd ever spent Halloween anywhere else.

"Huh?" she said, trying to reign in her attentions as they reached the bottom of the hill.

"I'm saying that any day now, Mary is bound to bring up the fact that we eat more of her food than we sell."

That did it. She had Minorie's full attention now.

"You mean she resents feeding us with the food we grow for her?" asked Minorie, hoping she had misunderstood. That wasn't a lecture she was sure she could handle. It reeked of Dad and his food bill.

"It's always around the time of the full moon. It's like she's been holding it in all month and then it comes spewing out. And it'll be worse this time, with you not having *given back* yet…."

"Whaddaya mean I haven't given back?" she said, her cheeks flushing to match her unruly, scarlet hair. "What am I doing working a stall today if not *giving back*?"

"Oh, it's different. Never mind. You'll see," said Omelia, trailing off disconcertingly as they reached their stall.

She'd been right about the fruit. Two bags of apples had been emptied along with one bag of lemons, and half the strawberries had been taken from the box in front. The vegetables hadn't budged. Minorie was relieved to see the cash-box fuller than before with coins and the odd paper note. Thankfully, Mr. Magee seemed to have disappeared, as had half his chocolate-covered onions.

"So seriously, what are we working for if not money or food?"

"For fun, I guess," shrugged Omelia, that devilish smile returning to her face. She looked around for her next source of entertainment and locked eyes on a shadowy figure that had manifested as if from nowhere in front of the stall. Minorie's stomach tumbled as she realised it was Blaise. Here she was, fraternising with the enemy. How could she ever face Na-nan again once Blaise told her where he'd found Minorie? When his month of silence ended, he'd be sure to blurt it out at some point. Or would he even wait that long? Perhaps he'd write it down on a sheet of that rough, flowery paper and place it in front of Na-nan for her to read. *Or maybe he doesn't give a shit.*

"Well hello, tall dark and handsome," said Omelia, in a treacle-mouthed manner that Minorie hadn't expected. It brought out a sort of territorial urge in her.

"Hi Blaise," she said, forcing herself to look directly into his soft, brown, thousand yard stare. When his eyes connected with her own, she forced herself to smile through the shuddering shame. To her surprise he smiled and nodded back.

"Oooh," said Omelia, appearing to swoon, "And the strong silent type to boot!"

She was adoring every minute of this. *She'd be licking his face by now if I wasn't here,* thought Minorie, trying hard not to feel left out. *Or maybe she doesn't care that I'm here and she'll do it anyway....*Omelia stood up to come out from behind the cart, and Minorie could have sworn Blaise looked more than a little alarmed as he shoved a note into Omelia's hand and began indiscriminately packing lemons into a small cloth bag.

After reading it, Omelia's flirty attitude turned abruptly to sneering. "What does she mean, 'Got a fine, big conch shell for you?' Doesn't she know we don't *do* credit, or....or bartering, or whatever this is...." She tried to push the note back into Blaise's hand but he managed to dodge her advances, raising his hand to a little wave at Minorie before hurrying off amongst the growing crowd of the marketplace.

"Oh great! That's just the kind of news we need to give Mary this evening. 'Hi Mary, yes someone stole your lemons, but don't worry, he says he'll give you a seashell for them.'"

She snorted her agitation out in bursts of steam from her mouth and nose, rubbing her hands together frantically, trying to bring the feeling back.

Minorie didn't know what to make of it all, and began to rub her own hands, which were slowly but surely filling with the icy tingle of being outside in late autumn. One thing was for sure, she wasn't looking forward to this evening. Omelia's predictions for Mary's mood were an early and unwelcome insight into the lives of those who live beneath the permanent sunbeam. Minorie had hoped living at the Merryweather's would be more like those sitcoms where a wacky bunch of housemates always get on swimmingly. But it looked like no matter where one went, domestic discord was just a given. Even Na-Nan had had to order Blaise to a month of silence to keep him from 'talking for the wrong reasons', whatever those were.

She was starting to feel a bit miserable. She was getting very hungry again and the cold was starting to make her muscles ache. She was happy to be here though, rather than wandering the streets wondering where she would sleep that night. And she was happy to have Omelia and Mary and even sickly-looking Grace. They were better than her father any day.

"So what's the story with Grace?" she asked, hoping Mr. Magee would keep his distance long enough for her to get some juicy nuggets of gossip out of Omelia.

"Well," said Omelia, perching herself back on the stool and shifting about as though she were a mother hen adjusting her feathers, "you can imagine what kind of a start she had to her life after her mother escaped from the laundry with her and went on the run."

"*That's* how they ended up here?" asked Minorie, saucer-eyed.

"Yes. Mary came here with no more than the clothes on her back and the milk in her breast to feed the baby she'd carried on her hip. Came up over the mountain pass she did, too. She said it was like reaching the top of Everest when she came up between the lips of Mount Vagina. And when she stood up there looking down on it all, she knew she would never leave the place again for as long as she lived, and so she hasn't.

She built herself a little shelter out of blankets she stole from the washing lines in people's gardens and then caught up in the trees of the forest. Some women out picking mushrooms in the autumn found her there and convinced their husbands to build her a decent home, which they did. That first humble little dwelling over time became the fine home we live in now. Though Mary has never since allowed a man to cross the threshold.

Grace was raised in what you could describe as unusual circumstances. For the first few years of her life, she would have seen only the women who had originally commissioned the house she was growing up in. The women still called with baskets of excess food they had left over from their own gardens, and Mary became increasingly resentful of their acting like they were better than her, like she was a wounded animal to be pitied, and like it was unfortunate that she'd had Grace, like she was just another mouth to feed."

"That's terrible," said Minorie, shocked to hear that Mary had received that kind of attitude from the women who had previously helped her. But then, didn't some people like to help others only because it then gave them a power over that person, like they own them or something?

"So for a while, Grace wouldn't really have seen another living soul from one end of the day to the next. Eventually, when Mary decided she'd had enough of charity handouts and the meagre scraps from more settled folk, she began to dig in her own vegetables. She started taking in young women who had run away to Carlinn, like herself. She needed the extra hands and I guess after what she'd been through, she could just never trust a man again, which I suppose is understandable. So then Grace had company once more, though they were mostly teenage girls or older. It's nice for her now to be the same age as the girls who stay, though I'm not sure she knows how to handle the competition," she finished, sounding both like she was being funny and like she was pleased to be considered competition.

"So do you reckon that's why she's weird about food?"

"Who is?"

"Grace. Because it was held over their heads when they lived on other people's leftovers? Do you think, like unconsciously, maybe- "

"Oh I wouldn't say she's *weird* about food.....She has just mastered her body to a point where she no longer needs it. I know I joke, but really it's just because I'm a little jealous. I still scoff down cakes and hamburgers at every opportunity. Can't help myself."

Minorie didn't want to push it any farther. If Omelia couldn't see how never eating might be considered strange by some, she didn't think it was her place to explain. Also, she didn't really want Omelia thinking that she was being disagreeable or naive. *Although wasn't that what Omelia was just saying earlier, about the Catholic Guilt?* This wasn't the right time to become self-righteous either, though. She was depending upon Omelia and Mary and Grace for a place to live, for food in her belly....

Almost as if she'd been reading Minorie's mind, Mary appeared before them, with a basket on her arm. She was in jolly form as she pulled down her hood and greeted them.

"How's it going, girls?" she said, pulling back the linen cloth from the top of the basket. "I thought you might appreciate some lunch."

"Oh *god*, yes," said Minorie, unable to contain her relief.

"Grace sent it," said Mary, pulling a sealed jar from the basket, along with two square plastic tubs, which she handed to the girls.

"Oh, tell her thanks. And thank *you*, for bringing it," said Minorie, tripping over herself at the thoughts of food, until she opened the first plastic box and found it full of fingers of raw carrot. The second lay unopened in Omelia's lap. As for the jar, it was full of a puke-coloured paste with oily bits floating on top.

"She made the hummus herself, from chickpeas she got especially for you. She thought the transition might be easier for you if we wean you off the normal food gradually. She's so considerate," said Mary, leaving Minorie wondering what they'd think of her food tastes back home if they thought this flaccid-looking jar of mess would pass for normal food. And just what in god's name was a chickpea?

"I hadn't actually planned on coming down to the village," started Mary again, "but I moved some plans about and I suppose I have some things I can take care of when I am down this far...."

"You are most gracious," Omelia said, again surprising Minorie with the authenticity in her voice when responding to Mary's disingenuousness. "Oh, Mary, I must show you this," said Omelia, producing the note Blaise had given her. "I tried to give it back to him and say no but he took- "

"It's fine," said Mary, in a manner that suggested the end of the conversation. Her mouth tightened as though she'd just sucked a lemon. Minorie could see why Omelia had been laying it on so thick before. Mary took the note and walked off without even saying goodbye.

"Is she for real?" asked Minorie in disbelief as Mary disappeared into the throng. She took a carrot stick from the box and unscrewed the lid of the hummus. It was much tastier than she'd expected but it would take a while yet for her to consider it *normal*.

"Best not to think about it, Minorie. It'll only make your red hair blaze between now and dinnertime. And speaking of Blaise," she said, suddenly perking up noticeably with the promise of gossip, "I'd almost forgotten that you know Mister Tall Dark and

Handsome! So you got yourself a *friend* or two before you made it to the sunbeam......" She was ecstatic with the juiciness of it all, winking and nodding and making Minorie giggle.

"No, no....it's not like that," said Minorie, not wanting to give the wrong impression, even if she did kind of feel like Blaise was *hers* first. "He stays with Na-nan. She's making him do this month of silence thing...."

"Oh, that's *awful*," said Omelia. She paused and munched thoughtfully at a stick of cucumber from her own box. "Though maybe silent snuggling could be fun too...." she said impishly. "He might be at the festival......"

"*Snuggling?* Really?" said Minorie, thinking again of that night, of Keith and his face straining and sweating as he came. There was nothing remotely *snuggly* about it. "Anyway," she continued, "Doesn't Mary have a 'No boys' rule?"

"Well of course it's no boys *in the house*," said Omelia, diplomatically. "But she can't tell us what to do when we're down here, or anywhere else, for that matter."

That made Minorie even more eager about the festival. She couldn't believe she would be spending Halloween at the famous Festival of the Dead, and that none of those losers from Findair would be there. She was even delighted that Keith wouldn't be there. He didn't deserve to be. *No, he'll probably be between Bunny Ears' thighs....*She mentally pushed the voice and the images away with protests of *So what? So what?* whilst chomping down stick after stick of raw vegetables piled high with hummus.

The rest of the afternoon passed largely without incident, except for the turbaned musician returning from his liquid lunch and falling asleep mid-song, which gave the nearby stall owners a great laugh, though the shoppers and tourists had mostly assumed he was meditating. Mr. Magee had come back and told them loudly and repeatedly that there were seven cheeky thieves out there eating his chocolate onions right now. He was so pleased he gave the girls some more biscuits and tea, and he told them funny stories about villagers they didn't even know, and the tricks they had been involved in in previous years. Then Omelia had begun talking loudly about periods, which made him go away. Minorie had confided that she was praying her own wouldn't come yet, to which Omelia had replied that she shouldn't be at all apprehensive, that periods were a time of celebration in the Merryweathers', and that if her period came it might even cheer Mary up. This had struck Minorie as rather peculiar but then, so did most things at The Merryweathers'.

The temperature began to drop rapidly with the onset of the night. The other traders began to dismantle their stalls which marked the signal for them to do likewise. There wasn't much to do, just packing everything back up into the cart before covering it over and setting off. Minorie was glad to be moving again, it warmed her muscles a little, though they had begun to ache quite badly.

Omelia talked mostly about the festival as they pushed the cart back up the hill to Mary's - who might be there, which traditions were the most fun, and how excited she was to wear her new dress. Indeed, she talked at length about the dress, which surprised Minorie. She didn't think someone who was so worldly wise would still care so much about her appearance and how others perceived her. But then, looking at the clothes Omelia had worn since Minorie arrived, it was obvious that style was important to her.

It reminded Minorie that she would probably never see her own clothes again. All she owned now was the stinking pile she'd worn in Na-nan's and a dress that made her look like a crow. She missed the woolly jumpers her mother's mother had knitted her, which she had been ashamed to wear in public back home. It made her miss Mam again. It gave her a sickly feeling in her stomach. Then with the sickly feeling came a familiar cramping pain. *Uh-oh.....Could that be my period?* She tried not to pre-empt the embarrassment of asking for a pad or a tampon, especially since Omelia had warned that Mary would soon be making her begrudgery known. *Although maybe Omelia is just overstating things....She does tend towards the dramatic.*

As they finally crossed the hump of the last hill the sunbeam came into view. It was indeed eerie in the darkness, spilling out of blackness and showering the Merryweathers' with unnatural daylight. She thought back to her spotlight moment during the mushroom trip and shuddered. Hell, it was trippy enough to look at sober, never mind with a head full of psychedelics.... No wonder they ignored it at night time. *Though if they can put it there in the first place, why not just put it there part-time, like the real sun?* But maybe it didn't work that way. After all, what did *she* know about magick?

She helped Omelia pull the cart into the Merryweather's laneway. Minorie was relieved to be home again, but was nonetheless anxious about Mary's mood. It was pitch black outside the sunbeam now and freezing, though once beneath it the cold was far less severe. Minorie's breath had once again turned to huge puffs of steam. She helped Omelia put the leftover vegetables back into their places in the shed. She was starving as they entered the front door, which allowed a shaft of golden light into the cosy darkness within and made Mary screw up her nose, though she greeted them otherwise warmly.

"Welcome home, girls," she said, swanning from the living room to the kitchen table, which was set for dinner and even had candles lit on it.

"This is great, Mary," said Minorie, noting the distinct smell of cooked food, which in this house was thus far unusual. "Oh and thanks for lunch today," she said, not taking any chances at seeming ungrateful. "It was.....awesome." Now she was lying through her teeth, but pandering seemed to work for Omelia, and Minorie was really hoping it would work for her too, at least until she could learn what this *giving back* was all about.

Omelia took their coats off to one of the bedrooms and Mary motioned for Minorie to take a seat at the table. As she did, Mary flicked the lights off and the fluorescent-lit kitchen became a candlelit bistro. Minorie watched her shovel ladlefuls of a soupy-looking substance into bowls and carry them to the table, just in time for Omelia's return. It looked and smelled delicious – a tomatoey soup with great big lumps of vegetable and other kinds of sprouting things....She didn't mind that there was probably no meat in it. What would her father say now if he could see her eating vegetarian food? *He'd probably say I need my head examined. Ha!*

She wolfed down heaped spoonfuls of the stuff, delighted to find a plate of thickly buttered bread which was brown and tasted funny, but it went down a treat all the same. She and Omelia both told Mary at least a half a dozen times that the food was delicious, though Mary didn't respond once to their flattery. Each compliment was met with stony, awkward silence. Finally, she took a deep breath and said, "Yes, it took more vegetables to make this than you actually sold today."

As soon as the words had left Mary's lips, Minorie gasped with the gushing feeling in her pants. She just knew it was a bad one. She stood up immediately and looked at the pristine white cushion she'd been sitting on, which now had a pear-shaped stain of deepest blood red on it. She gasped again.

"Oh Minorie, it's your moontime!" said Omelia, sounding delighted.

Mary extended her arms towards Minorie suddenly. Minorie's flinching was barely perceptible, but Mary noticed it.

"Now come with me dear girl," she said, suddenly sympathetic and nurturing to a tee. "Don't feel ashamed at all, I beg you."

She led her to the bathroom where she lit the tall taper candle inside the door and went to the little cupboard in the corner. She opened a small drawer in the top of it and produced a small linen bag from it. Out of the bag she drew a rubber appendage that looked like it belonged in a laboratory. It was shaped like a cup, or rather, like a wine glass. It even had a little stem on the bottom of it.

"What we do is fold it like this, you see," said Mary, folding the thing carefully in half and making a vague, upwards inserting motion with it.

"You mean you want me to…."

"Yes dear. And what we do after a few hours when it's time to empty is, we place it in the bottle, oh I'll have to refresh the bottle….Well there'll be a bottle of liquid here, and you can just empty your cup in there when it's full, then give it a little rinse and it's good to go again!" she said, as casually as those women on television ads telling you how easy it will be to clean your oven if you just use this new and improved spray. But cleaning ovens was never easy, not even if you used *all* the sprays. She knew this because at home, cleaning the oven had been her job since the first time she'd asked for pocket money.

"Got it?" asked Mary, apparently expecting a response. Minorie took the cup which was being offered to her and copied that inserting motion Mary had done. "You mean I…."

"That's it. Good luck!" she said, smiling broadly before leaving Minorie there, bemused and overwhelmed on the toilet seat.

Minorie looked at the thing she had been given and gulped. She felt another rush of blood coming. There was no time to lose. The cramps were growing worse even as she fumbled with her layers of clothing in the darkness.

When it came time to do the deed, Minorie held her breath. This made her whole body tense and the realisation dawned on her that she would have to be relaxed in order to succeed. How in god's name she was going to relax, she hadn't quite figured out yet. As she practiced her folding and imagined how this might work, and how it might utterly fail, she took deep breaths and tried to think calming thoughts. Getting lost in one of Mam's big chesty hugs, fleecy socks on freshly washed feet, a huge slice of homemade apple tart, still warm from the oven....For a moment she thought about Keith and it just made her tense up all over and she had to start again.

Finally, she decided to take the plunge. After two failed attempts, the panic and shame began to rise again rapidly, but she told them to fuck off and returned dutifully to her breathing exercise. The third time was a charm, though she wondered if she'd done it right because she was very *aware* of it.....After quite a while of deliberating whether it was safe to stand up, she did. She inspected the huge bloodstain she'd made on Omelia's dress and went beetroot red with embarrassment, just as someone knocked softly on the bathroom door. *Oh god, how long have I been in here??*

"Minorie darling, don't worry about the dress. It's yours anyway, once I've shown you how to remove bloodstains. And here, I have some lovely soft pyjamas for you," said Omelia. With that, she let herself in. Minorie stood frozen, unable to meet Omelia's gaze.

"Did you get it in alright? I remember how difficult it was on my first try, and how awkward it felt....That'll totally go away in a few days. You won't even know it's in there. Just remember to *pinch* when you're removing it.....All that suction....Anyway, do get these pyjamas on....Mother sent them last

Christmas and I haven't worn them much. They really are as soft as a cloud."

Minorie changed whilst Omelia reiterated what Mary had said about the bottle. It all sounded fairly frightful, and right now all she wanted to do was get comfortable somewhere and feel sorry for herself until she fell asleep. When she had changed, Omelia held the grey woollen dress over the sink and said, "Now spit on it."

Minorie wasn't sure she'd heard her correctly.

"Go on, spit right on the stain. It has to be your own spit for your own blood. It works like white wine on red. That's Hedgewitchery 101."

Minorie was stunned, but nevertheless she gathered up the saliva in her mouth with her tongue and dripped a long, slow stream from her pouted lips onto the vile stain below. Even by the candlelight she could see the blood separate where her spit had landed.

"Hit it again!" said Omelia, "Then rub it gently into itself and when it's all loose, give it a quick rinse. I'll be in my bedroom rolling a spliff for us, though we'll have to smoke it out the window. Ooh, I should make some tea too. Just hang the dress over the shower rail when you're finished and come join me."

That was just the thing Minorie wanted to hear. She beamed at Omelia as she was leaving, and spat on the dress again. Omelia's tip did work like magick and in no time at all she had completely removed the stain.

This time, when feeling around the darkened hallway, Minorie only opened one incorrect door before finding Omelia's bedroom. It was quite a different affair from her own rather plain lodgings. Omelia looked up at her and smiled before placing the freshly-rolled joint between her lips and rising from the bed.

Above her head hung expensive-looking lengths of richly coloured fabrics with gold patterns stitched into them. They looked like the saris of elegant women, in teal, turquoise and maroon, draped from point to point on the ceiling and in places on the walls. Everywhere there were candles of all shapes and sizes and colours, making the room, which was really only slightly larger than Minorie's, seem more like a Bedouin tent than the poky bedroom of a teenager. *Magick,* thought Minorie.

She made herself comfortable on Omelia's bed, which was piled high with silky-feeling sheets of gold and silver, with plush cushions of purple and cerise pink scattered around it. She noted how much easier it was to feel like a goddess when surrounded by opulent luxury.

"So what's the story with the bottle and the holy grail?" said Minorie, feeling that this month's round of PMS seemed to be bringing out that acrid, hormonal side to her that had so impressed the boys of Findair, who had mistaken it for quick wit.

Omelia giggled. "Oh it's nothing, just our little monthly…..gift." Pulling back the curtain, she let an errant sunbeam into the otherwise shadowy room. Seeing the sun this late in the evening still surprised the hell out of Minorie. *It's just all wrong….But then, who am I to say what I would do if I was Mary and I could capture sunbeams and make them shine all night?*

"Gift to *who,* exactly?"

"Oh you know, just like, to the *place*. For nurturing us and sustaining us. That kind of thing."

"So what, we pour it on the ground or in a stream or something?"

"No, no. Mary takes care of it all. Don't worry about it, all you have to do is get the hang of the cup," said Omelia, taking a final drag of the joint before holding it out for Minorie.

"It's kinda gross," said Minorie, shuffling on her knees across the mattress to the window.

"Gross is a state of mind, Minorie," said Omelia, smiling sarcastically whilst placing a stick of incense in the curled trunk of a decorated wooden elephant. "Besides, you're back in Mary's good books now that you're giving back. We really dodged a bullet tonight."

"I still bled on her white cushion," said Minorie, unable to even look at Omelia as she the words came out of her mouth. She offered her back the joint and threw herself face down into the mountain of cushions.

"I'll convince her it was a good omen," said Omelia, leaning out the window and lowering her voice. "All the same, you should spit on it before bedtime. Then she'll forget all about it and the weekend will be smooth sailing. Perfect run-up to the Festival on Wednesday."

Maybe it was the hormones talking, or maybe she secretly fancied Omelia just a little, but she felt moved to mark to moment. "I'm really glad we're friends, Omelia," she said, cautiously peering up from the cushions.

"Oh, so sweet," said Omelia, much as one would say about a kitten playing with a ball of yarn. "It's always so nice to have new girls in, especially ones who are as much fun as you are. Sometimes it gets a little tedious with just the three of us here."

There was something altogether too ominous about the way she had said it. Minorie, rolling onto her back, pondered at the sentence's possible meanings and watched Omelia, who had produced a shining crystal pendulum from her pocket and was apparently checking if it was working or not.

"Will we have a dry, still night for the festival?" she asked it.

It answered her by swinging clockwise in a circle.

"That's my *yes*," she said to Minorie. "And will there be boys lusting after us?" she said, once again addressing the pendulum.

It repeated its clockwise motion.

Omelia clenched her free hand in a fist and made an excited squealing noise.

Minorie wondered how a girl who identified as a *Soon-to-Be-Priestess* could be so gaga for *boys*. When invisibility and eternal sunbeams were a possibility, why was getting attention from boys still the most important thing to a teenage girl? It struck her as being kind of sad. She liked to think if she had all that capability she'd be using it to help homeless people, or to take down corrupt governments or something useful like that....*Yeah right,* came a voice from just below the surface. *You know you'd just use it to show Keith what he's missed out on. Maybe if you had time you'd teach your dad a lesson too. You are as self-absorbed as any other teenage girl. Don't fool yourself.*

She feared the voice may be right. She tried to blow out the fear in huge clouds of green-smelling smoke. She watched them elegantly holding their shape in the freezing air of outside, their vivid hues shifting as they made their way across the shaft of untimely sunshine towards the sleepy darkness beyond.

# Now You See It

The next few days had gone pretty much exactly as Omelia had foreseen. Mary had generally been in good humour. She had given the girls Monday off and had even lent Minorie a hot water bottle for her cramps. Minorie had hoped it was the beginning of a beautiful friendship but Omelia's darting glances and awkward murmuring noises had suggested otherwise. At least she'd gotten the hang of the cup thing and had even mastered emptying it into the bottle.

Minorie wished she could have some real privacy with Omelia so she could find out once and for all what all the tension in the Merryweather household was really about. However Mary and Grace were never too far away. Even going out for walks had been completely out of the question, considering the torrential rain which had beaten down non-stop the entire time.

On Tuesday they had been instructed to tidy out the vegetable shed which had at least provided a welcome change of scenery if not an ounce of warmth, since the constant rain had reduced even the house on the sunbeam to a chilly, squelching mess. Minorie had stuffed the hot water bottle into the waistband of her pants which made working in the damp shed almost bearable. Omelia had fortunately turned a blind eye the few times she had needed to collapse into the bags of

173

rejected vegetables which were kept for feeding animals. She had almost gotten rumbled by Grace at one point, when Grace had floated in the shed door and caught her just rising from the piled up bags. Fortunately a girl can get away with pulling some pretty strange shapes when she's menstrual.

As it turned out, Grace had only wanted to gloat about the likelihood of the festival celebrations being a washout. She had apparently spent the morning meditating for an accurate weather forecast, out of consideration for Minorie and Omelia *naturally*…..She had described in detail her deep relationship with the local weather spirits who had seemingly told her that it would certainly rain right throughout the festivities. Grace had cited this as *yet another* reason she wouldn't be succumbing to the festival throngs and had left them to their tasks without so much as offering a hand.

In truth they had been glad. Minorie had made exaggerated facial imitations of Grace once she was well out of earshot. Omelia had pretended to stifle a laugh but Minorie had seen the fear in her eyes. *She is scared of me mutinying,* she had thought to herself, though she had hidden her own fears behind jovial expressions.

For the rest of the day she had tried to push the dark thoughts out. Those thoughts seemed to manifest into reality just a little too easily, and she didn't want to have to run again. She was tired of running. She just wanted a home.

All had seemed well as the evening had settled in. Omelia had tried on her dress for Minorie again, and then she had tried on Minorie's too, since Minorie hadn't felt up to costume changes. Minorie had been a little concerned about Omelia looking better in it than she did but Omelia had been self-deprecating to the last, pointing out how she was too short for it and how it really was more eye-catching on a pale-skinned red-head.

Grace had knocked at Omelia's bedroom door at one point and invited the girls to join her in the meditation room. Omelia had given her some spiel about having been instructed by her spirit guides to stop meditating for a time, which Grace seemed to buy. In fact she had seemed a little intimidated and even awed by it.

Minorie had just responded by saying she was too tired from the day's cleaning to sit still and concentrate. Grace had hit back quick as a flash by saying that it would then be the perfect time to learn. Minorie had noted how fluidly the words fell from Grace's lips, even though since she'd arrived, Minorie hadn't seen her lift a finger to do anything remotely resembling work, bar to make some sprouting salad or other, which seemed as patronising as it was useful.

Omelia had thankfully stepped in to Minorie's aid, which had prevented Minorie from saying something she would later regret to Grace. She gently reminded her that a tired student was no student at all. Minorie was fairly certain this wasn't even a real saying but the way Omelia said it had given it an air of timeless authority. Grace had eaten it up as a piece of ancient wisdom and had left the girls alone to smoke joints out of Omelia's window.

They had bedded down early, since Mary had wanted them to be up at dawn to harvest the cabbages, which they had been. In fact they were still sawing at cabbage stalks with bread knives when Mary rose from her bed and came to check on them several hours later. She had cast a vaguely approving eye over the stacked boxes of harvested cabbage heads and instructed Omelia that they were to begin moving boxes down to the root cellar once the cabbages were finished with.

"Lucky to have gotten such a dry morning," she had said, before turning on her heel and disappearing back into the house.

Minorie pondered this for a bit before saying, "Didn't she think it would be raining today?"

This prompted an absentminded 'Hmph?' from Omelia.

"Grace forecasted rain," said Minorie, hacking at a particularly stubborn cabbage. "Mary thought it would be raining this morning and she didn't care," she continued, now becoming positively furious with the cabbage, which was absolutely refusing to budge from the bosom of its ridiculous leafy nest. When she finally ripped it victoriously from the ground she said, "For all she knew, we'd been out here labouring in the rain for fucking hours while she was snoring in her bed." She threw the cabbage at the pile with a little too much force and the whole thing tumbled down and sent cabbages spilling over the ground in every direction.

"Come now, it's hardly what you'd call *labouring*," said Omelia, trying unsuccessfully to distract Minorie from her course. When she saw that Minorie wasn't helping her to pick up the cabbages and was instead standing with one hand on her hip and the other holding a knife, she hastily added, "You won't even notice the afternoon passing and we'll be finished and it will be time to party. Ok? Just please help me pick up these cabbages before Mary spots them rolling all over her garden…"

"Precisely," said Minorie. "*Her* garden. Though she never seems to do any work on it. Grace neither, for that matter." She could hear herself saying it but she still didn't quite believe it was happening. Here she was, fecklessly throwing away her chance of calling Merryweathers 'home', when only yesterday she was almost paralysed with the fear of being kicked out. "Why are we out here slaving away," she continued, "and they're in there all warm in their beds or their meditation rooms or wherever they are….?"

"A few days of helping out and you feel like a slave already?" said Omelia, sounding more exasperated than annoyed. "I work six days a week most weeks and you don't hear me complaining…." Omelia wiped her forehead with the back of her muddy hand, which left a long brown streak above her eyebrows.

"You're right. I *don't* hear you complaining, Omelia. And why is that exactly?" said Minorie, letting her hand drop from her hip as she turned away from Omelia's bemused stare and picked up a stray cabbage. She hoped it would be enough to counter the uncontrollably slicing tone of her attack.

Omelia seized the opportunity to rein in the conversation. "Oh Minorie, love. One of the things I have learned here is that there is great liberation to be found in acceptance," she said sort of wistfully.

"Which means?"

"Well, look at Mary for example," said Omelia, placing the final cabbage atop the rather impressive pile. "She couldn't just start a revolution when they sent her to the laundry. No-one believed what had happened to her in the first place and so she would have just been beaten back into line and treated as a troublesome liar. She said girls like that sometimes even went missing from the laundries…"

"They probably ran away."

"Some maybe. But Mary said she had actually seen one of them being dragged away in the dead of night once. The things that happened there were what some would call evil. There are still some she won't even talk about…." She paused out of respect. It added a real dramatic quality. "And then there's Grace."

"You mean to tell me she's evil too?" Minorie quipped. It was a welcome break in the tension.

"Of course not. It's just that she didn't ask to have a mother who was affected by such frightful circumstances. No doubt it has taken its toll on her too over the years. Yet she has accepted it…."

"Ah yes, that's what we were talking about," said Minorie. "*Acceptance*. Well I think I'll take a little time to decide whether or not I'll just *accept* this as my home or not. I don't have perverted priests and family ties to worry about. I'm a free bird, baby," she said, clicking her tongue and pointing her hand like a gun at Omelia.

"Indeed you are, Ms Minorie Raine. And I do believe it's the very thing that makes you such a complementary addition to our little homestead," said Omelia, feigning officialdom. "And hey, if it doesn't work out we'll run away to the peak of Mount Vagina and establish a new homestead of our own, right?" There was a cheeky glint in her eye as she said it. Minorie almost believed her. She really wanted to. Instead she settled for just keeping her mouth shut. She followed Omelia to the clump of trees which surrounded the entrance to the root cellar and watched her throw back the heavy wooden door and disappear down into darkness.

Moments later, with a scratching sound and a flicker of light, the stairs gradually became illuminated enough by the glow from the gas lamp below for Minorie to easily descend. At the bottom was a simple, stinking room with shelves built in along the walls. It was the most bunker-like place she'd ever been and the idea of it being below ground level both excited and terrified her.

Omelia was standing there, looking rather out of place in her brightly-coloured faux-Victoriana. She was lighting a joint from the flame in the lamp. As she took the first few tokes, she explained to Minorie that she would be wheeling over boxes of vegetables to the top of the stairs, and that Minorie would have to slide the boxes down the stairs, or lift them if she was able, and stack them in rows along the cellar floor. She handed the joint to Minorie who took a cautious pull.

"Won't Mary or Grace catch us smoking down here?"

"They never come down here. Mary especially. The energy of being in the earth is too heavy for them. Besides, we haven't got time for smoking, we've work to finish before it's getting-ready time." She smiled excitedly and took the smoke back from Minorie's outstretched hand.

And then she was gone. And Minorie was all alone in the cellar. Suddenly she was hyper-aware of the decrepit look of the bricks in the walls, and every crack in the wooden beams overhead. Even the cobwebs seemed more sinister down here; as though the spiders that live in them might be some kind of super-arachnids, growing as large and as fearsome as the shadows they hid in, drinking up blood and human joy for their sustenance.

*I can't stay here*, she thought.

*But where else can you go?* asked a smug voice from inside of her.

*Omelia and me will find somewhere*, she answered defiantly.

*Omelia won't go anywhere with you. She's lying. You know this.*

This was a very uncomfortable thought. She fought it with everything she had.

*Omelia's NOTHING like Keith!*

With that, she could hear the sound of boxes being dumped on the ground above. She ascended to the daylight to find Omelia had already returned to the vegetable shed and she had left behind boxes of carrots. She lifted it to chest height, remembering to lift from her knees as her father had once instructed her from the sofa when she had lifted a box of books that was much too heavy for her. With manageable difficulty, she made her way down the stairs and placed the box neatly against the back wall before returning for the next one. This time it was onions.

*Actually Omelia's quite like Keith, if you think about it....* came the voice again.

"I don't want to think about it," she said aloud in the dim light of the stairwell, hoping the echo of the words through material existence would put a forceful end to the spiteful little saboteur in her head.

*He promised to run away with you so you would like him,* it continued. *So did she.*

"Seriously, just fuck off, ok? You've no idea what you're talking about. Keith said that so I'd sleep with him. He didn't care if I liked him or not. And Omelia doesn't want to sleep with me, ok? So just drop it."

*Oh yes she does,* it said. *But that's beside the point. Keith did want you to like him. He wanted you to think that he knew everything. Omelia does too. They want you to think that they are brave. Braver than you. But they are not.*

That last bit surprised her. She hadn't thought of herself as being brave because she'd been scared shitless most of the time since the night she'd run away from home. But it was true that she had done it anyway. She had made it. It gave her a feeling of worldly wisdom that she rather enjoyed.

Lifting boxes of cabbages, apples, beets, potatoes, leeks, carrots and onions from the daylight above down into the belly of the earth seemed more enjoyable after that. She felt simultaneously humbled and proud of herself for being humble. The voices told her that it wasn't true humility if she was proud of it. She struggled with them even as she put the last box in its place. They disappeared as soon as Omelia appeared down the steps, pulling her wools around herself and squinting at the joint in her mouth as she lit it.

"Time for lu-unch," she said with an exaggerated chirp, as though she were trying to interest a child in a dish it detested.

Minorie hadn't realized how hungry she'd become since the breakfast of sprouted oats this morning. She had never craved food so many times in the day as she did in Merryweathers. Apparently that was what hard work did to you. Hard work and eating nothing but vegetables.

By the time the joint was finished Minorie was ravenous. She followed Omelia into the house, where she was surprised to find all the blinds open with light pouring in. To further add to her confusion Grace was stirring what appeared to be a soup of some description and there was also a decadent looking chocolate cake on the counter. The oppressive vibe in the house seemed to have entirely dissipated. Mary even appeared with a set of curling tongs in her hand and began excitedly explaining to Omelia how to get the best results with them.

Minorie approached Grace and had an inconspicuous glance at the contents of the pot. Not a single sprouting thing to be seen, just an array of rainbow coloured vegetables.

"I thought you girls could be doing with something hot and heavy in your bellies for when the rain comes on later."

Minorie rolled her eyes behind Grace's back. But this wasn't fair. After all, she and Mary had taken Minorie off the street and into their own home. They were feeding her, sheltering her and teaching her magick. Well, she hadn't actually *learned* much magick in the time she'd been here, now that she thought about it....And she still sort of felt like Mary begrudged her the food....But there was no doubt that she would otherwise be sleeping in a rowboat if the Merryweathers hadn't opened their door to her.

"Will you not come with us Grace? It's going to be great fun."

"Oh no," she said, grabbing a bowl from the counter with one hand and ladling thick spoonfuls of creamy vegetable soup into it with the other. "Tonight is an important night for my meditation. It's the time when the veil between life and death is at its thinnest. I like to meditate upon my own mortality at this time of year. It's really helped speed up my evolution, you see....." She pushed the bowl into Minorie's hand.

"Mm-hm...." said Minorie, narrowly overcoming her thinning patience whilst poking at the soup with the spoon. Was she more annoyed that Grace was evolving faster than her or that she was just *implying* that she was? She didn't know. She tried not to care. "Well at least sit with us for lunch and tell us more about the veil. You know, the dead? And the meditating on it and stuff...."

Grace looked at her like a hole had opened in her forehead and a little person inside was waving out at her. "I no longer require that kind of sustenance," she said, deadpan. "You know, with all the meditating and stuff?" She added an almost convincing little laugh at the end.

But Minorie had caught it - that subtle betrayal of Grace's true feelings. The revulsion which lurked beneath. She could see it in her eyes. Though Grace was roughly the same height as her, her stare carried with it the distinct energy of *looking down* at you, though she was trying hard to be seen to be jovial....Minorie forced a smile and took a bowl to the table for Omelia along with her own.

Mary disappeared with Grace into the bowels of the house leaving the girls alone together again. They slurped at the soup and chattered about how they would wear their hair, and which shades of Omelia's makeup would suit Minorie, and how odd it was to wear makeup beneath a mask and yet at the same time, how important it was. The conversation spilled over as they washed the dishes up and found themselves in Omelia's room, itching to put their costumes on. They agreed it was only sensible to beautify themselves first.

As they squeezed onto Omelia's boudoir stool and began experimenting with dabs of this and squirts of that, Omelia suddenly asked Minorie if she'd like to have a boyfriend. Minorie had to concentrate to stop her mouth from bobbing open and shut in a most unflattering way.

"I....I guess I wanted Keith to be my boyfriend," she said, feeling the knot in her stomach do a back flip at the mention of his name.

"You're not over him...." said Omelia, opening out the braid from her hair and running a thick paddle brush through it.

Minorie dropped her gaze to the expensive looking tube of moisturizer she was holding in her lap and shook her head.

Omelia paused for a moment and tousled her hair gently with her fingers. "You know you mustn't ever tell Mary or Grace about Keith, ok?"

It had never occurred to Minorie to mention him to Mary or Grace. She hadn't felt close enough to them at any stage. But the fact that Omelia had actually *warned* against it was rather shocking.

"I know you said she didn't want boys around here but......what? Does she want us to be virgins or something?"

184

As she said the word *virgins* she caught Omelia's reflection looking right into the eyes of her own reflection.

"Oh god, she *does*, doesn't she?"

"Minorie no, no...It's not....It's just that, you know, she doesn't like to *think* about us being with boys. It brings back awful memories for her."

"Oh for the love of *god*," said Minorie. "If Mary likes to pretend that sex never happens, let her. I for one have popped my cherry and I'm damned proud of it!" she hissed in whispered tones.

"You know Minorie, there's such a strong energy about you. I love how you speak your mind," said Omelia, bunching her hair up loosely at the back of her head and inspecting it carefully from both sides in the mirror. "In fact, you could say I'm sort of in awe."

Minorie had never had anyone say that about her before. It made her heart beat a little faster. It was of course followed up by the inevitable slew of inner critics: *You're such a whore for flattery....You know she's only saying that to shut you up.....Imagine a priestess being in awe of you....*

She knew they were right. Priestesses, she imagined, much like goddesses, wouldn't often declare their being in awe of ordinary things or people, particularly *her,* unless there was some overarching agenda. But then Omelia didn't really act like a priestess. She dressed like one, certainly. But Minorie hadn't really seen her do any actual *magick*, or priestessing, whatever that would look like....She thought back to that night in Nanan's; how she'd been dancing wildly in the moonlight, calling the names of spirits Minorie had never heard of.

Perhaps that was real "Priestessing". Perhaps she'd missed her chance to truly learn....

"Are you really in awe of me?" asked Minorie timidly, dabbing small blobs of moisturizer on her nose and chin and watching for a reaction in Omelia's reflection.

"Are you joking?" said Omelia, leaning in close to the mirror and plucking some errant mousey brown hairs from the space between her eyebrows. "You stood up to your bully of a father and walked away from your asshole boyfriend, all before you braved the ocean to make your way to Carlinn.....I mean, it's so epic somebody should really be writing a song about it."

"It's not really an ocean, just a sea. And at least half of the trip wasn't even sea, just Lough...."

"You're so humble on top of everything else. You really have no idea of your own power."

Minorie was truly beaming inside now. She also wished Omelia would elaborate on what this *power* might consist of exactly, but Omelia seemed utterly lost in the world of open pores and placement of hypothetical ringlets. Interrupting her would have seemed desperately egotistical.

The stillness of the house was suddenly tangible, particularly here amongst the rainbow colours of jewellery and makeup which were usually a precursor to a night of celebration.

"Don't you ever listen to music when you're getting ready to go out?" asked Minorie.

Back in Myrtle's house in Findair, Myrtle had always let her choose the songs they listened to as they layered on black skirts and even blacker eye shadow. She was partial to some of the weirder stuff Myrtle had

– her brother was always making mix tapes of obscure dance tracks from years ago and together they had discovered some hidden gems that their other friends often thought were some exclusive new releases.

Mostly before a night out she played the ass-kicking rock stuff though. That way, when she and Myrtle stepped out into the big wide world of Findair's alternative underage music scene, they carried the attitude that all the boys liked, the 'don't fuck with me, I bite' kind of gait that always left them wanting more.

She missed being looked at like a piece of meat. It had been almost a week now...

"Music is a rare luxury in this house I'm afraid," said Omelia half-heartedly. "It's agreed that a quiet, contemplative air is the one most conducive to spiritual evolution."

"Wow," said Minorie, starting to dot concealer on all the red blemishes both small and gruesome which routinely invaded her face each month. "If I'd closed my eyes you could have been Grace there for a second."

Omelia made a sarcastic half-laugh noise. "Yes well....I like my tunes as much as the next girl but I'd like to think if I wanted to undertake a week-long silent meditation, there'd be a peaceful space here for me to do it in."

Minorie couldn't decide if Omelia was kidding or not. She made up her mind not to probe. Instead, Omelia took the initiative of breaking the insufferable silence with the first few bars of a song. She sang it in a strange accent that made certain words difficult to understand; though Minorie managed to gather that it was about two sisters.

However in the third line came the distinct mention of her name. It was unmistakable, even when sung in the peculiar accent which may have been Scottish. *Minorie, oh Minorie....*

She was dumbfounded. She knew her mother had named her after an old song she'd heard once. The chances of Omelia knowing the song in its entirety seemed astronomical. Yet here she was, singing it in sweet, lilting tones whilst dabbing at her own blemishes with concealer.

Verse after verse tumbled out, carrying Minorie off on a journey to a faraway time and place where a jealous older sister killed the younger one because she was the prettier of the two and had attracted the attention of the much sought-after local miller boy.

The mournful melody was heartbreaking and somewhat suggestive of dark intent. It was still nevertheless a shock when the younger sister, having been thrown into 'the dams of Minorie', turned out several verses later to have actually drowned before the vengeful eyes of her own sister.

Minorie had pretended to sample makeup shades until almost halfway through the song. By the time Omelia finished singing she was spellbound.

"H...how did you- "

"My mother insisted on my learning as many place-specific folk ballads as possible. She says the energy of the songs and the stories they carry is an extremely potent tool to have if one should find oneself in one of these places, or even just when dealing with someone from one of them. The more far-flung the area, the more potent the knowledge of its songs. Though obviously it's quite a rare occurrence actually getting to sing one of them."

"Why didn't you tell me you knew it before now?"

Omelia stopped blending the pink liquid blusher into her cheeks and turned away from the mirror. Her gaze hinted that she was about to say something awful. Minorie took a deep breath and braced herself.

"Didn't you hear what it was about?"

"Of course. Two sisters going all mental over a boy. What's your point?"

"Don't you think it's rather poignant?"

"Omelia will you just spit it *out*??" The promise of juicy new knowledge was starting to get the better of her but mostly she just didn't want Omelia to discover that she didn't know what poignant meant.

Omelia heaved an exasperated sigh. "Minorie, the song you were named for revolves around a theme of lethal jealousy between two sisters. Doesn't that creep you out?"

"Why should it? I don't have any sisters."

"Oh for the love of goddess, Minorie," said Omelia, totally losing her cool for the first time since Minorie had met her. "Haven't you ever heard of a metaphor??"

"Ok right," said Minorie leaning into the mirror and experimenting with a cheeky copper tone on her closed left eyelid. "So the sisters represent what, exactly?"

"Well, you know women in magick circles will often call each other sister."

"Well I'm not in any of those either, so consider that bullet dodged."

"You're in *our* circle," said Omelia, with a surprising tone of tenderness. "And don't you sort of feel like *we're* sisters? What with being the two adopted non-Merryweathers and all...."

The bigger picture was starting to come into focus. Omelia had been talking about herself and Minorie. Minorie decided the copper was very fetching and proceeded to go to town on both her eyelids with it.

"I don't think I'm jealous enough of you to kill you, Omelia," she said matter-of-factly.

"Most likely the death is symbolic too. In magick, death represents an ending."

Minorie was familiar with this concept. Mam had brought her along to a tarot night in one of her friend's houses when she was little. Minorie hadn't wanted to go play in the other room with the children, and so had sat in on the first few readings, including Mam's. The psychic, a very ordinary looking woman, had drawn a hanged man card amongst her mother's spread. Mam's dismayed gasp had heightened the curious and macabre atmosphere as each graphic little image was revealed in turn. The psychic had explained that the hanged man card meant an ending, like shedding a skin.

Minorie had spent much time after that considering how little deaths happen to everyone every day, though mourning some was much more socially acceptable than mourning others.

She had been told "It's ok dear, let it all out," the time she had cried uncontrollably at her grandmother's funeral. Her distant aunt Dolores had rubbed her back and given her a handful of tissues. Conversely, Myrtle had fallen out with her for a few days when she had cried at the news of Myrtle's newfound veganism. Burgers in The Booth on Saturday afternoons had been their thing for almost a year, which in teenage terms was practically forever. Myrtle had taken her reaction as a lack of support. In truth, things hadn't quite been the same between them since then, especially after Keith had come on the scene....

"So what kind of death do you think one of us will cause the other?"

"I don't know," said Omelia, now applying her own eye shadow rather methodically. "But death is death, right?"

"Hm..." said Minorie, now turning her attentions to her hair.

Omelia had stopped dabbing at her eyes and was now staring fixedly at the side of Minorie's face. Minorie turned and looked at her. As soon as she had registered that this was one of those 'moving in for the kiss moments', Omelia's lips were on her own, soft and voluptuous. They hadn't been friends long enough for it to seem truly weird, and there had been that unmistakable chemistry from the get-go. Minorie had just never actually thought Omelia would go for it. But she had. Minorie closed her eyes and kissed her back. Omelia had just slipped her tongue between Minorie's lips, turning on all kinds of fabulous new sensations inside Minorie, when approaching footsteps could be heard in the hall. Minorie's heart was still palpitating as the door handle turned, but Omelia went immediately back to her eye-dabbing, as though nothing whatsoever had happened.

The door swung open to reveal Grace, who came in and announced that the spirits had requested that the house be brought alive with music. She scurried off to retrieve the CD player. The steadily increasing sound of tribal drums and chanting choruses indicated that she had found it. Minorie and Omelia finished their beauty rituals before ceremoniously slipping on the dresses and masks which transformed them into goddesses of the night; Omelia like the moon, taking a different coloured glow with each subtle movement and Minorie, the fearsome feathered face of death itself. Grace intermittently danced in and out of the room, throwing out shallow compliments and occasionally twirling one of them across the limited floor space between the bed and the vanity table.

It was almost like being in Myrtle's, but it was different. It was *strange*. But this was her circle now; her *magick* circle..... These were her sisters. *You don't always like your sisters, but you do love them....*

When all the final preparations had been made and the mood in the house appeared to climax, Minorie and Omelia made for the front door, bidding goodbye to Grace, who presented them with a carved turnip, complete with a rudimentary handle stuck into the top and a candle burning inside. It had a hideous little face, and was, according to Grace, for warding off evil spirits, as well as lighting the way, obviously. It wasn't yet even fully dark outside the sunbeam, but carrying a creepy turnip lantern certainly did add to the effect of moving into the unknown, once they had left the supernatural warmth surrounding Merryweathers.

The landscape looked as though it too had dressed for the occasion. The sky had turned the most tremendous shade of purple and glowing streaks of pale yellow still hung around the peak of Mamon where the sun had descended. Dark, foreboding clouds loomed above the Lough and threatened to engulf the sky, its lingering daylight and even the mountain itself.

The cold air on the winding mountain road quite literally took Minorie's steaming breath away. She emitted a gasp of consternation at feeling it penetrate even the velvet shawl Omelia had lent to her. When they had rounded the first bend and found themselves beneath the shelter of several aggressive-looking hawthorn trees, Omelia paused and pulled a small silver hip flask from the corseted bodice of her dress. Minorie couldn't contain her amusement. Even though she'd done mushrooms with her, the vision of a priestess drinking from a hip flask was blowing her mind.

She was still giggling when Omelia handed her the flask and said, "Go on. It'll put hairs on your chest," as she wiped her lip carefully with the back of her golden glove.

Minorie took a few swigs and resumed giggling. It was whiskey. She remembered the same smoky warmth from the whiskey given to her by the sailor who'd roused her from the boat that morning in the harbour, and from the whiskey Na-nan had drizzled on her porridge on her first day in Carlinn.

Omelia started off up the road again and Minorie followed after her. They sipped as they walked and Omelia assured her that they would soon be able to refill the flask.

"There'll be no shortage of booze for two divine beauties like ourselves," she said.

Minorie couldn't wait to show off her divine beauty at her first official social event in Carlinn. She could hear the echo of the drums already, rolling up the mountainside, beckoning down creatures of all sorts to join in the merriment and mischief. The glow of firelight could be seen amongst billowing clouds of smoke in the near distance, licking the black sky wantonly and challenging the dead to rise again in an eternal dance of ecstasy.

Flashes of the fire in her dream. *Misyeu Snake and Misyeu Fire are wanting to make your acquaintance....*

*.....And I'm wanting to make theirs,* she thought.

# Now you don't

Coming down the hill towards the village was far more surreal and vibrant than her dream of dancing around the fire had been. The waning daylight made the sky look as though it had been set alight by the enormous fire in the village square. The low stone wall which separated the road from the stream that ran alongside it was lined with candles glowing fiercely in glass jars, carved pumpkins and lanterns. Omelia placed their turnip in an empty space beside them before leading Minorie down to the otherworldly frolics below.

The first thing they met was the mass of costumed festival-goers. A Chinese-style dragon writhed past them, with the man at its head blowing great streaks of fire into the night sky. Demons circled wildly around the place banging drums and shaking rattles made from tin cans. Ghosts and wild animals danced furiously around the fire and a scary clown waltzed past whilst balls of fire swung from his revolving arms. A fearsome witch stirred one of several huge cauldrons. The steam which was heaving from it made the air smell like citrus and spices and alcohol. Omelia and Minorie automatically gravitated towards it. When they reached the witch Omelia simply nodded her head slowly at her and she began pouring huge spoonfuls of dark liquid into goblets for them.

Minorie felt uncomfortable trying to tell which parts of the witch's deformed old face were real and which, if any, were makeup. She let her gaze fall instead to the young boys at the next cauldron over. One of them had removed his mask and was trying hard to keep one foot on the ground as he leaned over, face-first into the cauldron, which was evidently full of water and apples. His friend, who was holding his mask and who was dressed like an imp, was keeping some older boys back with a stick, whilst they tried persistently to get past him and push the apple bobber into the cauldron. Just as the witch handed a steaming, aromatic goblet to Minorie with a spotty, wrinkled hand, the bobber emerged victorious with an apple between his teeth. From it he pulled a shiny gold coin. He and his friend briefly celebrated before running into the crowd and leaving the bigger boys to take their turn.

"Drink to the dead, ye bright young things...." said the witch.

Omelia nodded again and Minorie said thank you, and they turned to leave. As they rounded the bobbing cauldron, Minorie lifted her hand to the bigger boy who was currently face down in the water and pushed him sharply into the cauldron. He made a huge splashing sound and sent a wave of water over the edge of the cauldron and onto the shoes and legs of his friends. Omelia looked at Minorie, half-accusing, half-amused.

"That'll teach him to pick on smaller kids," she said, sipping casually at the hot drink in her hand. It was mulled wine. It had a slice of orange floating in it and was utterly delicious.

They glided on around the circumference of the square, taking in all the supernatural sights as they went. Two people dressed as some kind of elemental spirits were balancing and swinging off each other in a gravity-defying dance which saw several drunken bystanders take unexpected blows to the head from random flying limbs. The circle tried desperately to move with the erratic dancers but those who had begun partying too early just weren't quick enough. Minorie saw one particularly stocky man in an eerily lifelike pigs mask take a roundhouse kick to the head. He swung around as fast as he could with fist clenched. The only blow he landed was to the ground when he fell upon it. Minorie laughed out loud.

Omelia had found them an empty space on the makeshift bar to lean on. It overlooked a smaller fire which was tucked into a quieter corner of the square. It was being used to cook a selection of ghastly looking snacks. A costumed samba band was preparing to play. There was a huge, pelted man with dreadlocks and braids in his hair. He had a heavy-looking drum hanging from his belly. He was taking shouted instructions from a short woman who wore a long narrow drum slung over her shoulder. Her hair was wild and she had what looked like mud and blood streaked all over her skin. There were also a few zombies with little drums that looked like tambourines and a great horned bull with a cowbell. Hobgoblins and devils and even a six foot tall black cat appeared from the shadows to join them with bongos and whistles and rattles. They began sporadically warming up with short bursts of rhythm here and there, and numerous sips from steaming tankards.

Minorie turned her attentions to the swarming crowd before them and the hijinx taking place all around.

There were vaudevillian ghosts on stilts throwing what appeared to be balls of dung at each other and at random passersby. One of them was wearing a sign that said "Shit Happens" around his neck. Minorie nearly spewed hot wine out her nose when the drunk in the pig mask, having apparently escaped the trajectories of the aggressive dancers just to be hit in the head with one of the aforementioned dung balls, came charging at the stilted man with the sign and knocked one of his stilts out from under him, sending him crashing down into the surging mob below. His "Shit Happens" sign was sent flying into the ceremonial fire at the centre of the proceedings. Minorie exploded in laughter at the irony just as one of the sharper sounding drums found a steady rhythm and the rest of the troupe picked it up.

When all the instruments kicked in at the first break, the noise was deafening. It made Minorie's head vibrate. Though she couldn't say it was entirely unpleasant. The rhythm penetrated her entire being and shook her to the core with every strike of the big bass drum.

"It's LOUD!" she roared at Omelia, who smiled back at her.

"The noise is meant to keep evil spirits at bay!!"

"Does it work??"

Omelia shrugged and nodded in the direction of two foxes wearing smoking jackets who were subtly but swiftly moving towards them. They were standing in front of them before there was a chance to escape.

Omelia didn't look entirely like she wanted to escape though; one of the foxes had stepped in very close to her and was whispering into the bunch of golden ringlets which hung around her ear.

Surely a priestess would be put off by the obvious desperation of these two? *Swooping down on us when we've barely just arrived.....and wearing smoking jackets of all things....*

But Omelia was talking into his ear now, the whole thing being made all the more sinister by the fact that everyone was masked. The fox was raising his hand to Omelia's bodice now....*Dear god, he's going for it. And she's letting him!*

The second fox appeared to be checking Minorie out with his glassy yellow fox eyes, though he was standing at a much more appropriate distance.

She was somewhat relieved to see that Omelia had merely instructed her companion to remove the flask from her bodice. He had done so and was now filling it from a bigger bottle he'd been carrying in the pocket of his smoking jacket. It was still a fairly sordid scene, all considered. The fox put the flask slowly back into Omelia's bodice whilst looking intensely at her face, clearly enjoying every filthy moment of the encounter. Omelia was staring directly at Minorie from behind the eye holes of her shimmering mask. Minorie hoped she could sense her discomfort.

And then at once Omelia jerked her head backwards in the universal girl signal for 'Let's get the fuck out of here....' And they were off, blending effortlessly into the maelstrom of samba rhythm, moving with the procession which now appeared to be picking up stragglers. The pilgrims were writhing wildly to the beat, clanging a cacophony with their drinking vessels, with sticks or just with their voices. The foxes weren't following.

Suddenly the procession carried them into the front door of The Mussel Inn. The people inside, some of whom were sat drinking at the bar and others who were sat at tables eating huge plates of greasy food, were rather stunned at this gross invasion of the relative silence inside. Alewise, the landlord, was screaming incomprehensibly from behind the bar at the noisemakers as they passed through. Minorie could swear he was firing teaspoons at them too. This made the partiers whoop and bang all the louder and the vibe really began to take on a life of its own.

The section of the procession which encircled Minorie was now passing through the little low-ceilinged snug at the back of the bar, presumably towards a side exit. At the only table in the nook sat a non-costumed family of two parents and two children, whose horrified expressions seemed more exaggerated than the situation really called for. The blood had drained completely from their faces and the father had half a hamburger hanging out the corner of his open mouth. Minorie looked behind her to where she expected Omelia to be, but instead there were just the legs of a huge shining black horse. She looked up to its head, which was ducked to just below the level of the ceiling and saw alongside it the form of a terrifying demonic woman who had an unruly mane of black and grey hair and was clothed in draped black rags. The countenance on her mask was so terrifying that it took Minorie a moment to realize it was false. It took her a further moment to work out how such a huge beast could fit in such a confined space.

But there wasn't time to find the answer; Omelia was pulling her along, out the side door of the inn and out into the alleyway where the driving pulse of the band and the tinny rhythm of the stragglers echoed up the walls and erupted out over the village like a musical volcano. Minorie was dancing now too. She couldn't help but move along when the band began making their choreographed movements between beats of their drums, waving their arms from this side to that, then up and down.....It was infectious and Minorie was getting lost in it, howling to the night sky every so often amongst uproarious fits of laughter and allowing her pelvis to follow the bassy throb of the song.

The procession passed onto a little road she didn't recognize now, its numbers still increasing steadily. Now and then eggs would explode as they hit random costumed revellers thrown by a passersby or some trickster in the crowd. Some of them didn't even seem to notice when it happened. Minorie was grateful that she had thus far avoided all such embarrassing calamities, but she was all too aware that there was still plenty of the night left to explore yet.

The horse was still with them. Every now and then the rider would allow it to rear up on its hind legs and let a whinny at the sky, sending up shrieks and squeals of terror from the people around.

Minorie and Omelia had moved away from it and found themselves amongst a small crowd of strangely contorting dwarves, or perhaps children, who were beating bells with bones. They had pointed cloth boots on their feet and cone-shaped hats made from large folded leaves on their heads. Their paper masks had little black pinpricks for eyes and wide, smooth, unsettling smiles. They were scurrying around the feet of a Viking who was occasionally blowing into the enormous horn of a cow which had been wrapped in leather thonging for grip. He was mostly ignoring them.

One of them pretended to bump into Minorie, and then did it again, and again....She expanded out her feathery, cloaked arms and cawed loudly in its masked face. It bounced away. Minorie flapped her arms a couple more times, just because it felt good.

As the high stone walls which lined the street gave way to tall black gates, Minorie realized they were entering a graveyard. The music clattered on, and the horse had somehow made its way to the centre of proceedings. It was pacing furiously up and down amidst lunacy let loose. People were getting into a frenzy now, convulsing and wailing. Minorie wondered what her father would have thought of the scene. In fact she was still wondering what she thought of it.

But Omelia was enjoying herself, as was everyone else including Minorie. Nobody seemed to think that having a rave in a graveyard was in any way inappropriate or disrespectful. As she danced deliriously around the nearest tombstone, Minorie pondered how the dead might even enjoy the celebration. After all, if any part of their consciousness was left floating around here, it would be a terribly boring and dreary place for it to exist in. She drummed on top of the tombstone as if to say "Wake up! Wake UP!" to the ashes of the bones that lay beneath it.

All at once, a stream of fire dancers flowed in the graveyard gates, spinning balls of flame around their heads, and fiery wings around their bodies, and shooting great rivers of it out their mouths. They looked like the last indigenous tribe of some mad country people hadn't even discovered yet. They made frightening faces which glowed by the light of their flying fire. They surrounded the horse, who didn't seem frightened at all, merely charged by the energy of the jumping burial ground.

The rider stilled it completely and in one swift movement, moved to a standing position atop the horse's back. The horse stood eerily still as a storm of cheering rose from the thrashing crowd. The rider rose its arms up into the air and the horse slowly dropped its two front legs into kneeling position. The rider stepped down onto the ground before moving like a spider to the centre of the graveyard, surrounded by the whirling fire dancers.

*Like a spider.....where have I seen that walk before....?* Minorie slowed her own dancing now and spied more closely on the rider. Omelia had stopped dancing completely and was leaning against a tall stone crucifix and sipping from the hip flask, watching the entire proceedings. She offered Minorie a swig. Taking it, Minorie observed that the horse had been led away and its rider had now joined in the hysterical dance, stopping only occasionally to scream out words she couldn't make out. *The voice sounds familiar too....*

Suddenly the rider's hideous wig came flying off and Minorie saw the silhouette of dreadlocks swinging in a wide arc against the surrounding firelight. Before long the rider's mask had fallen away also. The rider seemed unperturbed. The rider was Na-nan.

Minorie saw now that she was dancing amongst a ring of skulls which lay in the clay and the grass around her. Just as she turned to Omelia to suggest going elsewhere, Omelia turned to her and said "Want to see what's happening outside?" with a devilish smile on her face. Minorie smiled devilishly back at her and sipped again from the flask.

At the gates of the graveyard, they were met by a cavalcade of exclusively costumed carousers. Not an inch of flesh was visible amongst them and they carried lanterns and small rudimentary drums and rattles. When they passed right by the gates, Omelia exclaimed "Oh! It's the Procession of the Dead! Let's go!"

It was a markedly quieter procession, and the rhythm of the music was more chaotic, and the other revellers kept coming up to them and pawing at their hair, which Minorie found infuriating. Omelia told her quietly that they were meant to have covered up any distinguishing features to be in this procession, but that tonight was the night when rules should be broken. They sipped intermittently at the flask, getting woozier as they went. It was strong stuff that tasted of aniseed. Minorie detested the taste but appreciated the heat it was generating inside her.

The first house they'd seen since Merryweathers lay just before them where the narrow street widened out to meet the main road in the village. Its front door was wide open. The procession entered. They danced from the tiny hallway into the large kitchen, where several costumed people were sitting quietly around the table drinking tea by the light of a candle. The other revellers began to pull their scariest poses. Minorie took the opportunity to flap her wings and caw some more.

Omelia was making silly clawed hands at the house's inhabitants and hissing pathetically. She wasn't very good at being scary. It was like watching a really upbeat kid's television presenter struggle with the

Halloween Special episode, complete with half-assed 'Boos!' and wimpy snarls.

*Well, not everyone is born to scare.....Stop being so judgmental.....*

But she couldn't help but think of Na-nan and her command of the frenzying legions back in the graveyard, her utter abandon when dancing to the honour and memory of the dead, her fucking *authenticity.....*Not to mention how badass she was, riding a horse through a pub, then stepping down off his back like some mythical being.....She wondered if that wasn't really what made a priestess, or at least what ought to. When Na-nan wasn't communing with the moon or the spirits of the dead, she was gutting fish and stirring stew and rescuing suicidal girls from their miserable lives....As she rallied with the pack out into the back garden of the house and across into the back garden of the next house, Minorie began to feel pangs of guilt for how she had treated Na-nan, for how quickly she had written her off as insane.

They passed through house after house in the same manner. Some houses had costumed inhabitants like the first house, some apparently had no inhabitants, or at least they were hiding upstairs. Sometimes the revellers played tricks, like taking a handbag or a dish of food from one person's house and depositing it in their neighbour's house. Sometimes the residents of the houses were lying in wait for them with tricks of their own, such as throwing handfuls of flour at them, which only made them look more otherworldly.

Minorie gathered that they, the revellers, were playing the part of the spirits of the dead and they were to be welcomed into the homes of the village dwellers.

They passed in and out of each house, many of which were small and cozy, some of which were larger and more modern, creating only as much harmless mischief as the spirit of the festival called for. She wondered how the small-minded people of the countryside around her father's house would react to such a procession making its way to their front doors. Not only would they be closed but more than likely the police would be called. Minorie mused on how she hadn't seen a single police officer since she'd arrived in Carlinn, yet Findair was habitually swarming with them. Yes, this was certainly a place she could get down with.

As the main village road led them back towards the square, there was one more house to visit. It was bigger and much newer than the tiny fisherman's cottages which preceded it, but it clearly hadn't been cared for for some years now. With its patched up windows, its grass-filled guttering and its slimy black doorstep, it looked like an abused rental house of the kind they gave to students. The kind she had partied in several times.

The procession stepped up into the once impressive hallway, with its now worn carpet and its scratched and chipped dark panelled walls, and as they moved into the living room to a waiting bunch of young partygoers, Minorie's heart stopped.

Sitting back in an armchair with a hot zombie nurse perched at his side was Keith. He was preaching politics at Nursie with hypnotising hand gestures, even as the tempest of unearthly music and restless spirits poured through the room. But he spotted her straight away. He knew that silky, curled cascade of fiery hair from every fantasy he'd had in the months since they'd met. *My goddess.....* he had said. *My goddess......* he seemed to say now, across the room full of surreal festivities, across the pain in her heart and the sickness in her belly, his unmasked stare seemed to slice through all of it, calling, '*Minorie......*'

She turned to face the oncoming tail of the procession behind her. There were dozens of heavily costumed bodies still squeezing unceremoniously through the front door, grabbing at her hair and shaking rattles in her face. The harder she struggled to get out past them, the more she panicked at the apparent futility of it.

All of a sudden, Omelia appeared beside her with the hip flask to her lips. When she took it away, a huge spray of misted alcohol came bursting from her mouth and into the faces of the revellers in the doorway. In the time it took them to wipe their stinging eyes and proceed forward, Omelia had pulled Minorie through the doorway and out into the freezing air of the street. Minorie gasped in great lungfuls of it. She looked back and saw Keith struggling to follow her out the door past the revellers. She grabbed Omelia's wrist and ran, not knowing where they could even run to without *him* finding them....

When she stopped running it was because they were surrounded on all sides by wall to wall costumed partiers. It would have been difficult to spot him, even unmasked, amongst the ebbing and shifting crowd but the feeling in her belly told her they lost him before they even hit the square.

"Come with me," said Omelia loudly into her ear over the throb and wail of the drum-fuelled gypsy music which was pumping from a stage Minorie couldn't even see. As they squeezed towards the far edge of the mob she said, "I know just the place for a quiet smoke and a top up." She took the flask from her bodice and jiggled it in the air before necking the last drop of cold mulled wine from it.

When they finally made it off the square, having both been splashed by the remnants of a nearby landing egg and narrowly dodging a bloody row at the centre of the throng, Omelia led them around a ruined old stone castle and up a little laneway towards the waterfront.

"We're not going too far, are we?" asked Minorie, still eager to soak up as much of the festival as possible whilst avoiding Keith. *Let him have my virginity. Hell, let him have Nursie's. But he won't take this night away from me.*

Omelia simply turned to her mid-step and touched her index finger to her forehead, smiling knowingly. Everyone in Carlinn seemed to smile knowingly. Minorie wondered how long it would be before she could pull it off that convincingly.

When they crossed the road to the short stone wall which separated the heaving waves of the Lough from the village that was tucked in behind them, Omelia proceeded down a little set of steps beside the only house on this whole stretch of the waterfront. The house was totally hidden behind high wooden fencing, although a discreet gap between its panels gave way to the uneven and winding stone stepway Minorie now found herself descending.

"Omelia, aren't we on someone's property here?" she whispered, darting glances over her shoulder to ensure they hadn't been spotted.

Just as she said it, she could hear an accordion striking up a tango. Omelia didn't even bother to answer. Minorie's eyes were wide behind her feathered mask. The feathers were really beginning to irritate her, tickling her face and grabbing tiny strands of her hair....

The carved stone steps wound down around their final bend and into a sheltered alcove where a large, crackling fire had been lit and was currently surrounded by human moths. They danced in pairs, drinking, laughing and.....wasn't that *sobbing?*

As they drew nearer, Minorie saw a large wooden crucifix had been stuck into the ground a short distance from the fire. A woman and a man cried before it. The man's shoulders were shaking and he was grabbing up handfuls of sand and releasing them in streams to the sharp breeze, stopping only to wipe his face with the back of his sleeve. The woman was letting forth great, sighing wails, which could have been the call to prayer at some exquisite place of worship, but they signified that this was absolutely a funeral.

Minorie thought better of demanding answers from Omelia this time. She simply followed her to the nearest empty seat – a ledge on a particularly shelf-shaped boulder which had been covered in thick layers of blankets – and chose a ledge to sit on. She was both surprised and relieved to see Omelia smoking up. She looked more closely around her for clues to what kind of messed up funeral this actually was.

The musicians, mainly accordion players by the sounds of things, were stabbing and striding their way through the verses of their maudlin sounding tango. Minorie recognized some of them from The Cat Dragged Inn.

The crying man at the graveside had risen from his knees and was dragging the female mourner in a grotesque dance around the crucifix. She was struggling with both of her arms against him, even when her forehead was touched to his ear, yet every now and then she would look directly into his eyes and flick her leg around his, as though she were threatening him with the dance itself.

"So what happened back there, Minorie? Are you ok?" came Omelia's voice over the heathen din.

Oh god. She was going to have to *talk* about it....*Ick*.

"It was Keith," she said simply.

As Omelia slipped off her mask, her mouth made an 'o' and her eyebrows knitted into a deep 'v'. "Back there?"

"Uh-huh. Some zombie nurse all over him. I don't really want to talk about it, to be honest Omelia. I'd prefer to just get really fucked up, if that's ok."

She slipped off her own mask with a huge sigh of relief that threatened to bring a little vomit up with it. Omelia's eyebrows shot back into an upwards-pointing arrow and her round mouth curled up at the edges with amusement. She turned to the rowdy, but thus far self-contained group of sailors who had taken up residence on the next boulder over.

"Hear that boys?? This goddess wants to get FUCKED UP! Could you please assist us?"

Minorie was simultaneously appalled and delighted when the troupe began stumbling towards them amongst a symphony of lecherous roars and spilling mugs. They left the scrawniest and drunkest behind on the rock to hold down the fort.

Omelia squealed with glee whilst they were still out of earshot. As they came nearer she lay back coolly, extending a leg along the edge of the boulder and adopting an air of teasing coyness.

Minorie's presumption that this was merely a ploy of fakery to obtain free booze turned out to be unfounded. As the tallest, fattest sailor – he had to be a sailor; he even wore an eye-patch for chrissakes! – slimed his way right up to Omelia, the pair automatically met in an embrace. For a fleeting moment, Minorie's tiny voice of perpetual optimism screamed *'Thank god, they are old friends!'* It was quickly silenced by the quite frankly gruesome display of him shoving his tongue down Omelia's throat and Omelia's body rising readily from the rock to meet him.

His thinner, drunker second-in-command was now rounding the rock towards Minorie with an expectant look on his face.

"Uh, Omelia?"

Minorie's panicked words were falling on deaf ears. Omelia was making disgusting noises and Fat-Man's friends were already asking him if it was their turn yet.

"Omelia??"

She flashed back to her attempts to rouse Keith from his psychedelic stupor and the voice this morning telling her how similar Keith and Omelia were. The sickness in her stomach propelled her from her little ledge on the rock through the three or four men who had been closing in on her and onto the sand beyond. The tango had finished now and some of the musicians had begun to knock each other's lights out. A singular accordionist struck up a stirring song in a minor key. She looked back to see if the sailors were following. They weren't. Willing prey was apparently a tastier meal. Omelia had been completely swallowed by the swarm.

Minorie walked up behind the bench the swaying accordionist was sitting on and stepped over it, taking a seat far enough away from him so as not to distract him, but close enough that he might offer her a request. His tune was full of emotion. It sounded all French and sad. She remembered the joint was in her possession and leaned forward to light it from the fire. The tangoing mourners had disappeared from the scene, although Minorie was quite sure those were their limbs wriggling around behind that rock over there.

When the song ended, and a very drunken singer took up the initiative and started a bellowing lament, the accordionist turned to her and said, "Aren't you a little young to be smoking weed?"

She cocked her head to the side and replied, "Fine. Got any vodka instead?"

His face softened to a laugh. The lines around his eyes were actually quite attractive in the firelight. "Yeah sure," he said, reaching to lift a bottle and looking up almost seductively at her. "I'll let you swig whilst I eat out that ginger little pussy of yours."

Though his face hadn't changed her perception of him had. Instantly. That flirtatious look was offering more than she had bargained for. He looked like a monster to her. A monster, just like all the rest; just out to take from her whatever he could by any means necessary....

She stood up and stepped over the bench and walked away from the fire's glow towards the moonlit tide amidst a chorus of jeering from the musicians, who had apparently reunited in their amusement at her. Even the drunken singer had forgotten the song and was joining in the renewed swell of music. This time it was a sea shanty with dirty lyrics.

The couple had reappeared from behind the rock and were now staring lovingly into each other's eyes as they walked towards her in the direction of the fire and the music. Every now and then one would stop the other mid-step to take their face in their hands and kiss them passionately. She thought about telling them to get a room but decided their pathetic attempt to conceal themselves behind the rock had at least trumped Omelia's nauseating display, performed atop her very own silver platter.

"What the hell is going on here?" she asked the couple when they were close enough.

The woman answered. "It's sort of a funeral."

"Well it's either a funeral or it's not, right?" she asked, perplexed.

"He was alive when we put him down," said the man. "Hopefully he'll be alive when we dig him up again at dawn."

Minorie had heard of stuff like this amongst stuntmen and Indian gurus, but she was still at a loss to explain the outrageous behaviour of this pair.

"And you two are what; the pretend mourners?"

"Oh we're not pretenders," said the woman, being groped feverishly by the man now. "We're dancers." Apparently that was meant to clarify everything.

The couple slinked onwards towards the music and the fire and left Minorie standing in the harshening sea air and the dark of the night. It was freezing out here but the cave walls had felt like they were closing in on her. When she went back it would be to grab Omelia and get back to Merryweathers' as quickly as was humanly possible. Unless of course, the opportunity for actual fun of the Keith-free kind came along on the way.

Off in the distance, from the corner of her eye, she could have sworn she saw a bolt of white lightning touch down on the horizon. The rumble which followed confirmed it. The thunderous hiss and slap of raindrops hitting land and sea was fast approaching, as was the wave of the horrified screams of women who couldn't stand to have their hairstyles ruined.

The moon disappeared as Minorie moved briskly back to the cave. She wondered if it was really *her* who was causing it to rain like Christy had said. She wondered why she hadn't been able to make it rain the day she'd embarrassed herself in the school sports day in first year, or the time she and Myrtle had bunked off to hang out in the pool hall, but the pool hall had been closed....

She looked to the boulder where she'd left Omelia and was relieved to see that one of the two remaining bodies entangled atop it was hers. At least she hadn't disappeared. *I'll be home in no time.*

A reserved and cynical voice in the back of her mind said, *'That's a big, brave statement for a homeless girl....'*

She noticed a familiar face at the bottom of the cove steps. It was Pig. At least it looked like him. No it definitely *was* Pig.....And there was Sal and Groovy, and that guy who'd been talking politics with....

*Keith.*

Minorie looked back to Omelia and the body she was entwined around.

"Hey," shouted Pig. "That IS Red! Keith, man, you could *not* have timed that better!"

The writhing bodies ignored them. But Minorie knew already.

"Omelia....?" she said when she was just close enough.

Omelia rose a little from the body beneath her, still kissing its face furiously. It sat up, knocking her aside and Minorie could see that it was Keith.

She managed to gasp a 'No' before the air left her completely and she felt like she'd never breathe again. Pig's filthy guttural laughter began surging through the grotto above the obnoxious racket of bawdy songs. She turned and ran towards it, pushing through Pig and the rest of his henchmen and taking the steps behind them two at a time.

At the last bend before the top she almost lost her footing due to the increasingly slippery rocks and her inability to see through her tears. The heaving sobs threatened to come and overwhelm her before she was safely hidden away. She looked back at the empty steps below. She looked up to the street above. She was taken aback to see a guy dressed as a mime standing with a concerned look on his face. She searched through the white paint and deceiving eyeliner and saw the face of Blaise. His mouth opened and closed but said nothing.

Minorie charged forwards up the stairs. "Get out my way, you mute freak," she barked, moving around him and breaking into a run just as the slicing sound of the rainfall turned truly torrential, almost angry.

# Compus Mentis

A mile from the ruined cottage, he could feel them approaching him at great speed from behind. He thought back through his actions of the past half an hour. *Candles lit......check. Circle opened......check. Blood dripped upon the ground.....check. Bottle left open......check.*

He had left everything exactly as it was supposed to be back at the cottage. *What more could they possibly want?*

Being called upon monthly made the demons feel important, especially when it occurred at the full moon, and on festive occasions. So tonight was particularly auspicious. Their power would be great.

They had been floating around the ether of the earth and other planets for a long time, searching for an opportunity to manifest and to rise above the level of their fellow demonic nonentities. When the man had first called them they had rushed to his side much as they were doing now.

He had tested them with simple tasks such as lighting the thing the woman was smoking with fire that would not burn her, then making the glass bubble in the corner light up the room for them. He honoured them that first night by mating with the woman there and then in an attempt to give them a little baby body to inhabit.

The moon had turned almost two hundred times since that first night. The man had assured them that despite their consistent failure to create a baby, he and the woman were still trying very hard. He had offered them the blood of her womb each time she had bled as an evidential gift, although they would still sometimes demand of him that he mate with the woman in front of them to prove he was truly trying to impregnate her. He would then occasionally offer them a turn with her using his body as a good will gesture.

He had renovated one of the rooms inside the cottage to serve the ritual purpose. It had been obvious from an early stage that having the woman call to his own house for this work was not going to be at all desirable, what with her.....*instability*.....and her own house wasn't ideal either. Of course he had endowed the little rendezvous room with all the creature comforts she was used to, and some very careful and inconspicuous boarding up of the windows. From the outside, the place looked decrepit. No-one had ever bothered to investigate the cottage and for sixteen years it had remained their little secret.

During those years he had gradually trained his servile entities in more difficult tasks such as making particles big and crashing them together to make lightning, and in assisting him with his experiments on various living cells. Then he had asked them about directing the light of the sun. He had spoken of making pathways and portals through which the energy could travel and be stored and poured forth upon the earth at a fixed location.

Mostly they were happy to indulge and carry out the requests of the human man. It empowered and strengthened them to have their existence validated so.

Each month the gifted womb blood had secured their loyalty for the coming cycle. They said it tasted warm and satisfying. Sometimes they remarked on strange hints of unusual flavours in it. He accounted for this with lifestyle, mood and hormonal variations, which his servants accepted. The man had worried that someday they would find out the truth.

They had just about caught up with him now. He could feel their searing, spine-tingling presence. The one among them who the man knew as Maldaron spoke.

"With such great heat in your blood, why should you require *us*?"

The man stopped walking and looked confused. The man spoke. "Has the blood not pleased you this month, Maldaron?"

"No. It has burned us with a passion we are not sure belongs to that woman."

"Check her then," said the man. "Look inside her head and see that the blood is hers. See what caused the passion of which you speak."

Maldaron thought on this for a moment. "This we shall do."

With that, he felt them leave his side, soaring across the dark landscape in the direction of Mary's house. Her shrill cry cut clean across the mile of blackness that stood between them and he knew he couldn't go on. He was duty bound to help her.

They could feel the sickness inside her belly as they entered. They moved right in alongside her mind and saw the untruths hiding behind the thick, clinging cobwebs of panic. Inside of the cobwebs and the lies, at the very heart of it all, they saw hair that shone brightly like fire.

# Non Compos

Stomping up the hill, out of breath and horrified, Minorie could hear Omelia screaming her name from the still frenzied party below. She pushed harder to try and pick up more speed but the hill really was quite steep and the rain and wind were driving down mercilessly upon her. Omelia's frantic calling drew nearer, along with the rapid slaps of high-heeled shoes running through the streaming wet.

"Minorie, PLEASE! Come back! I didn't know!"

That made Minorie furious. For Miss Oh-So-Wise to suddenly not know something just seemed all too convenient. She spun around, sending a halo of water droplets spraying from her saturated hair. She was horrified to see Omelia's legs were largely bare and she was clutching Keith's overcoat around herself.

"What the fuck is *this??* Are you NAKED under there??"

"Minorie, my dress.....the witch......she cursed it....."

"Oh so it's the WITCH'S fault you kissed Keith? Is it??"

"Minorie please....."

"It's her fault you shoved your tongue in *MY* mouth just a few hours ago??"

Omelia was trying hard to explain. That was just making Minorie madder. Though the dress *did* actually seem to be melting away from Omelia's body even as she stood before Minorie now, pleading pathetically and shivering violently...... Clumps of it were just dropping to the ground. It was a good job Keith was fond of longer length coats really.

"I really didn't *know*," she said, stepping closer to Minorie, but not so close as to be eye-level with her. "And then when I ran out into the rain to explain, the seams just gave way.....oh, that old *witch*!" she said, sounding like she was about to cry with annoyance as she pulled the remainder of her right sleeve out the neck of the jacket and let it sop down into the stream below her feet where the road used to be.

Omelia just looked at her, appealing silently for forgiveness and peace. Standing there with her skin and the fronds of her soaking hair glistening, wearing Keith's heavy grey jacket, she looked at once like an angel and like the whoreiest daughter of Satan himself.

Minorie could see Keith and the gang below, walking out from the crowded square and beginning the ascent towards her and Omelia.

"Why him, Omelia? Of all people, why did you have to kiss him and wear his jacket when you're naked....?" She couldn't hold back the tears now. The fury and the shock and the grief came flowing down her cheeks, indistinguishable from the torrents of rain which made her feel so painfully wet and cold that she thought she just might die.

Omelia somehow managed to avoid getting carried off in the swell of Minorie's emotion, but there was still an authenticity about her words that was almost soothing. "If it counts for anything, I wish this was someone else's jacket too...." She looked behind her to confirm the cause of Minorie's distraught expression. "I have to give it back to him though. They'll have to come with us."

Minorie was frozen to the spot, unsure of what to expect. Would Pig mock her? Would Sal laugh? Would Keith put his arm around Omelia?

"Besides," said Omelia, now eye level with her, "he wants to talk to you. He really loves you, you know...."

Omelia began to move on up the hill just as Keith was getting close enough to make out the whites of Minorie's eyes. Pig and Sal were idiotically trying to push each other over the near-bursting bank of the stream. They ignored Minorie completely.

Keith walked straight to her, if a little slower than she'd have liked. He stared intensely at her the whole time until he was standing almost toe-to-toe with her. The expression on his face made her want to cry again. He was so strangely beautiful, like an angelic vampire. He was a creature of the night, a capturer of souls. He looked as though he ached for her and at the same time, as though he couldn't care less about anything, let alone her. She wondered if it wasn't that same heartbreaking look that had her so dangerously wound around his little finger. He said nothing at first. He merely stood there in the pouring rain, his dirty blond hair stuck to the sides of his face and his forehead. He lifted his hands a little towards her, as if to offer her the softness of a hug in penance for the arseholery he'd been guilty of in the past week. She didn't want to hug him, but she didn't want to stop him from hugging her. As he wrapped his arms around her and she fought the desire to return his embrace, he pulled her tight and spoke into her ear.

"My goddess......I can't live without you."

She thought the shifting of his frame after this statement meant he was going to lean back a little and interpret her reaction from her face. Or at least that he wanted to look into her eyes as he told her he was sorry.

In fact, he was merely positioning himself to kiss her. As his tongue forced its way into her mouth, she made a grunting moan of disgust. She tried to free her mouth to ask him if he was crazy but he wasn't letting her go. His tongue licked hungrily at her lips and her clenched teeth and his arms were closing in on her in a claustrophobic sort of way she had never experienced before. She tried to wriggle free from him and failing that, she began to panic. She lifted her arms and dealt to his torso the almightiest blow she could muster. It was barely enough to separate them, but that was all she needed.

"Fuck you, Keith. Just....fuck you," she said, trying unsuccessfully to wipe the memory of him from her lips with her hand.

"I thought that was what you wanted. Really I think you're just annoyed you can't have me all to yourself."

His smug expression made her want to smash his face in. He walked casually past her up the hill with long strides. Her blood boiled as he disappeared around the first bend without once looking back.

She wanted to rush up the hill past them all to Omelia; to tell her Keith was a complete asshole; to tell her to just give him the jacket and send him packing. No-one would see her naked. Maybe they would though. It was the Festival of the Dead after all. There were probably perverts lurking everywhere. Plus it was an awfully cold and wet night. And Merryweathers wasn't really so far away. By the time she'd have caught up with Omelia they would probably be there anyway.

Instead she just walked behind the tittering gang, at a safe enough distance that she wouldn't catch their attention but not so far away as to be seen to be afraid of them. She was utterly distraught. Her stomach churned wildly, reminding her that everything was all wrong. Her beautiful flowing, feathered dress looked like roadkill. She kind of hated Omelia. She just wanted this night to be over. She prayed neither Mary nor Grace would be skulking around when they arrived back. The last thing she needed now was a hundred questions about the forbidden boys they'd smuggled onto the property. The forbidden boys her mother had tried to protect her from. She thought of her mother. She thought of Sr. Xavier. She thought of Na-nan. She was too sad to cry any more.

Finally Minorie could make out the door of Merryweathers. Something was amiss. Something was.....*darker* than usual.

The sunbeam!

It was gone! No longer the artificial spotlight. No longer a ray of hope. Only chasmic blackness, folding in around her.

She saw Omelia disappear cautiously in the front door. She saw Keith slink in after her and Pig following them without hesitation. Almost immediately, Keith and Pig reappeared, running at speed. They grabbed Sal as they passed him and shot towards Minorie, not even acknowledging her as they darted back in the direction of the village.

She turned to watch them for a second before proceeding slowly towards the cottage. There was no noise from within. The rain tore down relentlessly on the smooth gravel around her.

As she stepped over the threshold, there came the loud, unsettling sound of buzzing flies. *Strange for this time of year,* she thought.

Over the buzzing, Minorie thought she could make out growling and whimpering. She hoped she was imagining it.

As she turned into the living room she spotted Mary, standing quite still in a beam of moonlight which was glowing in through the window. There was something strange about her gait. It seemed somehow more *bent* than usual. The flies were swarming disproportionately around her.

The words of greeting she'd summoned for Mary dissolved on Minorie's tongue as a loud voice from within told her *Shush now.....Be still and listen.....*

The growling was indeed coming from Mary's general direction. It was a moment later before the whimper came again and led Minorie's attention to Omelia, huddled atop shaking legs in the farthermost corner of the room away from Mary, like a terrified animal. She didn't even seem to notice the flies landing on her face and legs.

"Omelia?" Minorie whispered.

Omelia looked at Minorie as though she'd just fallen from the sky, then fixed her gaze quickly back on Mary again, her chest rising and falling at a rate Minorie was sure would make her pass out. In fact, it almost looked to Minorie like Omelia was *trying* to pass out.

Midway through her thought, as she looked again at Mary's face, Minorie was struck by the curious disfigurement which was staring at her with gleaming black eyes. The grimace upon Mary's face was profoundly horrifying. The knot in Minorie's stomach spoke to her now:

*That's not Mary,* it said, as if Minorie even knew what to do with that information. She prayed silently to Lady Macbeth and whoever else was around and tried hard to avoid joining Omelia in fits of pathetic sobbing.

She looked back to Omelia for something, anything to make the situation seem a little less like a real-life nightmare.

Suddenly Mary took a deep and unsettlingly wheezy breath before she finally spoke. "I'm not like you tramps," she said, in someone else's voice. It sounded similar to her own, except there seemed to be another, deeper voice speaking alongside it, like some creature living in Mary's mouth.

Minorie froze to the spot. What Mary had said was as startling as the manner in which she had said it. In all the transformations she had seen in her father when he'd been drinking, she had *never* seen the likes of this. This was like, some real demonic shit....

"You filthy fucking tramps," spat the Mary thing again. "I never asked for his hands!"

"Excuse me?" asked Minorie, not quite able to believe that the words had actually slipped from her lips.

"Oh, of *course* you didn't," said Omelia, seizing the opportunity and taking Minorie by surprise with the random ingenuity that was her trademark. When Minorie shot a glance at her, she was even more taken aback by the fact that Omelia had let go of Keith's jacket to offer her arms to Mary in an embrace, though she was trying hard to conceal as much of her bare breasts as she could behind her elbows.

"Stay away from me, you vicious Mother Superior bitch!" hissed Mary through clenched teeth.

Omelia's hands shot back to the jacket about her. She dropped her gaze to the floor and huddled deep back into her corner, almost knocking the lamp from the end table beside her.

"And as for you," said Mary, her gaze now burning into Minorie, "I asked you to cut his fucking baby out of my belly and where were you?? Off riding the postman's son behind the van, that's where! You know I asked him too and he said he'd do it if I kissed his *thing*...."

The words were coming fast and hot and hard like lava into Minorie's ears and down into her chest and her belly.....She wanted to puke.

"He didn't think you were special," she continued. "Not even with your fucking red hair!"

Minorie knew Mary's words of ranting bile were probably sweet fuck all to do with her in actuality, but she couldn't help feel the sting of them anyway. They spoke directly to her own inner voice; the one that told her she wasn't good enough; the one that told her she shouldn't be at all surprised by Keith's taking a proverbial piss on her. Why should she think she was special? *Not even with your fucking red hair......*

Mary cackled sadistically. She wasn't done with Minorie just yet.

"Oh yes, you're *so* special. Red-haired bitch! Interrupting me when I'm doing my crossword. No respect for anyone but yourself! You know we were happy here before *you* showed up....."

That last bit had sounded more direct, as if it had actually been Mary speaking to Minorie. Minorie wasn't waiting any longer to find out. She felt a rage bubble up inside of her, the rage which had pushed her to threaten her father's life. She allowed it to erupt inside of her.

"You know what, Mary?" she said, in a dangerously challenging tone. "You're afraid of the dark. You're afraid of your own power! You hide away up here doing god-knows-*what* and making everyone tip-toe around you like you're a queen! Well I've had enough!!"

A shot of Na-nan flashed into her mind like a blinding vision as Mary flew at her. Omelia shrieked. Just as Mary's hand closed around Minorie's throat, she saw a figure step out from the shadows of the hallway and into the moonbeam where Mary had been standing.

"MALDARON!" he shouted in a deep, authoritative tone.

Mary's hand momentarily tightened around Minorie's throat and Minorie could just about make out the crazed look on her face in the reflecting moonlight. For a moment she could have sworn she saw the face of her father where Mary's should have been.

"I command you to STOP!" said the man again.

When Mary's hand loosened again, Minorie stole a glance at the man who was speaking. He was dressed from head to toe in sweeping black robes, and flashes of scarlet red satin sliced through them

Mary began to growl again. She let her hand fall to her side and hissed menacingly at Minorie before turning to address the man.

"And just what makes you think you are still our commander?" the Mary thing said.

"You know fine well what," said the man. "At the least you might find yourselves back rotting in the limbo I dragged you from." His voice was cool and even, but Minorie detected the slightest hint of bitter fear on him. He continued with confidence, not giving the Mary thing time to react. "At worst I can leave you to roam this world with all of your knowledge but none of the blood or the prayers to sustain you. I can make your names disappear from the tongues of men forever."

The frame of the Mary thing slumped visibly.

The mention of blood made Minorie's skin crawl. She thought of emptying the little cup of her blood into that foul little bottle and prayed that this wasn't the blood being used to fuel this sorcery. She looked at Omelia. Omelia's face was buried in her hands and she was trembling violently.

"We could have done it though," the Mary thing said in a voice that sounded like a battered accordion which had recently been set on fire. "We could have kept sunlight over her house from sunrise to sunset without the blood."

The combined effect of the Mary thing's voice and its erratic movements was grotesque, like Mary was being used like a dummy by some repugnant ventriloquist.

"Maldaron, my dear one. Even our own Mother Nature can make the sun shine from sunrise to sunset. What mortal do you think would be impressed by this? It takes a sorcerer of rare skill such as myself to maintain the necessary conditions for the magick you have so faithfully performed for me these past years...."

The Mary thing slumped again and emitted a defeated sigh.

Suddenly the big picture came into focus in Minorie's mind. Omelia must have sensed it. She looked up from her hands and whimpered, "Minorie, no...."

"So what you're saying is that Mary could have still had guaranteed sunshine every day *without* the need to steal our period blood?? What kind of twisted fucking game IS this??"

The Mary thing began to cackle delightedly. Omelia sobbed uncontrollably. The sorcerer broke his rock-solid stance for the first time since entering. Minorie could see now that he had a long, pointed black beard, as if he'd watched one too many kung fu films and fancied himself an evil villain. He looked ridiculous. And right now he looked afraid.

The Mary thing began to twirl drunkenly around the room, knocking a lamp from the end table and making the chaise longue beside her squeak noisily across the floor by several inches. "Tra-la-la, you silly old fool.....The mortals in rainy countries shall kiss our feet for the want of the sun....Tra-la-la La-la!" It continued laughing to itself and fondling Mary's fingers through the air in its macabre dance.

They stroked Minorie's face as it passed her in a sweeping swirl which ended in the creature falling backwards onto the chaise long and wrapping Mary's arms around itself in an ecstatic fit of laughter which rang shrilly through the air and bounced off the thick stone walls of the cottage.

The sorcerer was grasping for words. Omelia made a break for her bedroom at the first possible opportunity, not looking once at Minorie as she bolted. The Mary thing was still taunting the sorcerer and had begun demanding gin now also.

Minorie felt herself being overtaken by the same nauseating, claustrophobic feeling which had consumed her in Pig's when she'd found Keith and Bunny Ears on the living room floor. She ran for the front door. Nobody in the room moved to stop her. She opened the top half of the door but the bottom half remained stuck fast. After a moment of frantically fiddling with it, just as the panic threatened to take her sanity for good, she managed to wrench the latch free and fall out the door onto the muddy ground outside.

She didn't stop to feel sorry for herself. As she ran down the dark path onto the even darker road beyond, she tried to think of somewhere dry where she could sit for a few moments and absorb all that had just happened. The torrents of rain pounded down upon her, forcing her to squint hard to see just a few feet beyond herself.

She wondered if she looked as cowardly taking off like this as Keith and the gang had done earlier on. She wondered how they would justify the horrifying vision of the Mary thing to themselves later. She wondered how she would justify it to herself. As paralysing thoughts of spending the night outdoors crept in, she began running again; around the first bend, then the second, then on towards the hill. Her breath began to run out.

This was it. This was rock bottom. There was nowhere else to go. Carlinn had chewed her up and was in the process of spitting her out. *I'm done* for, she thought, feeling the black hopelessness descend around her once more. It far outshone any temporary relief she'd felt at being safe from the *thing* in Merryweathers. It was like wriggling free from a noose only to fall into a freshly-dug grave.

The village had grown quieter now. The distant, dying rumble of drums was almost completely washed away by the loud gushing of rain. It covered Carlinn now like a soaking, smothering blanket. Many of the carved lanterns on the stream wall had gone out, and the good ones had all been lifted by passing festival goers who'd been sensible enough not to tackle the drunken and treacherous stumble home without a little light to guide their way.

Minorie slowed to a panting limp as she passed Madam Neige's bakery. She wearily began fumbling around in the ditch for the gap which would lead her into the hollow where Omelia had gone to meet Christy.

She prayed there would be enough leaves left on the trees within to keep the rain off her. As she found the gap and forced herself through the stinging brambles and grabbing branches (which ruined any remaining parts of her costume still previously intact), she discovered that it was just as wet inside the hollow as it had been out on the road. There was however, a familiar and friendly looking figure waiting patiently upon the tree branch for her.

"Blaise?"

His white mime make up had mostly washed off and he was giving her the most sympathetic smile she'd ever seen. She burst out crying and fell towards the branch he was perched on. He lurched forward to catch her and wrapped his thinly sleeved arms around her.

He felt so safe, so warm, and he smelled so nice.....Minorie raised her face beneath his chin, up to his cheek. She planted a tiny kiss there and moved quickly towards his lips to place another.

"Minorie, I'm gay," he blurted out suddenly.

She was speechless. *Of course you're gay. Of course it would have to be the first thing you ever actually said to me. Of course it would have to be tonight.*

She began to giggle. The giggling picked up and became belly laughs, which tumbled forth and became fits of roaring laughter.

Blaise laughed along, feeling he understood the joke quite well. He too had been a desperate waif, tumbling along at the mercy of Carlinn and the great mountain Mamon. He too had reached out for silly comforts which proved to be nothing at all compared to the untold majesty which lay in store for him. And he too had laughed hysterically.

He put his arm back around her as her almost maniacal laughter lapsed back into tired resignation. He led her back through the ditch and down the hill and across the no man's land that was Carlinn in the aftermath of its greatest festival. She never spoke a word the entire time.

# EMERGENCE

Back in Na-nan's the fire was lit. A cup of rich and decadent hot chocolate was shoved into her hand and a warm blanket was draped about her shoulders. Menew purred around her elbows. Her sobbing deepened when Na-nan appeared in her thick woolly layers, smiling warmly and putting her heavy, loving arms around Minorie.

Stroking her head and rocking her softly by the fireside, Na-nan explained to her how the sunbeam was powered by blood magick, dark magick; and how those who lived too much in the light never saw the dark creeping up on them.

Minorie wailed and nodded her wet face against Na-nan's cushiony shoulder. She squeaked about having no friends and no family. Na-nan soothed her pain with melodic chants of "Sha bébé, it's as natural as autumn leaves....."

Through the gushing sobs, Minorie could feel the layers stripping away; all the pain, the regret, the fear, the hatred......It poured out her eyes and when it wrenched itself free from her belly, Blaise held a bucket below her face and caught it.

In her mind's eye she saw Misyeu Snake winding and whipping in his extraordinary dance, shedding his skins over eons and not even noticing the loss of a single one. She saw herself dance alongside him in

Misyeu Fire, who licked and singed away the layers of deadness that had kept her rigid and still for so long now.....She saw herself rise from the flames like a phoenix and be reborn beneath the silvery light of the moon, radiant and strong.

The exhaustion of her journey so far reminded her that she was a long way from healed. It felt as though she had been completely broken just to be rebuilt.

Her head ached from the unsightly cocktail of liquor she'd consumed throughout the course of the night. Her body was sore from running hard and fast for the past week since her father had taken a notion to flatten her skull into the wall. She imagined that a branch losing its leaves might understand the pain that was in her heart – the achievements of an era ripped mercilessly from one's desperate clutch. She didn't see the trees crying about it though. But then they couldn't see her either.

She let it all flow from her until her body could literally take no more, and she passed out in a nest of cushions and blankets in front of the fire, with Blaise curled around her like a shield and Menew nestled at her belly.

Outside the wind howled and the rain turned to hail. Carlinn's ghosts faded uneasily back behind the veil of reason, and the bleak threat of dawn lingered ominously across the Lough, where not even the seagulls dared go.

The visiting tourists in their hostel beds had each, in turn, vowed never to return to Carlinn. The locals had mostly fallen asleep thankful for the end of the festival chaos and the approaching peacefulness of winter.

Minorie Raine slept like the dead between the mountain and the sea and dreamt of nothing in particular.

Tine, Flight of Fire

238

# submergence

On a wild mountainside Nicholas Crowther struggled onwards against the wind and lashing greenery which fought him every step of the way. He never once lost his place on the path though he couldn't see it at all. In truth he was just glad to not be struck down by a well-placed bolt of lightning. They were more than capable of it by now.

He knew Maldaron was with him and he could only hope that Jezelu and Branalok were following. He hadn't expected they'd be brave enough to make a move for Mary's body. They were getting too strong, even for him.

And that little red-haired vixen had only gone and validated them *exponentially*.... How high and mighty they had become when she lauded their pathetic abilities! *From sunrise to sunset indeed.....*

He wondered whether Mary would again call on him to reinstate the sunbeam. He wondered whether he'd be able to maintain his hold over his servile companions much longer. In truth he didn't care much either way.

His filthy nights with Mary over the years had come at a high price. She refused to see him only at the arranged ritual times and so every time she had a problem or got dreadfully drunk, or both, she would come to his home shouting about vengeance and power and if he didn't respond in an agreeable manner, she would begin the sad process of taking off her clothes and whining desperately. To say it was a turn off was an understatement, but on those occasions only fucking her would get rid of her.

He had long since considered her both a tiresome client and lover and was secretly grateful at the prospect of losing her business for good. This had been the foremost thought in his mind earlier as he'd locked her into her bedroom and handed her care over to that little waif daughter of hers, once he'd finally found her crouching in the shadows of her meditation room. He had almost laughed at the vision of her trying to protect herself from him with her two quaintly crossed index fingers.

Tonight though, as he pushed on in the fading darkness towards his home in the rock, it wasn't Mary the priest-bait that dominated his thoughts. It was that flame haired beauty.....

Her tenacity in the face of such power and her subsequent scrambling like a cornered mouse at the door – it was intoxicating, like strong wine infused with heady spices, flowing impatiently through his veins, making them throb. He *had* to see her again, to taste the sweet, fiery power that had made the demons wince.

He felt their presence as he approached the discreet entrance of his cave. It was a hollow which had been carved out of the mountain many centuries past by some unfortunate hermit. The idiot locals had long since believed the place to be haunted which in Carlinn, was really saying something.

He had felt pulled towards it shortly after he'd arrived in the village, when the rumblings of his supposed 'dark magick' began to circulate amongst the lesser lightworkers in the place. *Fools.*

Actually he'd found it suited him quite well. Finding just the right break in the trees to bring him to the mouldy green door in the side of the mouldy green rock and entering his silent and sacred sanctum always made him feel the full weight of the gifts which had been bestowed upon him during his life of torment.

There he was surrounded by rare magickal tools from all over the world, and books of such power that other, more cowardly magick workers wouldn't even dare hold them in their possession. It was where he could put all his most interesting spells to the test without being judged by small minded people. It was where the demons would never dare challenge him.

He was safe to rest for the night; safe to dream of her flowing red locks cascading down over his skin, followed by the sweet, butterfly kisses from her pouted pink lips.... Shudders of pleasure ran over him as he unhooked his outer robe and hung it up on its hanger. *She was looking for something when she came here. Looking for something that perhaps we can provide.....*

He lay back on the bed and closed his eyes, wondering if his otherworldly servants would have the strength to penetrate her fierceness and dominate her. He allowed the vision of her to take shape against his skin. *So soft.......so very soft.......Give anything......anything at all........It's yours.......*

"We may be able to help you there," said Maldaron from the thin air around Nicholas. "With the right blood, of course."

Outside the sun stretched its first thin arm across the landscape. The sleeping residents of the village had gladly missed the birth of winter, leaving the bakers, the sailors and the swans alone to witness it. The restless spirit of the seasons rolled over heavily in her bed and kissed goodbye to the autumn.

# KEEP GOING!

If you have enjoyed Flight of Fire, you'll love our other books and stories. Sign up to the Red Mantle list to get updates, freebies and information on new releases.

## Coming in early 2018, *'The Rapturous Moon'*, the second book in the 'Minorie Raine: Trials and Tribulations' Series.

"The moon brings strange desires….

Minorie Raine is on the move again, as an invitation from Lady Anna Marmaduke to live in her very own place at the decadent Darby House proves too tempting to ignore.

But other forces are bubbling below the surface, as her estranged friend Omelia is unwittingly playing into the lecherous schemes of Nicholas Crowther. As a result, Minorie's time in Darby House, like all magick it seems, is not what she expected it to be.

Her forbidden desire for Pierre and her fear of losing her best friend, Blaise, drive her into the arms of dangerous and unearthly forces who will stop at nothing, as long as Crowther is in control.

But who can stop Carlinn's darkest wizard, and how? And can Omelia redeem herself before it's too late?

With so many of the people who'd tried to help her ending up dead or with their lives destroyed, Minorie must fight through her guilt and shame to survive, but the night gets blacker with each turn of the screw…"

# About the Author –
## Tara D.W. Tine

Tara D. W. Tine hails from the borderlands of North Eastern Ireland and didn't graduate from anywhere.

Author, social activist, songstress and all-round scallywag, she spends most of her time commuting between dimensions and sending home postcards detailing her experiences. The rest she spends conversing with her cat and drinking tea.

Both Tine's music and her authored works draw heavily on themes of magick, nature and the lesser explored aspects of the human psyche.

"Tara Tines' vocal prowess delivers tasteful and infectious melodies, searing with undertones of soul and folk. Her bluesy lyricism conjures something spontaneous. The dog barking at midnight on the street; the chimes of the church bells; or the spatter of a heavy shower on your window. The sheer originality of this poetically textured musical patchwork will enthral all those who bear witness."
~ Dundalk Democrat, 2017

Tine's groundbreaking debut novel, 'Flight of Fire', from the Minorie Raine: Trials & Tribulations Series is due for release in September 2017.

She can be found on:
EMAIL: carlinnliteraturemusic@gmail.com
FACEBOOK: Carlinn, Literature & Music
WEBSITE: Carlinn, Literature & Music

Tine, Flight of Fire

# 'Omelia', Chapter One –

# The Rapturous Moon

# Book 2 in the
# 'Minorie Raine, Trials & Tribulations'
# Series

Omelia pulled her thick woollen jacket tight around herself as she stepped out into the freezing night and pulled Nicholas Crowther's front door closed behind her. The two and a half mile walk home would be difficult with the cramps, although the elixir Crowther had given her should be kicking in any minute now and besides, she knew the road like the back of her hand. The scattered bunch of glimmering lights that signified Carlinn village was not yet in her line of vision, but there was enough moonlight at least to make out the clumps of heather and occasional boulder which marked the edges of the dirt road back to Merryweathers. Her lessons from this evening swirled around in her head, trying to find the relevant memory banks to assimilate themselves into. She was thankful to have finished early; she had been in no fit state to extend the session and anyway, Nicholas had been eager to get to his 'experiments'.

She hadn't been sure at first why he had requested she bring the candles, particularly so many of them.

Things became a bit clearer when he then requested she bring the cushion and the hairbrush…..He had assured her that he was merely attempting to understand what it was about the blood which had so upset the demons. Omelia wasn't sure she believed him, and she had no desire to be an active part in anything which brought further harm or weirdness to Minorie. She still admired her bravery and in truth she missed her company. She had been so much more fun than Grace, a real kindred spirit. But in any case, Amelia preferred not to know the truth. The revelations uncovered by her stay with them had upset the apple cart, to say the least.

It had been revealed to Omelia that the weather magick in Merryweather's had not worked, as she had previously believed, by Mary's hands, but that in fact it had been Crowther's skills which had powered the sunbeam all these years. This had put a real dampener on her quest to find her power and to follow in her mother's footsteps in training to be a High Priestess of the Serpentine Sisters of Heart Hill. It proved to be one of the darkest times in her life thus far, full of uncertainty and misery. For a few days the sunbeam had ceased to function as Crowther had negotiated as hard as he dare with the demons, without whom its reinstatement couldn't have taken place. All hope had seemed lost during those days and Omelia had been faced with the very real prospect of having to go home to her stepfather's house.

It would have been impossible for her to stay beneath Mary's roof with the state Mary had been in. It took three full days before it was safe to even let her out of her bedroom. She'd destroyed it when she'd come to on the very first morning – shouting for her bottle of gin and smashing everything she possibly could. Grace had barred the shutters on her bedroom from the outside to prevent her escaping through the window. When they'd finally let her out on the third night all she could do was lie in Grace's arms in front of the fire and cry pathetically. She hadn't spoken a word to Omelia the whole time, other than to rant incoherently through the bedroom door. When Crowther's offer had come on the fourth day it was like a gift from Mamon.

Maldaron, Jezelu and Branalok had finally decided upon terms that pleased them. They would reinstate the sunbeam only on the promise that Crowther would immediately begin trying to make a baby with a new woman. They had settled upon Omelia as their choice. For her part in things, Omelia received the offer of an education in the *dark arts*, as Crowther was fond of calling it. It wasn't exactly the innocent-sounding weather magick her mother had envisioned for her, but it was much, much more powerful. Omelia had taken almost no time to think it over.

One definite pro to the new situation was that the demons no longer required the moon blood as evidence, deciding that its taste had so displeased them last time that they dare not take the risk again. Instead, Omelia was required to attempt to conceive at the end of each of her lessons with Crowther, barring days like today when she was menstruating.

She hadn't minded this clause so much at the start, particularly since Mary had given her some great tips on how to prevent conception. She hadn't felt she was ready for a baby just yet, and the longer she could string things out with Crowther, the more knowledge and power she could acquire. And besides, the regular supply of sex had really helped her to knuckle down and stop thinking so much about boys.

She couldn't keep it going forever though; the demons had placed a time limit on the new contract. If she hadn't conceived within the turn of twelve moons they would be released from their bond to Crowther and the sunbeam would be no more.

Additionally, things had gotten a bit strange when, just a month into their lovemaking, she had caught Crowther putting a glamour on her. Having red hair for an hour or two had been a kinky thrill on those nights during the first week or two since her discovery, but after that it did feel a little weird, especially when he'd say things like "Ooh, you fiery little cunt…." Omelia guessed he had some major mother issues. She wasn't really in any position to judge him on that front though. And besides, every little detail of information she gathered about him was just one more piece of assurance that he wouldn't try to pull anything funny with her. She'd learned a thing or two since having her moon blood misappropriated by a desperate woman and her dark wizard lover….

She felt lonely all of a sudden on the road. The glow of Carlinn was still a few bends away. She glanced around her to ensure no-one was about. *And why would they be?* People in Carlinn generally avoided this part of the mountain and in the months she'd been walking the road now, she hadn't passed a single soul on the way. Well, actually she'd passed many *souls*, just none which were still attached to human bodies.

The ghosts around here were legendary amongst the villagers and further afield. Outside visitors who came from the Findair side and who missed the turn for the mountain pass would often find themselves camping within earshot of Crowther's Crag and the noises they would hear were reputed to have driven most of them right back to Findair in the middle of the night. Some others were apparently driven clean out of their minds.

Crowther had taken certain special precautions to ensure Omelia would not be too bothered during her journeys – she had told him that ghosts still terrified her, and had immediately regretted giving him this window to her weaknesses. His only response had been to remind her that dealing with ghosts and even darker things besides was '*obviously an inevitable necessity of learning the dark arts.*' He had in any case held back some of the more desperate and angry spirits for her, although she felt that his efforts in this department may soon begin to wane, along with his interest in her. It wasn't her he wanted, nor was it even Mary. It was Minorie. Minorie with her red hair and the fire in her blood and the rain in her name…..Omelia knew that Minorie would never touch Crowther with a ten foot barge pole, at least not of her own free will. That was where her pondering on the subject would always cease.

The elixir was doing its job now, rapidly working tentacles of numbness through every part of her, soothing the pain until she felt as though she were floating – a perfect time to brush up on her skills. She cleared her throat. The noise startled her somewhat in the stillness of the night.

"Hesti? Your commander is calling you.
Hesti? Your services are required here.

Hesti, my love? I need you…."

With that, the ethereal vision of her little fire friend appeared as clearly in her mind's eye as if she were observing a real thing with her two everyday eyes. It was like a lizard made of flames, with a very distinguishable expression on its docile little face. It lifted its tail and heaved in a great breath before coughing out a decent-sized fireball which would serve as Omelia's lantern for the walk. She smiled and thanked it and sent it away with her mind.

Hesti had sort of been Crowther's first gift to her. Of course, she needed to summon it up herself under his supervision, but it was the thought that counted. "To light the long road home for you, my love," he had said to her almost tenderly, once the salamander had finally answered her call. It was the first useful thing Omelia had ever invoked.

Her previous attempts at summoning servants of her own had been embarrassingly amateurish. She had rescued some of her mother's books before her stepfather had sold them on for a fortune. With them, she had made several attempts to conjure up this helpful spirit and that servile demon but she always seemed to leave out some crucial element like reading the fine print first or cross-checking things she didn't fully understand. The result was that most of her attempts were complete failures, and some of those had gone horribly awry. One had even brought a reckless and angry entity into her stepfather's house which, for a good week and a half, had resisted both Omelia's and her mother's attempts to remove it. That had been the final straw.

Her mother said the whole thing had shown her that Omelia needed guidance and that she wasn't going to be able to give it to her under her stepfather's roof. She had contacted her friend, Lady Anna Marmaduke, to enquire about available positions for prospective students in Carlinn. Lady Anna had had a full house at the time but had arranged for Omelia to stay at Merryweather's. She had stressed that Omelia may wish to wait until a position in her own house became available but Omelia, her mother and her stepfather alike were all keen for her to depart as soon as possible. Of course, her stepfather still actually believed she was in boarding school on the other side of the country. Fool.

Omelia sighed as Carlinn's lights finally came into view and wondered at what could have been had she only waited for a place in Lady Anna's house. She wouldn't have had to hide every joint she'd smoked for the past three years, and she'd have been able to have all the boys she could manage over to stay. Plus there'd have been less work, more parties, no Grace to put up with…..She sighed again and wondered if she was mad to turn down the chance to stay at Lady Anna's now that it had finally come up. The invitation, when it eventually arrived however, was not as shiny and appealing as Omelia had once imagined it would be.

Some part of her had shut down on that fateful festival night last October. She could no longer live for the intoxicating mix of pleasure and submission which had been provided at Merryweather's and indeed, which would be magnified if she were to move to Lady Anna's. She wanted to show her mother and her stepfather and anyone else who doubted her that she was a force to be reckoned with. She wanted to learn magick that would make her mother regret sending her away. She wanted her stepfather to quake in his boots. She wanted Mary to be under obligation to *her* for a while.....*Yes....yes it's all falling nicely into place now.*

The sunbeam appeared in the distance now, lighting up the cottage like a freak show amongst the dignified dwellings which were snuggled around the edge of the village. Omelia smiled to herself as she drank in the vision. She felt in a way as though it was hers, like she was the one *earning* it. She knew Mary knew this too. She loved that she hadn't dared broach the subject with her. She loved how much more care Mary took to be nice to her and to swallow her rage and her cutting remarks. She *really* loved to watch Grace's face contort with futile disgust each time Mary instructed her to help out in the garden. She relished being the unspoken queen of the pecking order. And she glowed with anticipation of them pretending to be in bed asleep when she arrived home.

She sent her *wandering eye,* as Crowther called it, onwards to the house to look in upon her hosts. Grace was picking up on her nearing presence and was alerting Mary, who'd been crying into her wineglass in front of the fire. They were scrambling to make the living room look as though they hadn't spent the entire evening there. Omelia laughed as she observed Mary stretching up to shove the wine bottle into the antique toilet cistern before scuttling off, half-cut, to bed, and Grace positioning herself in lotus upon the floor of the meditation room, trying to look enlightened. *Fools, all of them. Useless, cursed fools.*

She pulled her coat tight around herself again and called the fireball a little closer, so that she might benefit from its meagre heat. She smiled, quite satisfied with herself. *Yes, it's all falling nicely into place.*

Made in the USA
Columbia, SC
24 September 2018